VILLAGE
IN THE SKY

VILLAGE
IN THE SKY

Jack McDevitt

SAGA PRESS

LONDON SYDNEY **NEW YORK** TORONTO NEW DELHI

SAGA PRESS

AN IMPRINT OF SIMON & SCHUSTER, LLC

1230 AVENUE OF THE AMERICAS, NEW YORK, NEW YORK 10020

Copyright © 2023 by Cryptic, Inc.

All rights reserved, including the right to reproduce this book or portions thereof in any form whatsoever. For information, address Saga Press Subsidiary Rights Department, 1230 Avenue of the Americas, New York, NY 10020.

First Saga Press trade paperback edition March 2024

SAGA PRESS and colophon are registered trademarks of Simon & Schuster, LLC

Simon & Schuster: Celebrating 100 years of publishing in 2024.

For information about special discounts for bulk purchases, please contact Simon & Schuster Special Sales at 1-866-506-1949 or business@simonandschuster.com.

The Simon & Schuster Speakers Bureau can bring authors to your live event. For more information or to book an event, contact the Simon & Schuster Speakers Bureau at 1-866-248-3049 or visit our website at www.simonspeakers.com.

Interior design by Erika R. Genova

Manufactured in the United States of America

10 9 8 7 6 5 4 3 2 1

Library of Congress Control Number: 2022948976

ISBN 978-1-6680-0429-6
ISBN 978-1-6680-0430-2 (pbk)
ISBN 978-1-6680-0431-9 (ebook)

For Ann and Ron Fleury
Friends of a lifetime

ACKNOWLEDGMENTS

Thanks to my editor, Joe Monti, and to my agent, Chris Lotts. To Walter Cuirle, Larry Wasserman, Michael Fossel, and David deGraff for scientific support. To Maureen and Christopher McDevitt for their oversight. Also I'm indebted to Michio Kaku for the inspiration provided by his 2008 book, *Physics of the Impossible*.

Dates not marked CE are from the Rimway calendar.
Action is set in the twelfth millennium.

PROLOGUE

1436, Rimway Calendar

There is no quality, no essence, no effect so distressing as the silence that pours out of the stars.

—Edmund Barringer, *Lifeboat*, **8788, C.E.**

I never thought the day would come when I'd settle in to write an Alex Benedict memoir in which Alex and I are the bad guys. It started when Quaid McCann took the *Columbia* on a routine mission for the Visitation Project. McCann was on the board of directors of the project, which was about to close down. Again. Officially, they were compiling a list of habitable worlds for eventual colonization. But, as everyone connected with the organization knew, they were really looking for someone to talk with. The first interstellar vehicles had been activated in ancient times, nine thousand years ago. They'd gone out into local planetary systems, and gradually moved on to distant stars, where they found nothing other than a few archeological sites, only a few of which had shown any sign of an advanced civilization. But they were all long gone. The evidence indicated that while life was not rare, intelligence was almost nonexistent. And when advanced civilizations developed, they inevitably destroyed themselves. Humans had come close to doing that, but we'd been lucky. The right people had shown up at the right times.

Human colonies were established around neighboring stars while we came gradually to accept the unrelenting silence that seemed as much a part of the natural order as starlight. Eventually we discovered the Ashiyyur, the only intelligent beings with whom we'd been able to sit down. But they did not have a speech capability. The Ashiyyur communicated by telepathy. They were the Mutes. And they read our minds as well as their own, so we were never comfortable in their presence.

Missions like this one seemed pointless. The scientific world supported the efforts of people like McCann, although they showed no confidence that he would ever find anyone. His wife, Edna, had given up hope that he would ever recognize it as a colossal waste of time. But she understood why he persisted. Though not enough to accompany him after his first effort.

The *Columbia* had been in deep space almost seven months, had visited nineteen planetary systems along the far edge of the Orion Nebula, examined twenty-six terrestrial worlds, and found absolutely nothing of interest. A few had jungles and whales, trees and grasslands, herds of creatures thundering across broad landscapes. Most were simply arid and windswept and, as far as they could see, lifeless. There might have been microorganisms down there somewhere, but they wouldn't be of any consequence for millions of years. The systems certainly hadn't seen anything that might have an inclination to say hello.

McCann's pilot, Robbi Jo Renfroe, had been a friend of mine since our early school days. She understood that even McCann had given up finally and was ready to quit. Just as well: they were running low on supplies. He surprised her as they approached the final system. "I'm ready," he said, "to find a more rational way to waste my life." He'd spent years on these missions. And he'd noticed that few of those who accompanied him ever returned for an additional flight. But she suspected that eventually he'd be out there again. He would stay with the project as long as he was breathing. The consolation was that the general emptiness would make success, if it could ever be achieved, even more compelling. He would become part of history. Though it wasn't the acquisition of fame that drove him. It was the Milky Way. It was just too big to be empty. There had to be others out there, and he was determined to find them.

Their last visit was to be in the system of a K-class dwarf star. They'd named it Korella, after one of McCann's uncles. They'd detected five planets in the system. There might have been more, but if so, they were too far out to be of interest. For that matter, only three of the five were orbiting in the Goldilocks Zone. One of those was a gas giant, and another was a barren world of rocks, methane, and ice. But the third one was a terrestrial. It had oceans and continents, always a good sign. And there was a green landscape. White clouds drifted through the sky.

McCann was on the bridge with Robbi Jo, leaning forward as if it would provide a better look. "Let's hope," he'd said.

Robbi Jo had grown to hate long, lonely voyages, but if they ever found anything, she wanted to be there. So she'd rolled the dice on this one. But she'd also given up and decided never again. So this was her last chance. But maybe there would be a payoff. That possibility occurred to her not because the world was green. That was not uncommon, but there was something about the appearance and the color that suggested they'd struck gold. Or maybe it was just McCann's desperation and a sense that something would happen to prevent his going home empty again.

They came in on the sunlit side. They were still too far out to see whether anything was moving on the ground or fluttering through the sky. McCann wasn't talking about radio signals, but that was what he was really looking for. Unfortunately, though, the receiver remained silent. He would have preferred to be on the night side, watching somebody down there turn on the lights.

)) ● ((

They saw no sign of any kind of structure. As usual, it looked as if there was nobody there.

We understand why intelligent species are not likely to appear even on worlds where conditions are perfect. The complexity of the molecular combinations required simply to produce life on a world with the right chemicals and conditions reduced the chances substantially. Add the nearly impossible requirements needed to generate brain evolution and the odds become extreme. "I wonder," McCann had asked a couple of times, "why we care so much? If the universe is really empty, except for us and the Mutes, it's a much safer place."

He was right, of course. With earthquakes and tidal waves, crashing asteroids, black holes and exploding stars, the Milky Way is already sufficiently hostile to its life-forms, its children, as the poet Tess Harmon had once described us. When finally we met the Mutes, we ended up in a war with them. Maybe that was the reason for the emptiness: there really might be a God behind everything, one who understood that intelligent beings are stupid, inevitably inclined to fight. So he keeps the numbers down. It makes sense.

It was just after midnight on board the *Columbia* when McCann went back to get some sleep. He left Robbi Jo alone on the bridge. The sky was filled with stars. After McCann left, she went back into the passenger cabin. Vince Reddington and Jason Albright were the only ones there. Vince was the backup pilot. Jason was tall and blond, a physicist who'd won a couple of major awards, though he looked too young to have managed anything like that. They were listening to a performance from their library by a late-night comedian. It was strictly audio. The view from the ship's telescope was on the monitor. She sat down where she could watch the screen. After a while she fell asleep. She was out for about an hour before the guys woke her. They could see movement on the ground. When they got closer, they were able to make out a few animals running across a prairie under a full moon. Robbi Jo moved the scope and saw mountains, rivers, and a forest. Birds or something flew through the night sky. A herd of four-legged creatures were making their way casually across a sloping plain near the base of one of the mountains, while a solitary beast that might have been a leopard watched. A pair of gator-sized lizards climbed out of a river. And something with multiple legs dashed across open space before disappearing into a cluster of trees. And then she saw a light.

Of course we all know what happened next.

The village.

)) ● ((

It was the discovery of a lifetime. Vince and Jason erupted with enthusiasm. The door to McCann's cabin opened and he joined them, yelling about not believing it and at last. They were still a substantial distance out, but the telescope locked on it. McCann was laughing and pounding Vince's back. He hugged Jason and Robbi Jo, who later described it as the wildest moment in her life.

It was a lot more than a village. The architecture was glossy in the moonlight, elegant, and somehow amicable. A place that welcomed visitors. There were log cabins and châteaus and villas. The light they'd seen came from a couple of lampposts and one of the houses. Otherwise everything was dark. The village was set along the edge of a lake. It looked like the sort of place that Mc-Cann's wealthier colleagues frequently built halfway up a mountain or along a shoreline. A place to which people could retreat and leave their mundane lives behind.

They saw movement. Someone was walking on one of the roadways. They weren't close enough to be able to make out anything other than that it was a biped and it wore clothes. It entered one of the houses. Not the one with the light.

The center of the village was occupied by a pair of large connected structures, possibly a school, or a church, or a town hall. Who knew? We've all seen the pictures.

The buildings had shafts, balconies, cupolas, arches, and domes. Most of the architecture was curved. It consisted of polished structures with balustrades and round-arched windows, cornices, circular entrance steps, parapets, and spires. They had pitched rooftops supported by rounded columns. The houses ranged from one to three stories. Everything gave the illusion of a rising symmetry, as if the design of the individual structures was somehow unified, more than simply a set of buildings separated by dirt roads.

They had almost an hour to watch, during which other bipeds wandered through the streets, before the planetary rotation took them out of view. When they were gone, McCann and his team went through another period of backslapping and exchanging congratulations. At last. It was hard to believe.

For Robbi Jo, though, and maybe for all of them, the sheer joy contained an element of disappointment. They weren't permitted to make contact. They were required by the Spaulding Mandate to do what they could to avoid allowing the aliens even to notice their presence. And they had complied accordingly.

They knew where the village was, so they had no trouble finding it. It was back in daylight again when they passed overhead. And they got their first good look at the aliens. They had bright green skin with a silver tint, faces with standard features. They couldn't determine how big they were. Ears and nose were elongated, and their eyes appeared to be set wide apart. They wore trousers and shorts and colorful shirts. And there was no sign of hair. They appeared to move with grace.

They were everywhere in the town. No vehicles, though.

"It makes no sense," McCann said. "Where's everybody else?"

They left the area and expanded their search across sections they hadn't seen previously. Nothing changed. Forests and plains and mountains and occasional deserts were all they could find.

The village seemed to be the only occupied location on the planet. They came back when night had fallen. Lights were on in most of the houses. The lampposts were also lit up.

Still nothing on the radio.

"They probably wouldn't have any use for a radio," said Vince. "Nobody's more than a few blocks away."

"So what do we do?" asked Jason.

"I guess," said McCann, "we go home and report it."

Vince didn't like the idea. "Why don't we take the lander down and say hello? They don't look dangerous."

McCann closed his eyes and shook his head. "Break the mandate and we'll all be in trouble."

"Mac," said Jason, "we can't just walk away from this."

McCann's eyes hardened. "Yes, we can. Suppose you go down and we scare them and they attack us? What do we do?"

"We have weapons."

"You really want to go home and explain that you killed a couple of these people?"

"Mac." Vince obviously thought they had no choice. "We can't just ignore what we've found. Look, we can go down in the lander, stay well away from the town, and keep out of sight. It shouldn't be all that hard."

"No." McCann wasn't going to budge.

The lights in one of the houses went out. They were outside lights, on the porch. And a post light. They all shut off together, so that removed any possibility that the aliens were using candles or gaslights.

In the end, as we all know, the *Columbia* just packed up and came home.

I rode into the dark, expecting to see my love in the moonlight;
But there was no moon, and not even a star.
Nevertheless, she was there.
I had but to find her.

—Walford Candles, "Ride by Night," 1196

It started on an early spring afternoon while I was playing volleyball. We were on an outdoor court at the Tara Center when somebody began shooting off fireworks. Sirens sounded and I heard a commotion inside the center. We stopped for a couple of minutes and looked at each other, and when nothing more happened, we resumed playing. I don't recall any more of the volleyball details, whether my side was winning or losing. I don't even remember whether it was a league game or just a couple of teams that we'd put together. All that disappeared in the turmoil that erupted that evening. We showered, and as soon as I got access to my link, I checked it to find out what was going on. We were informed that the research vehicle *Columbia* had discovered intelligent life. The only details were that they'd found a small town and that they'd seen the inhabitants, who were green-skinned. The town was a long way out. It was an exciting time. Real aliens. We were informed that plans already existed for a follow-up mission.

I was excited not only because of the discovery, but for another reason: Robbi Jo Renfroe had been piloting the mission. I hadn't known anything about it except that she'd been gone a long time.

There wasn't much detail available about the flight. They'd named the place Korella IV but released minimal other information. There was no data regarding the world's location. I tried doing a search for it, but I didn't know at the time that the name had been selected by McCann.

Robbi Jo and I had been out of contact for a few years, but I hadn't been surprised when I'd seen her name listed as the mission's pilot. I remembered standing with her under a starlit sky when we were both about twelve years old. Robbi Jo asked me if I thought it ever ended, the sky. If it did, what was at the edge? Was there a wall of some sort? Her mom had told her no, that the universe wasn't like that, that space was skewered. That was the term she'd used. So it didn't come to a stop, it just became circular in a way that seemed impossible to understand. But if you went in one direction far enough, eventually you came in from the other side. And she recalled her refusal to believe it when her mom said it was pretty much all empty out there. Nobody home. Robbi Jo made it her lifetime goal to find someone. Anyone. Which was more or less how she eventually got caught up with the *Columbia*. And she'd made it happen! Good for her.

Actually, we'd never been especially close, but we'd met as Girl Troopers during our grade-school years. We both played on our high school's basketball team, and for a time we'd hung out together. She'd always had a fascination with stars and galaxies. She'd told me once that she planned to become an astronomer. If anyone I'd known was going to be on that flight, she would be the one. The teachers loved her. She won the highly acclaimed Orion Award two years after high school for her article "Why Is It So Empty?" which appeared in the *Antiquarian*. It was a prize I'd have killed for, but I simply didn't have the writing skills. Or maybe I just didn't know how to dig into the cultural issues in a way that would hold a reader's interest.

I knew she wouldn't be home for a while, but I couldn't resist sending her a congratulatory note. "Wish I'd been with you," I wrote. And I added a reference to our basketball days in case she'd forgotten who I was.

The street was filled with people laughing and embracing and staring at their links. GREETINGS, ALIENS said the headline in the *Andiquar Sentinel*. There wasn't much detail on what they looked like, other than their green skin, but the hunt that had been going on for thousands of years, producing nothing other than ruins and the Mutes, was finally at an end. United Media had an anchor and two guests discussing the story and wondering whether we'd wind up in a war again.

Several of us crossed Weyland Street to the Akron Bar, where we could join the celebration while the reports came in.

The pictures of the town, which had arrived as part of a hypercomm transmission, revealed a village that might have been located outside Casper County. Modest houses, dirt roads, a long building that looked like a school. Despite the town's simplicity, there was a harmony and polish that underscored its unity. Everything seemed to be connected. It was somehow a single configuration rather than a group of individual houses and small buildings.

The mission also reported they'd found nothing else on the planet. Of course the assumption was that they'd probably sent the report immediately after sighting the village. But as time passed, we learned that they'd searched the planet and found no additional dwellings. How could that happen? It became the question of the hour.

The operation had been sponsored by the Visitation Project. The *Columbia* reported that in accordance with the Spaulding Mandate, they'd not made contact, would keep a respectful distance, and that there was no indication that their presence had been detected. They suggested a backup unit be dispatched to establish communications.

It was certainly not the kind of first contact we'd been hoping for, a lonely desolate village. But it was better than nothing.

)) ● ((

The Department of Planetary Survey and Astronomical Research (DPSAR) maintained an office in Andiquar. One of their primary responsibilities was to maintain a training program designed to create specialists who could establish friendly communications should we discover aliens somewhere, or if they showed up over the Melony River. That was the Xenocon program. It was a tricky business, since nobody had had any experience with communicating with aliens. I don't think anyone had ever taken the program very seriously, for that matter, but the lack of preparation led us into the war with the Mutes. If we came into contact with another alien species, we certainly didn't want to do a repeat.

It was inevitable, I guess, that the day would come. So when it finally did, we were prepared to do some bridge-building. Connect our AIs with theirs, if they had any. Speak softly. Smile. Don't do anything that could be interpreted as threatening. And don't tell anyone where the Confederacy worlds are located until we have a good handle on their intentions. And hope we had it right. There was also a branch of DPSAR people who maintained that we should just stay away and keep our hands off.

A few days after the initial *Columbia* transmission had arrived, we got word that the mission had started home. There was no indication that anything had changed. Since it took two weeks for a hypercomm signal to arrive from Korella, the *Columbia* by then was halfway back.

DPSAR called in its Xenocon volunteers. I was among them. Don't ask how I got involved. Even now I'm not sure. They had parties and the conferences were interesting, so I signed on. The director was Henry Cassell, who'd spent a lot of time with the Mutes. He started that first day by telling us DPSAR was looking for volunteers to travel to Korella IV and establish communications with the aliens. "They have electricity," he said. "The houses look good. But beyond that, they don't seem to have much technology. And one aspect that is especially curious is that they seem to be alone on the planet."

Henry was a middle-aged guy with a kindly appearance and amicable green eyes, though they had an intense appearance that night. He looked around at us and asked who was willing to go. *He* was going. They needed five other people, plus a pilot. They had no way of knowing how long they would stay in the area, but

Henry doubted it would be more than a few days. "But don't sign on if you can't manage a flight of at least three months."

There were only a dozen of us physically in the building. But there were probably twenty more electronically present. Most were positioned on other Confederate worlds, and even though they were locked in through hypercomm, there was a delay of up to several minutes while messages went back and forth. Meanwhile three of those present raised their hands. Jim Pollard, who'd always maintained he would love to be part of a contact mission, hesitated and then put *his* hand in the air. I was still thinking about it when the electronic results started to show up. There weren't as many as I would have expected. Aliens living in log cabins and stone houses just didn't cut it. Since everyone knew this was coming, I'd talked it over with Alex before signing on. He gave me an okay, with the comment that it didn't sound very exciting.

A woman on one of the electronic connections asked why we were taking only seven. "The *Harbinger*," she said, "can carry twice that many."

Henry delivered a tolerant smile. "Not for this distance," he said. "Aside from that, we should all be aware there's a degree of risk about this type of mission. We don't *need* twice as many people as we can carry. And, for the record, we expect to take one of the people from the *Columbia*."

The major question that dominated the meeting was whether we were actually going to establish contact. "We haven't decided yet," he said. "That's a difficult question. We'll go and take a look. And I suspect we'll decide depending on what we learn about them. And don't ask me how we're going to learn anything without talking to them. We haven't figured it out yet."

Three months in an interstellar. I had a decent social life at that time, which I did not want to leave for an extended period. But it was hard to just stand there and do nothing. My chances would have been pretty good to get picked had I known where Korella IV was. That was why they wanted someone from the *Columbia*. And preferably that would be either Reddington or Robbi Jo. In the end, I wasn't really that excited about a few hundred aliens in a town in the middle of nowhere. So I stayed out of it. The final count gave Henry twenty-two volunteers.

When it was over, he thanked us for our interest. "I'm sorry we won't be able to accommodate everybody. We just can't pack enough supplies into the *Harbinger*." He shrugged, pretending not to be surprised at the level of enthusiasm. "We should probably have gotten hold of the *Alhambra* for this operation." That got some laughs. We could have gotten half of Andiquar on board the *Alhambra*. He told us that it would take a while, a few weeks, to put everything together, and that he'd get back to the volunteers as quickly as he could.

)) ● ((

I spent the weekend mountain climbing with Chad Barker and a few others. Chad was a boyfriend at the time. We took our first break at Wiley's Bar & Grill, just south of Morley Canyon. We'd kept our links turned off, but the *Columbia* story was all over the news at Wiley's. I stayed with it for the next two days. The hosts on every major show had people in to discuss what was happening, whether we should be concerned about who was out there, and what effects the connection with a totally alien culture might have on our own lives. Would the aliens be hostile? Would they have a religion? Could we be sure the ones in the cabins weren't there to fool us into underestimating their tech capabilities? Transmissions from Quaid McCann on the incoming *Columbia* were arriving almost daily. And Greg Lindsay, the host of *Night Talk*, brought McCann's wife Edna in for an interview. Did she wish now that she'd gone along on the mission?

"No," she said. "If anybody was going to do it, I'd have put my money on Quaid. He's been trying to find someone out there his entire life. Most of the people we know always thought he was wasting his time. But he just couldn't be talked down from it."

"Edna, are there any plans to bring some of the aliens back here?"

"You mean to Andiquar? No, they wouldn't be allowed to do anything like that. Greg, you know there are laws against it."

"Sure. But if we run into something that seems friendly, who knows how we might respond?"

"I'd be shocked if my husband ignored the law."

Twenty minutes later Lindsay was talking to Clint Eliot, a historian whose area of special interest was the war with the Mutes. "Could it happen again, Clint? Could the aliens seize the ship's crew and learn where we are located?"

"Well, Greg, that's kind of a foolish question, since they're already on the way home and there's been no report of trouble."

"Maybe they're all at gunpoint."

For a moment I thought Eliot was going to throw something at him.

)   )   ❂   ((

When I got home, I switched on the Golden Network. The host, Morris Cassidy, brought in Jennifer Hancock to join the upcoming *Harbinger* mission. Jennifer had been on a previous flight, and she had a master's in astrobiology. She was tall with dark eyes and a voice that made it clear she was completely reliable and in charge. "Yes," she said, "of course we're sending a research team out. We're all trained for this kind of thing. We should be leaving within a week or two."

"Will you guys say hello? The research team?"

"Probably not. Unless the aliens find a way to say something." Her smile suggested she was toying with Cassidy. "We'll be concentrating on finding out what we can without making a connection. That's more for their benefit than ours. It looks like a pretty primitive culture." Cassidy started to say something, but she kept going: "I understand they have electricity, but they're living in a village. And they seem to be the only people on the planet." She shook her head. "I don't see any way they could constitute a threat."

"Jennifer, where is this place? Korella IV?"

"It's a long way out. In the Orion Nebula. Other than that, we won't be making details public."

"You don't want people going out and taking a look?"

"It could be dangerous, Morris. Not so much to us as to them. We don't want to scare a primitive culture. We don't know anything about who's there. So we'll just keep our distance." A warning had been issued that same evening that anyone attempting without permission from DPSAR to visit the place would be in violation of the law and subject to substantial penalties.

The Glynnville Archeological Society had its monthly conference two nights later. Gabe was scheduled as the guest speaker. I was pretty sure Henry Cassell would be there too. The last few days had been a major struggle. Henry had offered to include me with the crew of the *Harbinger*. I suspect my connection with Alex had something to do with that. I just couldn't make up my mind about it. The flight would be historical, and a golden chance to establish my reputation as someone other than Alex's assistant. Even without that, being present when we said hello to the aliens was a once-in-a-lifetime opportunity. And I should mention that I wasn't among those who thought the follow-up mission was just going out there to look around and not make contact.

But I didn't see anything particularly interesting about the village on the prairie. They were going to spend two months inside the *Harbinger*, say hello to the villagers, and presumably find out they just didn't reproduce much. Or whatever. My life with Chad had taken off and I didn't want to leave him. Especially since I'd seen how many of his bookstore customers were attractive young women.

Gabe planned to talk about some of the artifacts found during his recent trip to Morinda, a city at Point Edward that had been abandoned centuries ago for reasons still in dispute.

They traditionally do the event at the Acadia Hotel, adjacent to Oglebee Park. They'd turned on the force-field billboard that floated just a few meters above the top of the hotel, divulging the title and time of the event. Gabe's name was prominently on display, as well as his topic.

Chad was interested in going, so I offered to take Gabe as well. He passed because he was scheduled to sign books earlier at a Mount Barrett store. But he supplied me with two tickets. Chad picked me up and we rode his skimmer out to the hotel. We descended into the parking area, went inside the Acadia, said hello to a couple of people we knew, and sat down at a reserved table. The place was almost filled. I spotted Henry, who unfortunately was seated on the far side of the room. I'd have loved to find him at my table, but he was a VIP, so there was no way that was going to happen.

The dinner was good, a choice between salmon and pork roast. I couldn't help being happy that I wasn't there to talk to that packed house. Nothing scares me quite as much as public speaking. When I'd finished the meal, I decided to order a dessert. Strawberry short-cake sounded right. It was hard to believe that in the ancient world we'd killed farm animals to provide food. That, of course, was before we developed nutrient generators, which use cloned cells to provide all the meat, fish, vegetables, and desserts we need.

I was just finishing when the society's event secretary took her place at the lectern and spoke for several minutes about current projects. The society had selected a local high school student for its annual Jeremy Cranston Award. The winner was announced and came up to receive a plaque. She was also given passage to Dellaconda, where she could do some sightseeing, as well as participate in an archeological dig at a site near the ancient Kormite city of Barrakaia. After the applause settled down, the event secretary introduced the guest speaker, Professor Gabriel Benedict.

Gabe came onto the stage, bringing a drink with him. "Good evening, ladies and gentlemen." He looked out over us with a broad smile that suggested he would have made an excellent talk show host. "We're gathered together this evening in historic times. I know you were informed that my subject would be the recent recovery of artifacts found at Morinda, and that I would present a theory as to what really happened there. But I know, at a time like this, nobody really cares about a deserted city on Point Edward. This has been a fairly big week." He smiled as "fairly" drew a ton of laughter. "After all these years, we have apparently actually encountered some aliens.

"I can't help thinking that when we come back for the meeting next month, the *Harbinger* will probably already be on its way to Korella. And there'll be at least one more meeting before we hear anything back from them." He stopped, and momentary confusion wrinkled his features. "Bear with me. My physics isn't exactly up to date. I'm not sure how long those hypercomm transmissions take to get back to us. But anyhow, we might by then have some serious news about them. About the aliens. Maybe when we get into the middle of the summer, we'll have one of the aliens as our guest speaker. That's one we wouldn't want to miss."

He switched back to Morinda and spent several minutes on why artifacts matter. "They provide the only real way we can touch the past, and that's why we go to such measures to preserve them. Does the past really matter? Think what it feels like when you go back to the home you grew up in and everything's changed. The AI's been replaced by a stranger, the front porch is now enclosed, the house next door where the McClellands lived has become a tech shop." He paused, and his audience applauded until he held up a hand. "It's how we know who we are."

There wasn't much point that night in talking about anything other than aliens, however, so Gabe told stories from a couple of the expeditions he'd shared with Mutes. "Any archeologist will tell you that once the digging starts, they spend a lot of time hoping for what will be found. Maybe the lost body of the young Galatian hero Allie Moraas. Or Kim Marko's notebook."

Moraas had of course sacrificed himself to draw the savage Wakians away from the group of fleeing visitors at Tyro Falls. "It's hard to believe," he said, "that humans in an advanced society can still murder each other. Can kill strangers. But isolate them for a while, put them in an area seldom visited by others, and it happens.

"Marko's notebook was the reason we were there. It had disappeared shortly before his death. Marko is generally credited as one of the best playwrights ever. I'll confess I'm not a fan. His plays are a bit too complicated for me. But however that may be, the note-book, if we could find it, would be priceless."

But Gabe could not help returning to the *Columbia*. "The one thought I suspect we're all sharing this evening is how much any of us would give to have been with the people on that ship."

He finished his remarks a few minutes later, after getting more applause and laughs. Then he invited questions. The first one was usually the same at all his speaking events: How did he get interested in archeology? "It's hard to see how you can earn any money digging up ancient cities. Would you recommend it as a career?"

Of course the subject of the day surfaced quickly: "What about the aliens? Would you be interested in collecting artifacts from them? Would they be more valuable than stuff from Morinda?"

Gabe said he thought alien artifacts sounded like a good idea. That got more laughs. A few minutes later he wished us all a good evening.

)) ● ((

Henry was slow to leave his table at the end. He waited for Gabe to come down off the stage, and then he got up and headed in his direction. Henry and Gabe got together and talked for a few minutes. Then Gabe said a few parting words to the event secretary and turned back to Henry. They knew each other pretty well. Chad and I stayed at our table. They eventually began to walk toward the doors. I was hoping to get Henry alone, but it didn't look as if it was going to happen.

There were still a few people lingering at their tables, but most were now headed for the exit. Chad and I got up and joined them as bots began gathering dishes. We walked leisurely, off to one side, in plain view so Henry could see me. I'd told Chad that I'd been invited to join the *Harbinger* flight. When he asked about my intentions, I'd told him I hadn't made up my mind yet.

We preceded Gabe and Henry outside and I took the only course available, walking directly over to them as they came through the doors. "Hi, guys," I said. Gabe already knew Chad. I introduced him to Henry. When they exchanged greetings, I picked up a distinct coolness in Chad. He just wanted Henry to go away.

"Henry," I said, "I didn't know you were interested in archeology."

"Oh, yes. Especially when Gabe has the floor." He smiled at me but spoke to Gabe and Chad. "You probably both know she's a Xenocon."

"No," said Chad. "What the hell's a Xenocon?"

Henry smiled. "You just had dinner with one. They're people who've been trained how to respond during an encounter with aliens." He turned in my direction. "Chase, have you by any chance decided whether you're going to join us on the *Harbinger*? I don't want to rush you, but we're running out of time."

That was how the moment came. *Make up your mind.* "No," I said. "I'm going to pass, Henry. Sorry, I just can't manage it. But thank you." Chad's eyes closed momentarily. He looked relieved. But I could see the disappointment in Gabe's expression. He'd expected more of me.

Henry nodded. "I understand, Chase."

Gabe checked the time. "Got to get moving, guys. Chase, you need a ride home?"

"Chad's got me covered, Gabe. Thanks."

"Okay. See you tomorrow." He headed into the parking lot.

Henry watched him go and then told Chad he'd been glad to meet him. "Chase," he added, "I'm sorry you can't make it. Take care."

2

There's no question that the most significant scientific breakthrough in human history occurred eight thousand years ago, when Eugene Taimundo demonstrated that FTL travel was possible. It was an incredible step forward, in every way imaginable. But it came with a cost. We learned quickly that the universe was effectively empty. We've been looking for someone to talk with for thousands of years. And we all know how that's turned out.

**—Eleanor Zaraka, speaking at Salem University,
on Rimway, 1427**

Alex told me that if he'd been in Henry's place, I'd have been his first choice to pilot the *Harbinger*, and he wouldn't have taken no for an answer. Chad, though, was clearly happy. "I know you wanted to go, and I'm sorry it was such a difficult decision. I hope you didn't turn it down just for my sake. But I'll admit I wasn't looking forward to having you out of my life for the next couple of months. Worse than that, aliens are unpredictable."

A few days after the archeological conference, the *Columbia* finally arrived at Skydeck. The HV cameras were there, so we all got to watch in hologram format while its team of four emerged from the connecting tube onto the concourse. A crowd was waiting, and they wasted no time delivering enthusiastic applause. I had no trouble recognizing Robbi Jo. It had been a few years, but she hadn't changed at all.

The Hochman Network's Lester Wilkinson managed to corner Quaid McCann. "I know you weren't supposed to establish contact with them, but did you try?"

"No," he said. "We didn't."

"Did you receive any radio signals?"

"There was nothing. As far as we could tell, they didn't even *have* a radio."

"But they had lights?"

"Yes, they did."

"It's also been reported that they had electricity. Is that correct?"

"Yes."

"How could you tell? Did they have motors running somewhere?"

"The light in their windows was steady. It was clearly not candles."

"That sounds a bit speculative."

McCann looked annoyed. "We like to speculate, Lester. And they had lampposts that were steady. Electric, not gas."

One of the other interviewers got to Vince Reddington, the

backup pilot. "You guys actually were able to see the aliens in that town. Am I right?"

"That is correct, yes."

"It must have been disappointing that you couldn't go down and knock on a few doors. Say hello to them."

"It was."

"Why didn't you just do it?"

"It's against the rules."

"We're talking about something that happens twice in several thousand years. Why not bend the rules a bit?"

Reddington looked toward McCann. "That's a question you have to ask the boss."

The next morning I was back at my desk in the country house, tracking the authenticity of two artifacts that had been offered to us for auction. They were a link and a blaster whose owner maintained they'd once belonged to Christopher Sim, the legendary hero from the Mute War. Alex thought they were not authentic, which was probably true. There was no way to establish a connection with Sim. His initials were on the link. We knew that Sim's link had carried his initials, but nothing could prevent someone from taking care of that detail. There was no way to authenticate either object. I tried to track down what had happened to his blaster, but there was no record. The weapon matched one that Sim had used, but there was no way to connect it to him. I couldn't trace their sources, so the owner's claim could not be substantiated. He had gotten both artifacts from his great-grandfather, now deceased. The great-grandfather had served during the war. But there was no visible connection between him and Sim or his celebrated ship, the *Corsarius*. Artifacts don't matter unless you can establish their authenticity. I was just finishing the assignment, getting ready to send the results to Alex, when Jacob, our AI, informed me there was a story breaking on the Hochman Network that I would probably find interesting.

Mary Everson, one of the network anchors, blinked on. She was effectively seated behind a table in the middle of my office. Jacob had recorded it from the beginning: "DPSAR," she said, "has announced that the follow-up mission to the Orion Nebula will be leaving in eight days. As we've known for a while, they'll be using the *Harbinger*. Vince Reddington, who was one of the pilots on the *Columbia*, has joined the crew in the same role. They released the names several days ago of the other people who will be making the flight. And there's something else to add: I'm happy to report that the mission, which promises to be historic, will be covered in detail by the Hochman Network. Our longtime news anchor, Lester Wilkinson, will be on board the *Harbinger*. He'll be doing daily reports, so we'll all be along on the flight."

Alex came down a few minutes later. "You okay?" he asked.

"Of course."

))●((

Henry sent out messages to, I presume, everyone who'd expressed a desire to join the follow-up mission. He regretted not being able to accommodate everybody but explained again his reluctance to put anyone unnecessarily at risk. If another opportunity arose, he hoped we would not hesitate to come forward again. Another opportunity? Hard to believe he delivered that line with a straight face.

Robbi Jo called that evening. I'd just arrived home when she blinked on in my living room. "Hi, Chase." She was wearing the smile that had lit up schoolrooms, as beautiful as ever. "Good to see you again. I got your message. Thank you."

"Hi, Robbi Jo. Good to see you, too. You're having a pretty nice career."

"I guess we both are, Chase. You have a pretty nice job."

"It's not bad."

"I have to tell you, I'd have loved having you along on the flight. Most of it was pretty boring. Until we caught up with the aliens."

"It would have been nice," I said. "Next time you do one of these things, keep me in mind."

"Absolutely. By the way, I've enjoyed your Alex Benedict books."

"Thank you."

"Thank *you*. We could have used you to provide some PR for *us*."

"Are you serious? You guys discovered real aliens. The PR's built in."

"I'm not so sure. They're aliens, but they live in a small village on the edge of nowhere." She was leaning back in an armchair. "Not too much excitement there. It would have been different if Mac had let us go down and say hello. Anyhow, Chase, I've got to go. Maybe we can get together for lunch sometime?"

"I'd like that."

"I'll give you a call."

)) (((

The week passed quickly. We never quite managed to get together. Robbi Jo was being interviewed by everyone in sight. She was a speaker at events all around the Confederacy, and she was a guest on every talk show. Her life had gotten crowded, and I'd simply have to wait my turn.

Chad told me several times that he understood I was disappointed about not being on the follow-up mission, but that he was glad, as he put it, that I hadn't gone off into the wilderness. Hochman ran shows every night, interviewing participants, talking with people from the *Columbia*, and going on about how much everyone was looking forward to finding out what the village was doing alone on the planet.

McCann, appearing on *Night Talk*, reminded Henry Cassell and his team that the Spaulding Mandate was still in effect. That he would personally see that anyone who violated it would be prosecuted.

And finally the time of departure arrived.

I suspect everybody who could make it boarded the shuttle at the Andiquar Spaceport with Lester Wilkinson and the Hochman team and rode up to Skydeck that morning. Departure would be the following day. We watched them check into the *Harbinger*. Wilkinson interviewed Sam Carmody and Chuck Dumas. I'd never been in the same area physically with either of them. Both are Xenocons, of course, Sam from Dellaconda, Chuck from Earth. Vince Reddington said he was anxious to go back out to Korella and this time, he hoped, we'd at least get to say hello.

Two more Xenocons, both women, had not yet arrived. Autumn Ulbrich was from Saraglia, and Jennifer Hancock, from Rambuckle. Wilkinson pushed through the crowd on the concourse and let himself into the *Harbinger* passenger cabin.

Reddington and Henry Cassell were there, drinking coffee and watching a woman being interviewed on the HV. Wilkinson and his cameraperson arrived and took seats. They did a round of introductions, leaving the cameraman out. Henry told the Hochman host how much they appreciated his coming along. "I think," said Henry, "you'll find this a unique experience."

Wilkinson was in his later years, with a long history of bringing down corrupt politicians and anybody else who engaged in questionable activities. His most celebrated moment had come early in his career, when he confronted Margo Depierre, then president of the Confederacy, over using her position to control elections. It was an interview that led to her resignation a few weeks later. Wilkinson's name became a synonym for standing up to power. He told Hancock he was happy to meet her. "If you're able to talk to one of the aliens, Jennifer," he continued, "what's the first question you'll ask?"

She frowned. Apparently she'd been expecting something else. Hancock looked as if she'd been around the block a few times. Her eyes were riveted, not on Wilkinson, but on me as she considered her reply. And that was probably the surprise, discovering she'd just as soon get away from the cameras. "I guess my first question would be 'How are you doing?'" She was as tall as Wilkinson, with red hair cut short and an expression that suggested she had better things to do than talk to the media.

"And what would be the second question?"

"I guess it would be whether they are surprised to see us."

The second part of the show came on a few hours later, live from the Starlight Hotel, where the Xenocon team was staying. Autumn

Ulbrich had joined them. She was a late addition. Tori Hackleman, from Fishbowl, had pulled out during the last few days. Problem at home, she'd said. Autumn had been the replacement.

Wilkinson asked Henry Cassell about McCann's warning that if they violated the Spaulding Mandate, he would see to the prosecution. "I have great respect for Professor McCann," Henry said, "but DPSAR supports what we're doing. We have been preparing for years for precisely this issue."

We got to watch them eat, got details on the menu, and listened to a conversation about how anxious everyone was to get started. The table was set beside a long window that provided a dazzling view of Rimway, which dominated the sky. The hotel management had to be happy.

$$)) ● (($$

The following morning the passengers and crew made their way through a crowded concourse to the entry tube and boarded the *Harbinger*. We were able to listen in on the exchanges between Skydeck comm ops and the ship. Wilkinson was on the bridge when they separated from the dock. He signed off as they made their exit through the bubble that surrounds the space station. When he came back two hours later, he was still seated beside Vince Reddington. The two of them were looking out through the wraparound. We could see the control board and Reddington and, of course, the sky. "We're getting ready to make our jump into Armstrong space," Wilkinson said. "Vince, we won't be losing contact, will we?"

"We'll be fine." The pilot pointed toward Wilkinson's lap. "You'll want to buckle in."

"Yes, yes. I forgot." He took care of it and smiled at us.

I assumed Wilkinson had prepared what he hoped would be intriguing questions, and probably would have been for his viewers, like *How does it feel when you go into Armstrong Space and all the lights in the sky go out?* Or *What were your thoughts coming on board, knowing that you would be contained inside these bulkheads for a couple of months?* The problem is that you can only ask each question once, and it's probably not something the viewers haven't heard before. This was the first HV series of its kind I'd ever heard of, and they were only a half hour into it when everything started to sound repetitive. "I suspect," Alex said, "nobody will try this kind of coverage again."

On a flight with a one-way four-week duration, they were all going to be sitting around reading, doing puzzles, playing computer games, and watching movies. And sleeping. None of that amounts to good entertainment when it's nonstop. To make things even worse, aside from the fact that there's nothing to see through the windows when you're traveling through Armstrong space, there's also an absolute sense of stillness that takes over. The vehicle does not seem to be moving. Riding an interstellar, somebody once said, is like sitting in a hotel under a dark, gloomy sky. The normal routine is to surface roughly once a week to give the passengers a break. They made their first exit after only four days. Whatever remorse I'd felt about staying behind was gone.

Chuck Dumas was probably the oldest person on board. He'd been a high school teacher for a while but eventually just decided to do physics research and play chess. "I miss the kids," he told Wilkinson. "I'd like to go back and live those days again. But I just don't have the energy for that kind of thing anymore."

"Says the guy," replied Wilkinson, "who's sitting in an interstellar going out to the Orion Nebula to say hello to aliens."

He interviewed Reddington twice during the first few days.
Mostly he asked questions about the *Columbia* mission. How did
he feel about having an opportunity to meet aliens on that flight
and coming away with no contact? "Ask me," he said, "after we get
home from this one."

During the second week, there were reports that the audience had
shrunk almost to nothing. People were going back to watching *My
Life with Sally* and *On the Edge* and *Party High*. *The* Harbinger
Show, which had been playing for an hour each evening, slipped
back to thirty minutes and then to occasional fifteen-minute
break-ins during the late-night talk shows. Usually the setting
was the passenger cabin, although Wilkinson interviewed Sam
Carmody inside the lander on a Sunday afternoon. Carmody
admitted to a fascination with aliens from his earliest days. "I was
disappointed," he said, "when I found out there was nobody out
there. Or almost nobody. I loved Rack Gomez. My father watched
it with me when I was about five years old. I remember getting
annoyed because Rack had an interstellar that could go anywhere
in a few minutes, and all he could think of to do with it was pick
fights with a guy who looked like my uncle Brock."

"You're referring to Sharah the Pitiless," Wilkinson said.

"Yeah. Years later I went back and watched the show again. I
realized the interstellar didn't have an air lock or a washroom."

Wilkinson was visibly amused. "Not good when you're going
to Andromeda." That was where Sharah lived.

Fortunately, the *Harbinger* had a pretty good library, most of the popular games, and an excellent selection of vids. The team members recommended favorite shows to their invisible audience, talked about what they were currently reading or watching, and even staged a couple of games that probably sent what was left of their watchers to bed.

Wilkinson's guests usually avoided personal issues, like relationships with friends and partners that had been put aside to join the mission. "Were there any problems? Maybe a romantic attachment you hadn't seen coming when you signed up for this mission?" If anything like that had happened, no one was admitting to it. The only thing they were committed to was getting to the target world. We couldn't help noticing that no one ever mentioned specifics about the flight, anything that might assist someone who wanted to visit Korella IV.

Wilkinson was good at his job. It didn't seem likely he could have foreseen the difficulties that came with the assignment, but if that was the case, he adjusted well. He asked his guests whether they would recommend this type of mission for their friends. And given a similar opportunity next year, how would they respond? There was occasional hesitancy, but in the end they all claimed yes, of course they would go with it. "No question," said Autumn.

Alex asked me about regrets that I had not gone. "I never really had any," I said. I don't often lie to him, but that one was somehow automatic. And I could see he understood that.

"If the contact evolves into a major event," he said, "I'd expect you to feel some serious frustration. But the odds of that happening are minuscule. These aliens are likely not much more than advanced savages. We'll probably discover there are a few villages in the area, nestled within forests and consequently easy to miss.

But whatever, it looks as if they'll be a long way from any kind of serious tech advancement."

"They have electricity," I said.

"Based on the steady light theory. I have some serious doubts about that. But even if they do, they're going to be relatively primitive. If we actually get to do a conversation with them, I bet it will be every bit as boring as Wilkinson's interviews."

On their tenth day, the team surfaced again and just looked out at the stars for several hours.

)) ● ((

Chuck Dumas is an Earther, from Africa. He's written several books about scientific research, on topics like how telepathy works or why time travel will not. He looks good and was obviously enjoying the flight. In fact, I'd guess he was the only one on the ship who hadn't gotten tired of the daily routine. When Autumn mentioned that to him while they were sitting with Wilkinson, trying to come up with a topic that might draw some interest, he propped his chin on folded hands and smiled at her. "It's probably because of your presence, Autumn. You and Jennifer. No way we can be bored with beautiful women on board." He said it as if he was kidding, but not really. He's tall, with friendly eyes, black hair, and a killer smile. "I'm also hoping," he said, "to get a book out of this experience. But to make that work, the aliens will have to be interesting." Wilkinson frowned. He didn't like the path the conversation had taken. But Chuck kept going: "They need to have a characteristic that makes them radically different from us. Like the Mutes."

Autumn smiled. "And what might that be?"

He grinned back. "Maybe they'll have X-ray vision. Be able to see through our clothes."

"That wouldn't be good."

"It's not as unsettling as a species that picks up whatever we're thinking." Autumn nodded, in full agreement.

"Or," he continued, "they might have IQs averaging over two hundred."

"I doubt that."

"Based on what?"

"Based, I guess, on my natural-born stupidity."

Wilkinson smiled, obviously happy now.

"It's probably a good thing," Chuck continued, "that the universe isn't filled with aliens. You get a lot of them and half *would* probably be smarter than we are, and some *much* smarter."

"Why do you say that? Because we're dumb?"

"Intelligence is an evolutionary trait, Autumn. If there are some civilizations out there, most of them are likely to be older than we are. And intelligence is an evolutionary trait."

)) ● ((

At the end of the second week the *Harbinger* team surfaced again simply to be able to look out at the stars. They waited a few hours before descending back into Armstrong space. I should mention that the interview we received from that occasion was almost seven days old.

They were doing the right thing by taking some time to look out at the sky. It helps raise the mood. Henry, speaking with Wilkinson, offered to take anyone who was interested down onto a planetary surface. But it would cost a few days instead of a few hours. Nobody wanted to do that. Sam Carmody commented that "a flight like this reminds me how much my family and friends mean to me. And the ordinary things we do and live with, walking through a park, watching rain come down. And since you're here, Lester, I should mention listening to the nightly news reports. And going out to a bar or a theater. I remember someone saying once that the secret to a happy life is lunch with friends."

Unfortunately, despite all the technology, including our ability to store friends and family online, to create their images and put them in the same room with us, to talk to them even after they're gone, it still doesn't work. We know they aren't really there, and we can't get around that reality.

3

Books are friends. They are good company, they provide warmth and pleasure, they introduce new ideas, they argue with us, and they never get angry, no matter who's wrong.

—Tulisofala, *Mountain Passes*, translated by Leisha Tanner

The *Harbinger* was into its third week when my birthday arrived. Alex took me to Claymont's Pork & Beef, across from Gardner University, to celebrate. We were in the middle of lunch when we got one of the biggest surprises of our lives. They were running soft music on the HVs when the newshawks broke in. "Report from Skydeck," said Julie Sylvester, an anchor on the Golden Network. She looked worried. My first thought was that something had happened to the *Harbinger*. "We've received a transmission from an incoming ship, saying that they are aliens. Not the Mutes. Somebody else. They are un-knowns. So far there's no reason to think there's any connection with the Korella mission. Maybe it's some sort of wild prank. Who-ever they are, they've been speaking to the station in Standard. There's been no visual exchange yet, so we have no idea what they look like or how they would have command of our language. In fact, the only reason we have to believe they're actually aliens is that they say they are. They've requested permission to dock. They are expected to arrive in about forty hours. Purpose of the visit is unknown. We will continue coverage as it becomes available."

The restaurant had gotten noisy. "They going to attack?"

"What the hell's this all about?"

"Maybe we better get home."

"How'd they get so close without our seeing them?"

The only other alien vehicles that have ever arrived in the Confederacy, as far as we know, belonged to the Ashiyyur, the Mutes. It became a problem when we got into a war with them. "What do you think, Alex?" I asked.

He picked up a piece of pork, or maybe beef. On his fork it was difficult to know. "If it's an alien invasion, it's probably best to fin-ish eating." He smiled, studied the meat, and bit into it. I've always enjoyed his dry sense of humor. And his ability to stay calm when other people are throwing up their hands.

We heard nothing more for about ten minutes. Then Julie was back: "They've been talking to us for about an hour. We still don't know what they look like. Our security people are saying there's only one vehicle. The visitors still haven't identified themselves. But they're asking if they can acquire some books. Hardcover books." Julie looked good and had a close resemblance to Maria Gordon, the actress who'd broken hearts across the Confederacy when she'd died during an avalanche. I'd often wondered why Julie hadn't picked up a movie career.

"That's odd," said a heavyset guy at the next table.

A woman seated across from us told her female companion that unless it was a joke, the person speaking for the aliens was an AI. She was almost certainly right. We heard more coverage but nothing new in the restaurant. I realized belatedly that Alex had picked Claymont's because there was a jewelry store next to it. He insisted we go inside, where there was a necklace he'd already selected. It had pearls and was lovely. Despite the day, I thought it was for his occasional girlfriend Veronica. That I was there simply to offer an opinion. But he surprised me when he turned and handed it to me. "Happy birthday, beautiful." He helped me put it on. I walked over to one of the mirrors and admired its appearance.

I thanked him and said he shouldn't have spent so much money. "Well," he replied, "if the world's about to end, we should go out with a bang." We embraced, left the shop, and strolled back to the skimmer, which was parked about a block away. A light rain was beginning to fall as we climbed inside.

He started the drive unit and glanced at the necklace. "Looks perfect," he said.

"It *is* nice."

"I meant *you*." We hugged and then he took us up. We ascended over Andiquar and turned in the direction of the country house. The rain grew intense. My link told me another report was coming in, so we switched on.

It was Julie again. "If it really is visitors, they say they're bringing some books, which they hope to exchange for some of ours. Skydeck has been in contact with people on the ground to try to set something up. The aliens are saying they would especially like to get some history and literature books." A few minutes later the Arcadia Network reported that we'd gotten a look at the vehicle that was the source of the transmissions and it was not one of any kind known to us.

Alex grinned. "I imagine Chad is happy today. You think he might be able to get involved in this?" Chad is the owner of the Collectors' Library, a bookstore in Salazar. Strictly speaking, it isn't a library. He specializes in making difficult-to-obtain hardcover classics available to collectors. In a way, he does with books what Alex does with artifacts.

"I'm sure he'd like to, but I doubt it. I wonder if they'll actually be able to read our books?"

"Sure. They apparently already have command of the language. In any case, I doubt they'd be talking about a trade if they couldn't."

"He'd enjoy becoming part of that," I said. "But his operation is too small to have much of a chance, even if they landed downtown."

"We're also hearing," said the Arcadia anchor, "that the aliens are bringing two kinds of books, some in their language, and others that are translations into Standard."

Alex's brow crinkled. "Sounds as if they've been prepping for this a long time."

))●((

We were inside the country house when further details emerged: "We still haven't gotten any visuals of the aliens. We've sent them vids of ourselves, but they haven't responded. Skydeck is saying that the aliens were excited to hear that we have live theater. There's been no comment on this, and apparently nobody knows how they found out. They may have picked up on some of the advertising for Lost in the Fog, which has transmitted regularly to incoming vessels. Makes us wonder if these guys might eventually show up to buy tickets." Lost in the Fog was currently playing in nearby Golem City.

"There's something I'd enjoy seeing," said Alex. "Can you imagine what would happen if word got out that some of the aliens would be in attendance at one of the theaters this weekend?" He was pouring coffee for us. "I'd love to see that happen."

I couldn't stop thinking about the difference between this first contact and the one we were trying to bring off on Korella. Lesson learned: Before you show up for a first contact, do some preparation. Learn the language. Bring books. And maybe prep for a party.

Arcadia went to commercial and we switched over to Julie on Golden. "Got more coming in," she said. Her eyes widened as we watched. "We've got visuals!" She blinked off and was replaced by something that looked like a *spider*. Its skin was covered with a short layer of fur. The eyes were located on appendages as long as its head was wide. The thing had four arms, all accommodated by sleeves. It wore a dark brown jacket almost the same color as the fur. No ears were visible, and we couldn't see its mouth until it spoke. "H'lo, homins," it said, raising one of its arms in a gesture that was probably intended to be friendly but looked threatening.

I couldn't recall ever having seen Alex go speechless before. And I couldn't stop staring.

The upper part of the jacket was open, revealing a white shirt with probably a zipper. We heard a woman say hello. "We are happy to meet you," she continued. She didn't sound happy.

The thing tried again to say something, but this time it was completely unintelligible. "What happened to their speaking perfect Standard?" asked Alex. The creature stopped and put a hand on the side of its head. It wasn't actually a hand. More like a set of clippers.

"Welcome to the Confederacy," said the female. "My name's Kayla. Where are you from?"

"I'm surprised they're carrying this live," I said.

Alex shook his head. "No way they're doing it live. This is a delayed transmission. Which is good news. The meeting must have gone well." His mood had shifted. He was trying hard not to laugh.

"Hello." A different voice. Something else was speaking for the aliens. The spider simply watched. "My name is not easily pronounced. It might be best if you simply address me as 'Ollie.'"

I looked over at Alex. "It's an AI." He nodded.

A second spider showed up on the monitor. "This is Neo," Ollie said.

"Greetings, Kayla," said Neo.

Ollie continued, "We are looking forward to meeting you, Kayla. You are the first species we have encountered with whom we can speak."

"Ollie, where are you from?"

The creature's dark eyes brightened. "I do not know what name you have given the area in which we live. We are not close. Your world would complete several hundred orbits before a light beam could reach us."

"You indicated an interest in live theater. Does that include you, too, Neo?"

There was a pause while they talked it over, apparently in their own language. Then the AI responded for Neo. "Yes. I have a serious passion for stage work."

"So you have live theater at home?"

"Yes, we do. We are pleased to find others who share our interest. We wish to establish relations with you. Our explorations of the galaxy have been continuing for many generations, and we are relieved finally to discover that someone else is here. We are on schedule to reach you in somewhat longer than one of your days. I hope that is convenient for you."

"Yes. That is good, Neo." Kayla had been replaced by another woman. "Is there anything we can do for you when you and your associates arrive?"

"Not at all. We hope only that you will be glad to see us."

"It's an interesting coincidence that you would arrive at the same time we've discovered aliens elsewhere."

"You mean Korella?"

"Yes. You know about that?"

"Oh, yes. We've known for a long time that you shared our interest in finding others. Over the last few years, your efforts have become more intense. It seemed like an appropriate time for us to make contact."

)) ● ((

Chad had invited me to a quiet celebratory dinner at Barringer's Bar and Grill, which looks out across the Melony River. But it turned out that the day's events had left both of us with much more to think about. The band was playing when we walked in. They seated us in the middle of the place, which should have warned me something was going on. Chad always preferred either being near a window or, if the weather was decent, seats outside on the veranda. The evening was warm and pleasant, with a slight breeze coming in across the Melony. We ordered our meals with a couple of glasses of wine.

Moments after our drinks arrived, the band finished its number. The bar's manager stepped up to the microphone. "Ladies and gentlemen," he said, "Barringer's would like to welcome the well-known author Chase Kolpath, on the occasion of her birthday. We have a piece of music titled 'Chasing Chase,' written by Chad Barker, who is seated with her this evening." He looked across the room at us and waved. Then he disappeared behind a curtain. A good-looking guy who'd been playing a viola with the small band that was present that night put the instrument down and took the microphone. He signaled his colleagues to start playing. They did and he sang:

"Love is the reason for all I do,
All I feel and all that matters and dream of and pursue.

In the end it is always and only about you,

Chase with the golden eyes, it is you."

Okay. I'll confess I was near tears right from the start. The rhythm was soft and passionate, and I loved the lyrics. And the guy had a warm, alluring voice. It was an overwhelming experience. When he'd finished the performance, the audience provided an enthusiastic round of applause.

"Beautiful, Chad," I said, trying to keep my voice steady. "I didn't know you could write music. Not at that level."

"I wish I could take credit for it," he said. "The music is from a song that was popular in the eighth millennium."

"That's a long time ago."

"It might even be older. We don't have the lyrics anymore, but the title was 'Love Is a Many-Splendored Thing.'"

"Well, whatever, it's beautiful. Thank you." He reached across the table and took my arm. "But you wrote the lyrics?" I asked.

He needed a minute to think about it. "William did it," he said finally. William was his bookstore's AI.

"Okay," I said. "In any case, I appreciate it. Nicest birthday present I've ever received." If we hadn't been in a public venue, I'd have moved on him. I got up and we exchanged smiles and embraced and kissed. The audience applauded again.

Finally it ended and we sat back down. "You know, by the way, my eyes are gray."

"Sure. But they have a way of lighting up. Turning to gold. I love you, Chase. But you've known that for a while."

They brought out a stand-up comic, who did jokes about how I look so young because I hang out a lot in the *Belle-Marie*, which moves faster than time. And he said that Chad was hoping to talk the aliens into giving him a few of the books they were bringing. "But if he gets to Skydeck," the comic added, "Chase won't be with him. He made it clear that he wouldn't let her anywhere near Ollie and the spiders."

I don't usually drink too much, but it seemed like the right night to let it go. At one point, Chad told me he'd taken a call from someone, but I didn't get the details until the evening had ended and Chad was in the process of delivering me to my cabin. The caller had been Sally McAndrew. She was a literature professor at Andiquar University and had been invited to join the group who would be selecting the books to be made available to the aliens.

She'd shown up at the country house a couple of years ago when she learned that we had found a copy of *Their Finest Hour*, the second of six volumes of Winston Churchill's *The Second*

World War. It had been reprinted on Earth in the ninth millennium. As far as we know, it's the only one of the six that has survived. She'd hoped that Alex would eventually come up with some of the others, but his efforts had led nowhere. She'd participated in the process where she could, during which she and Alex became friends. Eventually I introduced her to Chad, and she'd become interested in his library.

"So what did Sally want?" I asked him.

"She was calling from the spaceport. To ask me if I had any books that I thought would be good to make available to the aliens,"

"Good for you. What did you suggest?"

"I was kind of busy. I needed time to think about it." We'd left the receiver on so we could watch what was happening. Julie was gone, replaced by Morris Cassidy. The aliens were due tomorrow afternoon. "Sally was waiting to board a shuttle, headed for Skydeck. She's probably there by now." We were descending into my front yard. "I told her I'd get back to her." A full moon floated in the middle of the sky. The lights came on as we touched down. "They're scary," he said. "The aliens."

"Well, what do you expect? They're spiders."

"But they like books."

"Right." I couldn't resist laughing. "I never realized you were so open-minded, Chad."

I don't think I'd ever seen that level of disapproval in his eyes before. But I let it go. We went inside and watched Morris Cassidy interviewing a physicist and Kayla, who'd done the first conversation with the aliens. The physicist thought it was a dangerous time and we should be careful. He asked whether Cassidy would get close to the visitors. When he said yes, that he hoped to do so, the physicist inquired whether he would be carrying a weapon.

Cassidy tried to laugh it off, but the physicist shook his head and wished him luck.

I agreed with the physicist, but I said nothing to Chad. I didn't want to get into an argument with him. Not on that night.

I switched on the HV. I'd expected to see a large crowd gathering at the space station for a chance to get a look at the aliens tomorrow, but the coverage revealed an empty concourse. "They're probably not allowing anyone into the place without travel documents," I said.

After we got settled, I got us some coffee. Cassidy was talking with the Skydeck comm op officer, asking whether security was on alert.

She smiled. "They're always on alert, Morris."

"The aliens look like something out of a horror film."

"I hope," Chad said, "the aliens aren't picking this up."

We were sitting on the sofa. Chad asked me to stop the broadcast for a minute. I did and he bit his lower lip. "My customers have mixed views. They're interested in getting access to the books. The alien books. But they've all admitted to being uncomfortable with the way they look. That's easy enough to understand. Especially since they've been listening to us for a while. A lot of them seem to think they're planning an attack. They don't approve of our letting them come into Skydeck."

"Chad, they only have one ship."

"Who knows what they have? Some of them think there might be an invisible fleet out there."

"If they have an invisible fleet and they want us for dinner, why bother with the books?"

"That's what I've been saying. But why have they been listening to us?"

"Isn't that exactly what we would do in the same circumstances?" We were sitting staring at each other and then at the screen with its empty concourse. "So, Sally's in charge of the book exchange?"

"They have several people working on it. She's already begun contacting some of her associates about suggestions. She invited me to recommend two titles and deliver copies of them that can be turned over to the visitors. She doesn't necessarily want classics, but primarily books that show us in a favorable light."

"As in friendly?"

"More like as in not to be messed with. Like Belstein's *History of the Mute Wars*."

"Do you have a replicator?"

"No. It wouldn't be legal for me to print books. But I can get access to one for this project."

"Sounds good. What are you going to recommend?"

"I'm not sure yet. Probably Arlin Kramer's *Greek Drama*. It's a collection of a dozen of the greatest plays. And *The Old Curiosity Shop*. The Dickens novel." He'd recommended that to me a few months earlier. I'd read it and was impressed by it, but I couldn't see how it might suggest that aliens keep a respectful distance. "I was also," he continued, "thinking about Horace Carpenter's *Meltdown*. That would be a good pick."

"Carpenter's fairly recent, isn't he?"

"Last century. He's from Dellaconda." He downed some of the coffee. "It's a description of the kind of events that foreshadow governmental collapses. I wish we could find some of the other Dickens books. Only three have survived. Out of over twenty. The guy was incredible. Pretty much the only person I can think of who wrote a novel that's still being read after nine thousand years."

"How long does it take to make a copy of a hardcover?"

"About an hour."

We turned the HV back on. " — to be later getting here than we expected," comm ops was saying. "They'll have to find their own way in."

Chad frowned. "What's he talking about, Chase? You have any idea?"

"My guess is that we haven't been able to get control of their ship. When someone's coming into the station, they turn everything over to comm ops. The station takes control and brings them into the bubble and stays with them until they're docked. They probably discovered the links aren't there to allow it to happen."

"How much longer you think that'll take?"

"It depends on a lot of things. For example, the ship might be too big to get through the bubble entry." I shrugged. "That's unlikely, but it's possible."

It was approaching midnight. "We both have to be up early tomorrow." He looked at me and smiled. "I better head home."

"I'm a bit in the wind. You really not going to hang around?"

"That's the reason, Chase. You wouldn't be on full burners tonight."

)) ● ((

I was in the country house the next day, tracking some of our artifacts, when news arrived that the aliens were docking at Skydeck. I switched on the HV and got my first look at their vehicle. It was longer, wider, and flatter than any of ours. And spidery symbols decorated the hull. In addition, two spiders were looking out from the bridge. Skydeck must have established some communications between AIs, because they were able to shut down the ship's power and bring them gently into the commercial dock, which was probably the only one large enough to accommodate them.

I joined Alex and Gabe in the conference room. They were both fairly excited, a reaction I'd seldom seen from Alex. We watched four armed security guards and a Skydeck official enter the connecting tube. Lights came on and they followed it to the hull. The hatch was open when they got there. Two of the visitors stood waiting. Each held a box. Two more boxes had been placed on the deck. The official made no gesture but simply approached. "Hello," he said. "Welcome to Rimway. My name is Harrison."

A voice translated it into the alien language.

One of the aliens responded, and the AI voice interpreted: "Hello, Harrison. I am Ollie and this is Neo, the same two that your representative, Kayla, spoke with earlier." A third alien retreated out of sight.

That was the way the conversation continued, with the AI managing translations for both sides. The aliens were slightly taller than the humans. They didn't seem to be wearing uniforms. It was hard to make out any difference between their faces, if that's even the right term. Ollie was the bigger of the two, which was probably the only way anybody could have told them apart. Their eyes resembled dark bulbs. Each had its arms wrapped around one of the boxes.

The extra pair of arms was unsettling. But despite all that, the aliens managed to look almost amiable. Maybe it was the leisurely way they carried themselves. Or the way they talked. I just don't know.

"We're glad you got here okay," said Harrison. "Can we help with the books?"

"Yes," said Ollie. "Thank you."

The guards took them, including the ones on the deck. The aliens approached Harrison and each extended an arm, touching their fingertips with his. Neo said, "Hello to all. We're happy to be here."

Behind them the hatch closed. Harrison and the guards turned and escorted the aliens back through the tube. They emerged onto the concourse, stopped, and looked around at the walkways, the shops and restaurants. Everything looked closed. "Beautiful," said Ollie.

They handed off the boxes to other Skydeck officials, who led the way to a conference room. The guards were still present, along with three more officials, one of whom was Sally McAndrew. The boxes were set down on a long table in the center of the room. One of the officials said how pleased he was to welcome our honored visitors. He identified himself as Calvin Polgar, director of the Contact Relations Bureau, a subsidiary of DPSAR. The aliens were, by our standards, casually dressed, with frumpy leggings and pullover shirts.

The officials and the visitors took seats around the table; the guards backed off but remained in the room. Translations were managed easily by the alien AI. Ollie, in near-perfect tone, said, "We've been traveling through the galaxy for a thousand generations, but we've only twice before encountered living civilizations. I can inform you that the news of our discovery, of your existence, has caused major celebrations at home."

"Can you tell us about these other civilizations?" asked Polgar.

"We would prefer not to without their permission. If you wish, we will pass your query on to them."

"Maybe it would be best to let it go," Polgar said. "We can discuss it later." He glanced at his associates. They all seemed in agreement. Then he turned back to Ollie. "How long have you known about us?"

"I was relatively young when we were informed that your worlds had been discovered. It is probably not obvious to you, but none of my people would mistake me for being now in my early time."

One of the officials smiled. "You can travel faster than light?"

"Yes."

"May I ask why it has taken so long for you to make contact?"

"We have always been intrigued by the possibility of an encounter with intelligent beings." Neo was speaking now. "Caution, however, seemed like an appropriate response. We wanted, first, to learn whether establishing a relationship with you was a good idea. To be honest, whether it was safe. For both of us. As that was an obvious objective, we wanted to be sure we did not do anything that would alienate you. We wanted to show, from the beginning, friendly intent."

"That's why the books."

"It's part of the reason. But yes. Ollie and I hope we got it right." Ollie and Neo got to their feet and opened two of the boxes, brought out sixteen books, and stacked them on the table. They were all hardcovers, and over the next few minutes we got close-ups of them. Impossible to read the titles, of course. "These are all duplicates of the original editions," Ollie said, "obviously not convenient for your reading, but we thought you would appreciate having them. We also have copies in your language." They opened the other two boxes and began lifting more books out and placing them on the table. They were identical in design except that the cover print was in Standard. Polgar and his associates were staring at them. The director and one of the others helped empty the boxes. Then they passed copies from both sets around, and they all sat paging through them.

Neo held one up for the HV camera. Its title was *Living the Good Life* by Parqua Des. And a second one: *All the Time in the World*. The author's name looked unpronounceable. "These are historical, literary, and scientific," he said. "You would describe some as philosophical. All that are in your language may be reproduced at your pleasure and made available to any who wish them. We ask only that they be made widely available to keep the prices at a reasonable level."

Polgar held a finger to his lips. "And what is your share of the profits?"

"We want nothing." "To be honest, there'd be no easy way to collect a payment." He showed another title: *Why We Laugh*.

They never really stopped paging through the books. The ones in Standard drew all the attention. Polgar and his associates spent several minutes sorting through the volumes, obviously overwhelmed. They thanked the aliens, and this time showed no reluctance about clasping their hands. Sally approached Neo, and when he opened his arms, she embraced him. In that moment, we knew Sally had become immortal.

Eventually we got to see the other titles as well:

> *Skies on Fire*
> *Foundations of Civilization*
> *Discovering Rimway*
> *Last of the Grundis*
> *Facing Reality*

Footprints in the Sands of Time

Faith: Why Belief Still Matters

Chaela, Where Are You?

Sharik Sunset

Empty Skies: Why We're Alone

Meditations on Ethics

Once More unto the Breach

Moons over Korkorum

Apparently they'd been reading Shakespeare.

"You agreed," Ollie said, "to provide us with some volumes to take home."

Everyone looked toward Sally. "That's correct, Ollie," she said. "We're working on it now. We should have them up here in a couple of days."

"Excellent. Thank you."

"Our pleasure."

"May we leave our ship docked where it is?"

Harrison responded, "Of course. Are there others on board?"

"Yes. There are several of us."

"We can provide quarters for everyone if you wish."

"No. Thank you. Your accommodations would likely not be adequate. We have different requirements. But we appreciate the offer. Is there anything else we need to discuss?"

Polgar was still paging through the books, in both languages. "Perhaps," he said, "you can tell us the name of your home world?"

Ollie leaned forward, and for the first time I saw something that looked like a smile: "We come from Ulaka."

Sally seemed caught up in simply touching the covers. She glanced over at Ollie. "Was this your idea? The books?"

"No." He looked at his partner. "It was a committee decision. But it was originally Neo's suggestion."

Harrison aimed a wide smile at Neo. "I think we are all fortunate that he was part of the committee."

"We'll get the books to you as quickly as we can," said Sally. "I'll let you know as soon as we have them."

"Thank you," said Ollie. "There is something else of which you should be aware."

The humans were getting to their feet. "Of course," said Polgar. "And what is that?"

"Neo is not a male."

Harrison frowned. "He isn't? I mean, *she* isn't?"

"Neither of us is." They headed for the door.

))❆((

The network switched back to Morgan Cassidy and a guest I did not recognize. "That's a surprise," said Cassidy.

"What is?" asked the guest, a young woman identified on the bar as a physicist named Charlotte Smith.

"This is probably one of the most important missions in their history. And they put two females in charge of it."

Charlotte grinned. "Morgan, you're forgetting something."

"And what's that?"

"They're spiders."

4

The most significant invention in the history of humanity was the printing press. It made everything else possible. It gave us the Enlightenment, paved the way for every scientific advance, and provided human beings with access to unlimited knowledge and imagination.

—**Timothy Zhin-Po,** *Night Thoughts*

Alex left a message with Carmen at home, giving me the day off. His explanation was that I deserved it. I didn't know what that was about, but I was happy to run with it. I called Chad. His image blinked on, with a smile. "You okay, beautiful?"

"I'm good. Anything happening with you?"

"Of course. She called me earlier." Meaning Sally. "She wanted to know if I'd made up my mind yet about my recommendations. I reminded her that I'd already told her, and she said she was sorry, that there's so much going on right now that she's having trouble keeping it all together. I think she was pleased with my choices, though I doubt she'll go for Carpenter's book. At the time I mentioned it, she sounded as if she didn't think the books would be of much interest to aliens. And she's probably right. They're not very likely to care much about Greek drama or misadventures in early Britain." He picked up a cup of coffee and took a swallow. "She's probably gotten a lot more suggestions than she asked for."

"Do you know what else she's getting?"

"I've no idea. She's keeping it close. When this first started, she asked me to say nothing about the recommendations. I should have mentioned that to you. You haven't told anyone, have you?"

"No."

"They're going to release the titles in a couple of days. Probably when they present them to the Ulakans."

"Chad, do you have any feelings about what else we should be giving them? Other than Dickens and the other two?"

"There are just too many substantial books, Chase. I don't know how you narrow it down to a couple dozen. By the way, have you been watching Andy Prescott?" The late-night comedian.

"No."

"He's been having fun making recommendations. George Carver, for a start." Carver is a classic cynic who thinks that we're all idiots, and he has lots of stories to support it. "And Wyman Harper. That, of course, was *The Art of the Con Job*. Actually, every one of the late-night comics is recommending books."

"Have you heard yet whether you will get to say hello to them?" I asked

"To the aliens? Unfortunately not. It's a pity. I'd enjoy doing it. But I don't think it will happen. I could use the PR."

"Have they made the copies yet? Of the books for the aliens?"

"Don't know. But I'd be surprised if that's not all taken care of and the books aren't already on their way to Skydeck."

"So all that's left for you is to get to meet Ollie and Neo. Have you asked Sally about it? She could probably arrange it."

"Chase, I'd bet everybody she invited to contribute titles is trying to get her to give them a chance to say hello to the aliens. I'd just as soon not do that."

"It's not going to happen unless you make a move."

"Just let it go, Chase, okay?"

"Have we any idea why we haven't seen any males? They don't murder their husbands, do they?"

"Oh, come on, Chase. Keep it serious."

"Sorry. I just couldn't pass on it. Do you know anything more about them?"

"Not really. Despite their appearance, they seem to be easy to get along with."

"You haven't gotten access yet to any of *their* books, have you?"

"Not yet. Don't know anything other than what's been on HV."

"Sounds like good business ahead for booksellers."

"I hope so." He was seated in an armchair, his feet propped on a stool. "They certainly have the language down. At least the AI does. Sally thinks they discovered us years ago, probably another vehicle. Maybe another generation. And they went home and did some extensive prepping."

"It's been quite an experience."

"It has, Chase."

"I have one more question. You probably can't help with this one."

"What is it?"

"I have a list of the titles. Of *their* books."

"Yes?"

"What's a 'grundi'?"

He had no idea. Eventually I found out that it was a giant predator that had lived on Ulaka for millions of years until it went extinct during an ice age.

)）◕(（

That afternoon we learned that the media had gotten hold of some of the alien books. Several of the shows brought on people who'd had a chance to look through them so they could talk about their contents. Sharik Sunset turned up on The Ellen Klein Show. Ellen explained that Sharik was another world in the same system as Ulaka. It was lifeless. But long before the Ulakans developed the capability to visit Sharik, they had been fascinated by that world. It had terrestrial conditions, oceans, continents, blue skies, and warm weather. They always assumed it was inhabited and they created a number of fictional narratives, usually about invasions. One of the earliest was Sharik Sunset, in which the world's inhabitants invade Ulaka and are on the verge of killing everyone before being taken out by the difference in gravity, which introduced severe heart problems.

Once More unto the Breach was a strictly military history from ancient times. Ollie and Neo both claimed they knew nothing of Shakespeare.

Today had gotten a copy of *Chaela, Where Are You?* Chaela had apparently been an actual person, a young female, who'd gone out on a camping trip with several friends, wandered into a forest, and was never seen nor heard from again. She became a classic representative of the dangers presented by the natural world, and why those of early years should not venture away alone.

The third reader showed up on *Truthhunt*. She'd gotten a copy of *Moons over Korkorum*. Korkorum, we learned, was an island on which visitors who met inevitably fell in love. The book was a description of the power of romantic activities and environment and how easily they blinded us and led to unfortunate decisions.

Sally, Polgar, and the Ulakans were on full display on HV, mostly talking about a cooperative future. I had a hard time imagining people vacationing on Ulaka. We also got to see, from a book haven in Andiquar, enthusiastic buyers crowding the aisles to pick up copies of the alien volumes. They only had five titles available at that point, and they obviously weren't going to last long. One of the Corbin bookstores had a few copies of the books in their original Ulakan format. It didn't seem likely anybody would ever be able to read them, but it apparently didn't matter. The media were there when the store opened, and the shelves quickly emptied. The copies on display all had the same binding, dark blue covers with gold lettering.

"Pity," said Alex.

"What's the problem?"

"They'd be worth a ton to collectors if the number of copies had been limited."

"But it's not about making money."

"I'm not talking about money. I'm talking about value. I know you're going to say that's a fine point, but how would you feel about your books being made available to everybody strictly for the cost of manufacture?"

Three titles not mentioned earlier turned up a day or so later. Apparently the Ulakans had brought some other books with them and either forgot about them or decided to leave them out of the package and then changed their minds. Whatever the case, there were now nineteen volumes in both languages. One was titled *The Light's Not Going Anywhere*. Was it a book about astrophysics? Or about theology? It turned out to be astrophysics. There was also *Skies on Fire*. That one, oddly, was a collection of plays. And *Cosmic Content and Other Rides into the Night*, an anthology of science fiction stories about time travel, what happens when someone invents a method of extending people's lives indefinitely, and whether there's any such thing as being *too* intelligent.

Ollie and Neo offered no comments about the new books, saying only that readers should enjoy finding out on their own. "And yes," Neo added, "we were looking though the books we'd brought and just forgot to include them in the packaging."

)) ● ((

Finally we saw the other Ulakans. They showed up for a tour of Skydeck with Sally, two of the DPSAR officials, and a couple of guards. The networks covered it. Obviously there'd been some planning. The crowds that usually filled the concourse were missing. All the places they visited were empty, except for the people who ran the shops and entertainment locations. The conversation was ongoing, and there was a lot of laughter. Everyone was in a good mood.

We learned during the course of the tour that three of the aliens were males, all smaller than the females. The Ulakans showed considerable interest in souvenirs, several of which the station guys purchased for them. They played games with enthusiasm in the entertainment centers, collected some books and magazines, and even stopped to look at some of the clothing stores, as if they didn't have enough clothes already. The aspect of it that was most striking was that they bought several jerseys with *Skydeck* logos. One of the males held a jersey against his chest. Two sleeves, four arms. They all got a good laugh, although it was clear the humans weren't sure they should join in.

)) ● ((

Chad stopped by the country house a day or so later. He was happy because both his suggestions had been picked up and translated, and were to be passed on to the Ulakans that day. I congratulated him. "Is Sally still on Skydeck?" I asked.

"Yes. They tried doing lunch with Ollie and his friends. Took them to a restaurant that was kept clear for them. They didn't allow the media in because nobody was sure how it would turn out. They'd talked with Ollie and Neo about food and tried to follow the Ulakans' suggestions. But I guess the meal didn't work out, and in the end they went back on board their ship and ate there. But other than that, everything's gone pretty well. Their books have arrived—the ones they're getting from us—so I guess they'll be leaving soon."

"What do they talk about, Chad? Do you know?"

"In general, how happy both sides are to have found another intelligent species."

I heard Alex coming down the stairs. Moments later he wandered into the office. "Hello, Chad," he said. "I hear you've become part of the book exchange."

"Yes, it's been fun. I'm wondering where I can get some more alien books."

"It must have felt pretty good to be involved in the process. Chase tells me they picked up both your recommendations."

"Yes. I was surprised. I didn't think Sally would go with either of them."

"Why's that?"

"The aliens indicated they wanted history and philosophy. In the end she got overwhelmed with suggestions that she thought were a bit heavy."

"And you gave her Dickens and Greek comedy."

"Well, yes. Greek theater, really. Though there was some comedy."

"Well done."

Chad smiled. "It's always good to make a contribution to a serious cause."

"I have to admit," Alex continued, "I was hoping you'd pick one of Chase's books."

His face wrinkled. "They want classics, Alex. Maybe in a hundred years we could try one."

"I'm kidding. So what's happening up there? On Skydeck?"

"Not much. Probably getting ready to leave."

"Do we know yet where they're from? Where Ulaka is?"

"I don't think so. I don't know if Ollie and Neo are even able to explain where it is. They'll probably have to get the AIs talking to one another."

"Aren't they going to come down here? The aliens? Spend a couple of days with us?"

"I don't know, Alex. Probably not. Mostly they're just hanging around up there talking and listening to music."

"They like music?"

"Yes."

"What kind?"

"Sally tells me they love symphonies. Classical stuff."

"That's interesting. Do they have music of their own?"

"I don't know."

"What else do they do?"

"They went on a tour of Skydeck."

"I saw that."

"And they like chess."

"They know about chess?"

"They do now. Doc taught two of them how to play." Doc was the Skydeck AI. "They all went into the lobby at the Starlight Hotel. DPSAR provided some chess sets, and a couple of Sally's people sat down with them to help get them started. Sally tells me they picked up the game pretty quickly. We gave them the sets. A few people came into the hotel and watched from a distance. Eventually they got closer, and in the end it looked as if everyone was having a good time."

"I guess," Alex said, "they're not as scary as the Mutes."

"They don't read minds," I said.

Alex smiled. "As far as we know."

The media coverage continued. And it wasn't all favorable. On *Newsdesk*, Walton Camry interviewed Senator Ivan Haskin. Haskin wore a thin mustache and had an expression that always reminded me of bad guys in the movies. "How can we be so dumb?" he asked Camry. "They come here with some books and we assume they're friendly and harmless despite what they look like. I'll tell you what I think. Could it be a coincidence that right after we find aliens on — what was it? — Korella Six or something, aliens show up here? I'd bet these are the guys who were on Korella. They followed us home. And why are we getting all the crazy talk about books? They're planning on taking us down. And right now they're trying to find out whether we can defend ourselves. There's a famous story out of the early days of the Space Age about aliens who arrive with a menu that includes humans for dinner."

"You think that's what's going on, Senator?"

"It seems more likely than getting a sudden visit from another group of aliens who all seem to be bookstore owners."

Blanche McMurtrie, a prize-winning journalist for *The Scientific American*, got access to the alien vessel and interviewed a couple of the males. Ollie and Neo, they explained, were in charge of the mission. Were the females always in charge? Of course not, they said. The passenger cabin had wide seats to accommodate the extra pairs of arms. Otherwise it didn't look much different from the cabins we had in our larger vehicles. They surprised her by providing some chocolate chip cookies for her. She tasted one and told her audience they were delicious. The Ulakans confessed they'd gotten them from the hotel.

A psychologist commented afterward that we were learning a good deal about the aliens. About the interests we shared with them. They needed sleep. They had a concern for privacy. They liked games. And of course they read the same kinds of books we did. He stopped to wonder what other kinds of books were possible. There was also the passenger cabin, a place where they could all get together. Mutes normally had only private cabins on their vehicles or in their living quarters. "They don't look much like us," he said, "but otherwise we seem to have a great deal in common."

)) @ ((

We were losing track of the *Harbinger* mission. The media were concentrating on which books the Ulakans were receiving and what kind of information we were gathering from the books they'd delivered. At first there'd been an assumption that they had come with a list of preferred titles. But they claimed they had no knowledge of what kind of books even existed in our culture. We saw a brief interview with another Ulakan, Krondo Laria, who was identified as the ship's librarian. They were relatively small, but we never learned whether they were a male. In any case, Krondo said that they had assumed any intelligent civilization would have books concerning what mattered in life, what our existence was really about, where the universe came from, and so on. They assumed that social interaction, e.g., fiction and theater, would also be an essential part of any advanced culture. Afterward, sales of the books we'd given the aliens rose precipitously.

The Ulakans remained at the top of the news. Their books led to endless discussions: they believed in divine purpose, they'd fought wars among themselves, they had democratic systems of government, and they too were appalled at the emptiness of the universe.

And finally it was time for them to go.

Chad joined me at the country house on that final evening. Alex was with us in my office. "Sally tells me," Chad said, "that they are saying they'll stay in touch. She says they tried last night to explain where they came from. She thinks they don't really know themselves. That only the AI actually knows where the home world is. Or maybe they don't want to reveal the location."

"So where is it?" I asked Chad. "Did we ever find out?"

"I don't know. Somewhere over the rainbow."

Seven Ulakans said goodbye at a short ceremony in the Starlight lobby. People posed with them for pictures and wished them luck and an enjoyable voyage. They said that if it was okay with us, they would come back. A couple of the spectators told them to go home and stay there. That led to some pushing and shoving. The protesters were escorted outside. A few minutes later the aliens got out of their seats to a round of applause. Then they were gone.

5

Books are vehicles that transport us into worlds far beyond the reach of interstellars.

—**Vicki Greene,** ***Wish You Were Here,*** **1421**

Two days later Sally showed up at the country house with three alien books that Alex had asked for. Two of them, *Faith: Why Belief Still Matters* and *Foundations of Civilization,* had sold out so quickly he'd been unable to get copies locally. The other one, *Cosmic Content and Other Rides into the Night,* edited by Los Quendo, had been one of the titles that had shown up belatedly. "Los Quendo is still active," said Alex. "Or *she* is. I'm not sure about the gender."

"She's a woman," said Sally, handing him a portfolio. "This is the complete inventory, in case you'd like to pick up any of the others. We've tried to get a description of contents for each of them."

We were in the conference room. "Which have you read?" Alex asked her.

"Parts of several. Only completed one so far. *Facing Reality*." She was looking at something far away. "It's about handling failure and death. They really aren't much different from us. And I'm pretty sure they don't kill their males."

"How long is their life span?" Alex asked.

"We haven't figured out the numbers yet."

"You only read one?" I said.

"It's all I've had time for." She smiled. "I've started *Foundations of Civilization*. I'm only a few pages in, but I've already picked up something interesting. They don't think democratic governments are a good idea."

"Why not?"

"Because voters are too easily won over by corrupt politicians. In other words, they're dumb. The author hasn't said that straight out, but that's obviously what she's thinking."

"So how do they manage it? Put in a dictator? Somebody told me they have democracies."

"They do. But they don't work as well as a philosocracy."

"A what?"

Sally took a breath. "We don't have a word that fits the system. They install an AI, one programmed by a team of philosophers and scientists. The AI runs the government. Apparently it's a pretty good system." She asked whether either of us had read any of the plays.

I hadn't.

"One," said Alex. "*Kiyo*. A comedy by somebody. I've forgotten his name. It was written several thousand years ago."

"Did you enjoy it?" she asked.

"It was hysterical. I wouldn't have believed someone could be so funny writing that long ago, let alone a member of an alien race. I'll be shocked if we aren't running his plays live before the end of the year."

"It's that good?" said Sally.

"Oh, yes."

She was consulting her notes. "Zon Ockle. He's a male. He was writing at a time when they didn't think males could do anything that was seriously creative. Other than sex."

"Well," I said, "I guess you expect quality in something you're handing over to another civilization."

Alex put the play collection on the table. The title was *Skies on Fire*. I glanced down at it. "I originally thought it was a physics book."

"Or a bad science fiction novel," said Alex. He was concentrating on Sally. "Is there something else?"

A shadow crossed her face. "No," she said. "Why do you ask?"

"You look as if something's wrong."

"No. It's no big deal."

"What isn't?"

She was looking at the doorway. Biting her lower lip. "This is just an opinion. And I don't want anyone quoting me."

"That's okay. Is there something we don't know about these guys that we should?"

"I think they're smarter than we are."

"What? Because of Zon Ockle?"

"No. Of course not."

"Then what?"

"You know Doc, the Skydeck AI, taught Neo how to play chess."

"And—?"

"It took a while, but lately Doc can't win a game."

"You're kidding," I said.

She shook her head. "No."

"Well," said Alex, "has Doc been turned up to full throttle?"

"As far as I know."

"Okay. So we have an alien who's spent her life reading and it turns out she's unusually smart."

"It's not just Neo. They've all picked up the game." She was smiling like someone caught telling a dumb joke. "The AI here is Jacob, right?"

"Yes."

"Does he play chess?"

"Yes."

"Anybody ever beaten him?"

According to Sally, the Ulakans had shown interest in coming down to Andiquar, or possibly another city, if that was the recommendation of the authorities. But there was concern about their safety on the ground. There had been some animosity toward them, but it wasn't widespread. Nevertheless, one nitwit with a blaster could do a lot of damage. The problem led to a revival of the old debate about citizens' rights to own hyperweapons. We could have provided security, but the aliens wanted to visit public places, meet people, and generally enjoy public attention. There was no way we could take the risk. Consequently, it never happened.

I couldn't resist asking whether anyone had inquired of the Ulakans about the question that had haunted everybody. "No," she said. "We never went near it."

We exchanged a few messages with them after they were gone. But we still have no idea whether they spin webs.

The *Harbinger* team had no knowledge of the Ulakans. There hadn't been time for our HV transmissions to catch up with them. The program we watched on the day the Ulakans left depicted the *Harbinger* team getting close to the target star. But almost two weeks had passed since that signal had left the ship. They might have made contact, shaken hands, thrown a party with the aliens, and been on their way back.

That two-week-old program was set in the passenger cabin, where Lester Wilkinson talked with Vince Reddington about what lay ahead. They were still submerged. Lester was asking Vince how it could have happened that they were able to orbit the target world for a couple of days and see only one village. "Were you even looking?"

"Of course we were. We had the scopes locked in. There were no lights anywhere. And nothing out of the ordinary showed up in the sunlight."

"You must have wondered how that could be. A world with one village?"

"Well, sure, Lester. Nobody had any explanation for it."

"What did *you* think, Vince?"

"I just assumed we were missing them. That the villages turned out the lights when it got dark."

"Does that make any sense to you?"

"They're aliens," he said. "Who knows how they think?"

Henry Cassell signaled that he wanted to speak. "Vince is right," he said. "We need to just be patient. We should be able to figure out what's going on this time."

Vince nodded. "The village was on the edge of a lake, sur-rounded by forest. If it's really a world with primitives, my guess would be that's exactly the kind of place where they'd want to settle. They'd be less visible than out on a plain somewhere. And they'd probably get more life support from the woods. And there have to be other places. One village on a planet just doesn't work."

Wilkinson looked as if he was in full agreement. "Is that why you signed on to come back, Vince? To find the other towns? I mean, this is a long ride."

"Sure. I was never looking forward to another couple months submerged in Armstrong space. But yes. It's a primitive culture, but they're here. Someone is."

"You could have waited for the *Harbinger* to come back. Get the answers then."

"Henry needed a pilot. Either me or Robbi Jo."

Henry smiled. "I wanted something better than a set of direc-tions. One village on a planet the size of Rimway. With electrical power. You can't manage that if you're completely alone. They are probably a colony. From somewhere else."

"Another world?"

"Yes." He grinned at Vince. "That's why we needed you. Somebody who knew where the damned place was. If it's really the only settlement on the planet, we could spend a lot of time wandering around."

"I hate to bring this up," said Vince, "but there's a good chance we won't be able to find out what's going on unless we go down and talk to them. Whatever, we'll get it settled." An exchange of glances suggested that he and Henry had already discussed and probably failed to agree on whether they would put people on the ground.

I asked Alex if it was true that primitives generally hid their villages among trees.

"I've no idea, Chase. I've never really thought about it." He looked at the time and sighed. "These programs are a waste of time. We should stay clear of them until they get where they're going."

The network apparently agreed. They canceled all the *Harbinger* shows the following day, although they informed us that the *Harbinger* was expected to return to normal space during the approaching weekend. They promised to deliver complete coverage.

))●((

We knew they'd probably make their transition from Armstrong space and still arrive at a substantial distance from Korella IV. But of course they had a telescope, so even though it would probably be a few more days before they reached the planet, they should still be able to get a decent look at it. We'd already seen pictures, of course, so we knew it was a routine terrestrial world. It had a couple of big oceans, lots of mountain chains, large green forests, and wide plains filled with a variety of animals.

))●((

The network canceled everything connected with the *Harbinger* over the next two days, until the ship was ready to surface. That program was titled "Arrival."

Wilkinson opened the show by informing us that they'd received a shock. "We got a transmission earlier today from home reporting that aliens have arrived at Skydeck. With books. And speaking *Standard*. Magnificent." He was seated on the bridge with Vince. "I guess we should all have stayed home. But welcome back to the *Harbinger*. We're about to surface." He looked over at the pilot, who signaled they were ready to go.

Vince went through the routine of notifying everyone on board that they were returning to normal space in three minutes. They'd have known about it earlier, of course, but the threeminute warning provided some suspense.

Everybody checked in, and eventually they went to a thirtysecond countdown. Tension mounted. Vince took the countdown through the last few seconds: "Three, two, one, zero." The camera was pointed at the wraparound and the absolute blackness outside.

Then it was gone and the sky was full of stars. We heard some commotion in the passenger cabin, people shouting, "Yay!" and someone pounding on the arm of a chair. It took a while, but the AI was eventually able to point out a star, or what appeared to be one, and explain they were looking at Korella IV. That they could get that close made it obvious they'd come out of Armstrong space earlier, located the planet, and submerged again, and gave us some excitement surfacing so close to the target.

)‍)‍❁‍(‍(

It had a moon. It was small and gray, with obviously no atmosphere. No sign of any structures. They were approaching the planet on its sunlit side. "Two days to orbit," said the AI. Korella IV was green, covered with forests separated by mountain ranges and occasional prairies. Its moon drifted through the sky.

"Vince," said Wilkinson, "you know where this place is, right? The village?"

"Yes, Lester. It'll be easy to find."

"Great." He looked out at his audience. "We'll be back tomorrow with another report. Stay with us. You'll want to be there when we connect with the aliens. This has been *The* Harbinger *Show*."

They were back a day later. Korella IV had of course increased in size. Other than that, nothing had changed. The only memorable moment about the broadcast was a comment by Wilkinson: "Other than the green skin, the villagers have a fairly close resemblance to us. I have to say I'm glad they don't look anything like those spiders."

I saw Alex a few minutes later. He hadn't been watching, and when I mentioned the remark, he rolled his eyes. "I hope Ollie and Neo didn't pick up the transmission."

))●((

I quit early and wandered out to Chad's bookstore. It was about four o'clock when I got there, usually a quiet time for sales, but the place was full of customers. He told me it had been like that all day. Business was still cranking along at a high rate. Customers literally filled the store. Chad was gloriously happy. "They aren't just buying the alien books," he said. "They're picking up other stuff as well, especially the books that were made available to them. To the aliens. The only ancient-world material we used to sell was a few copies of Greek plays to people working on degrees. Now we're selling *Beowulf*, *The Iliad*, *The Divine Comedy*, and *On the Road*. There was a woman in here today trying to find something by Sophocles. Anything by Sophocles. Chase, we've never experienced anything like this."

"Were you able to help her? With Sophocles?"

"Not much. The only one of his plays that's survived is *Electra*. That's in Kramer's book, one of the ones we gave the Ulakans. She already has that."

"That's a pity," I said. "How many plays did Sophocles write?"

"More than a hundred." Chad closed his eyes. "Most of them were lost long before we got the printing press. You and Alex want to give us a serious breakthrough: find one of them."

"We'd need a time machine."

"I wish somebody would invent one." He almost got teary. "People have been telling me for the last few days how they've started reading Kramer's book. They love it." He stopped to answer a customer's question about Dickens, and then smiled. "You and Alex are in the right business. There's a lot of stuff in the past that we should have held on to. It's unfortunate that so much of it just doesn't exist anymore."

I hesitated. Then: "Technically, we have a time machine."

He looked at me and sighed. He was in no mood for kidding.

"If Henry Cassell had a giant telescope on the *Harbinger* and he turned it on us, what would he see?"

Chad needed a moment to think about it. "I get it," he said. "They're about nine hundred light-years out, so they'd see us during the Metropolitan Age. Whatever was going on here nine hundred years ago."

"Okay. Now take them farther away. Maybe a third of the way out toward the center of the Milky Way."

"That would be, what, about twelve thousand light-years?" He smiled. "If they timed it right, they'd be able to watch *Oedipus the King* playing onstage in Athens." One of the lost plays. Credited as Sophocles's masterpiece. "But they'd need a pretty big scope."

We heard nothing more from the *Harbinger* until close to midnight, when Carmen's voice woke me up. "You there, Chase?"

"I think so."

"*Announcement coming.*" She activated the HV. One of the Hochman anchors, Grey Whitlock, was seated in a studio. Carmen started the program.

Whitlock was frowning in his standard majestic manner, which removed any question whether the mission had arrived at a critical moment. "We've received an announcement from the *Harbinger*. They've made contact. No details have been provided yet, but we'll be joining them in a few minutes."

The news got me excited until we joined the interstellar and it became clear they hadn't actually connected with anyone. In fact, according to Wilkinson, they were "entering" orbit, although that was hours away. Whitlock apparently didn't understand the meaning of "contact."

I didn't expect to stay with them long. It would take a while to get to the site where the village had been. It was located on the only continent that reached almost from the south pole to the north, falling short by only a few hundred kilometers. It was on the east coast, about two hundred kilometers above the equator, near a small lake about the same distance from the ocean. It would still be a while before they arrived. I was thinking about turning it back over to Carmen but decided instead to call Alex. "You watching?" I asked. There was no visual exchange, since he was probably in pajamas too.

"Yes," he said.

A couple of the network commentators were talking about how it was the second time this month that we were making history. "Who'd have believed it?" Alex said. "I wonder if it might really turn out to be the Ulakans."

"What makes you say that?" I asked.

"It's just too much of a coincidence. I don't know. Maybe I'm wrong. But there's a decent chance they followed the *Columbia* mission. I know the aliens don't resemble each other. But who knows? Maybe they were looking for a way to have fun with us. They might be the explanation for a village with electric power on a world where there's nothing else."

"Alex," I said, "your imagination's running away with you."

We didn't hear any more through the early morning, other than that the *Harbinger* was still entering orbit. I was enjoying brunch with Chad in Ellie's Café. He was describing how popular Dickens had become since the alien visit. It was not only *The Old Curiosity Shop*, but everything else he'd written as well. With the problem of course that only two other books, *David Copperfield* and *Barnaby Rudge*, still existed. Even Ebenezer Scrooge had been lost, although everybody knew who he was. His name had become part of the language. Chad had been trying to persuade me to write a novel in which an archeologist "like Alex" is closing in on a copy of A Christmas Carol.

"And of course," he added, "it should be in the hands of deranged aliens."

The monitors came to life. Wilkinson was sitting up front on the bridge of the *Harbinger*. We had a view through the wraparound of the planet. "Do you know where we are, Vince?" Wilkinson asked.

"Yeah. We're close."

"Really?"

The globe below was mostly ocean. A coastline lay on the right. "We're headed south," Vince said. "We'll cross the polar region in about ten minutes and keep going. That'll take us north. We should be at the village in about a half hour." Vince bent over the control board and pressed his fingertips against his earbuds. "That's interesting."

"What?" asked Wilkinson. "You hearing something?"

Vince ignored the question and spoke into the mike: "Henry, you there?"

"Sure." Henry's voice sounded interested. "You got something?"

"Radio signal."

There was some commotion. Then the camera swung around and we watched Henry coming onto the bridge. "Where's it from?"

There was a momentary silence. Then Yara said, "*I'm not sure yet.*" She was the AI.

Wilkinson surrendered the right-hand seat to Henry. "So I guess that settles the electricity issue."

"There never was an issue," said Vince.

"Yara," said Henry, "you getting a location?"

"*Not yet.*"

Vince shook his head. "We'll need to give it a little time, Henry."

"*I can tell you,*" said the AI, "*the signal is not coming from the ground.*"

"You reading a spacecraft out there somewhere?" Vince asked.

"*Don't know. Something.*"

Henry put on a pair of earbuds and both men sat, heads bent, listening. "It's a repetitive signal."

We heard Wilkinson's voice. "The same signal, over and over?"

"Yes."

"What's the point of that?"

Vince was looking happy. "To get attention," he said.

Yara again: *It's probably coming from a satellite.*

"That's a surprise," said Henry. "Do we know where it is yet?"

"In orbit," Vince said. "Where else would it be?"

"I mean, can we get close to it? Get a good look at it?"

"Of course."

"Let's talk to it," said Wilkinson.

Vince passed the question to Henry. "Do it," he said.

They waited a minute or two. Then Yara said, *"Getting no response."*

"Okay," said Henry, "let's do what we have to. Go find it."

"If you want," Vince said. "But keep in mind it could be a manned station."

Somebody—it sounded like Sam's voice—said, "That's why we're here, isn't it? To talk to these people?"

"Not officially." Henry sounded annoyed. "We have to do what we can to figure out what happened here."

That could require some time. Chad said he had to get back to work. We both did. I rode the skimmer back to the country house. It was likely to be nothing more than an automated satellite. But of course even that was going to be a big deal. Shortly after I arrived and walked back in through the front door, Jacob informed me that was what they'd found.

The satellite appeared as I entered my office. It was drifting over near one of the windows of the *Harbinger*, shaped like a cube with rounded edges. A couple of solar panels were inserted on almost opposite sides. And an antenna.

Alex and Gabe were both out of the building.

))●((

So they had a satellite. Jennifer mentioned that at least now we could be certain that they weren't simply a group of lonely primitives. "Next," Wilkinson said, "we'll go drop in at the village."

They kept the camera focused on the view from the wraparound so the audience shared the sense of riding along. We saw a few animals wandering across wide fields. And an occasional flock of birds. A wide lake slipped into view directly ahead. An animal with four legs and a huge set of antlers was standing with two offspring, watching over them while they drank. "See anything you recognize?" asked Wilkinson.

"Not yet. We're still well south of it."

"How does it feel, Vince, being back here again? I suspect you never thought this would happen." Wilkinson was struggling to make conversation. Unlike the others on board, he never forgot when they were in broadcast mode.

The sun set well before they reached the equator. The moon was out of the sky, but there were plenty of stars. The ocean lay just off to starboard. The village would be easy to find. Even if there were no lights.

Vince was leaning forward to study the ground ahead. "I think we missed it," he said. "That's the lake."

"You sure?" asked Henry.

"Yes. No question."

"So let's turn around."

They had, of course, dropped out of orbit and decelerated. Nevertheless, turning around took some time. When they got back to the south side of the lake, there didn't seem to be anything on the ground other than trees, fields, and a few low hills.

"Hold on." Vince brought up an image on the monitor. It was the picture of the village that the *Columbia* had sent home. "Look." He pointed at the edge of the forest. They were trying to get the camera on it, but all we could see was his finger tapping on the screen. Where the edge of the forest was. "Damn. I knew that was the same lake."

Wilkinson was shaking his head. "What are you talking about, Vince?"

"You see this tree? The one that's down?" Yes, one of them was on the ground.

"It *does* look like the same one," said Henry. "But if it is, where's the village?"

Vince continued to decelerate. He took the ship to starboard and went into a long turn, crossing the lake and angling back in.

"This isn't it." Autumn Ulbrich's voice came from behind them. Probably she was standing in the doorway to the passenger cabin. "We must have missed it."

"This can't be right," said Henry. "There's no town down there anywhere."

Vince was shaking his head. "This is where it was. The coordinates are correct and we all noted the landmarks. It's the same lake. No question."

"I don't believe this." Autumn sounded frustrated.

Vince growled. "Damn it. Look at that." There was a broken ridge on top of one of the group of hills along the edge of the lake. It looked the same as one in the picture. The picture and the view from the *Harbinger* were identical. Except for the village.

Vince glared down at the controls. "What the hell happened to it? This makes no sense."

The area where the village had been was now only open grassland.

"Maybe the town was a hologram," said someone in the passenger cabin.

They were getting a lot of noise back there. The camera switched to Henry, who had gotten out of his seat but was still looking through the wraparound. Then he shrugged and sat back down. "Everybody needs to relax," he said, which was advice *he* should have taken.

"I don't understand this," said Vince. "This is ridiculous."

"Look, this can't possibly be the same location. Towns don't just go away."

"This is *it*," said Vince. "It *has* to be."

Henry was shaking his head. "Not possible."

"I know it's hard to believe, but—"

"Vince, something's wrong." Henry needed a minute to catch his breath. Then: "Let's do a search of the area. Maybe there's another section somewhere that looks like this."

Vince insisted it would be a waste of time. The village was gone. But Henry wasn't willing to give up. Nor was anyone else. Vince was obviously confused. He sat back in his chair and asked Henry where he wanted to go.

"North," Henry said. "Go north up the coastline."

))●((

The network broke in a few minutes later and announced that they would continue to follow the effort and if anything happened, the broadcast would go live again. There was no way to inform Wilkinson, of course, but he was probably aware they would stay with him, even if they didn't keep the broadcast live. Big Town would run at its regular time on Hochman Alt. Then two consultants and an anchor came on to discuss what had happened—or, as the reality was, what had not happened. Their conclusion was that they had no explanation. The *Harbinger* was supposed to have the precise location of the village, but villages don't move. Best they could come up with: "Planets are big, and the only explanation is that there are two similar areas near the ocean."

I went to dinner with Gabe. He thought that whatever was going on out there, the satellite would be a central connection. We finished and said goodbye to each other. He was going back to the country house, while I headed home. I stayed tuned in. I'm pretty sure he did as well.

I was descending into the parking area at my cabin when the network took us back to the *Harbinger*. Henry was asking whether it was possible they'd chosen the wrong continent. Vince and Autumn both maintained that was not possible. "We are where we're supposed to be," said Autumn. "They've moved the village. Somehow." Finally they started talking about taking the lander down.

Henry had apparently conceded that they'd have to do that. Vince, he said, would remain on the *Harbinger*. Sam would stay with him. Chuck, Autumn, Jennifer, and Hal would accompany Henry in the lander. And of course Wilkinson.

While all that was going on, I touched down, climbed out of the skimmer, went into the cabin, turned on the HV, and settled onto my sofa. Finally, while Henry and his team pulled their pressure suits out of cabinets, Gabe called to ask if I was still watching.

"Who's Hal?" he asked. "I don't recall anybody with that name on the research team."

"I've no idea, Gabe." It was the first time I'd heard the name.

Yara, the AI, informed the team that they didn't need pressure suits. They picked up some weapons and pushed them into their belts. When everybody was ready, they got into the lander. I saw Henry and Wilkinson, Jennifer, Chuck, and Autumn. Nobody else. Then our perspective changed. We were looking at the hull of the *Harbinger*, where we were able to watch the cargo door open. The lander was lifted outside on a cradle. They started the motor, and the vehicle was released.

Then we were back inside the lander, where Henry was in the pilot's seat. "I think I know who Hal is," Gabe said.

"Okay?"

He laughed. "Wilkinson's cameraman."

How could I have been so dumb? We watched them descend toward the lake. Nobody in the lander was saying much. They were trying to hide their disappointment over the lost village. I suspect Wilkinson had reminded them that they were probably broadcasting all over the Confederacy, so they needed to maintain a decent level of enthusiasm.

Except for Autumn, they suspected they'd simply arrived at the wrong place, despite the similarity of the pictures. As Chuck put it, "Sure, they could have taken off and gotten out of here for some reason. But how could they have moved the houses? And some of those buildings, the school and the courthouse and the church, or whatever they were, would have been something of a challenge." As they got closer to the ground, the reality of the emptiness seemed to become even more compelling. Nobody was there.

They hid the fact that Yara, the AI, was piloting the lander. They never actually *said* that Henry had the controls, but it looked as if he did. In any case, they came down and landed on open ground in the middle of where Vince maintained the village had been. They had plenty of starlight.

They climbed out, and everybody took a breath and looked around. "Smells like the woods back home," said Autumn.

I almost picked up the scent of roses, but I guess that was my imagination. Or maybe my open windows. They looked at the lake and at the ground. It was covered with grass.

They walked in circles for a while. Jennifer commented that they should have brought a couple of shovels. They used their boots to break into the ground but found nothing. "I think," Jennifer continued, "that there used to be a road through here." Maybe. It was hard to make out. Wilkinson thought he saw a connecting road, but it was just an area where the grass was thin or completely missing. "So where does this leave us?" asked Sam, from the *Harbinger*.

"There *was* something here," said Jennifer.

Henry was frowning. "What the hell happened?"

Autumn and Chuck were over near the edge of the trees. They were walking casually when they both yelled. "Look! Over there!"

They picked up a carryall bag with straps. A backpack. "*Somebody's* been here," said Chuck.

Henry and Autumn got into a debate about what the backpack meant. It looked like a good fit for a human. Maybe somebody from the *Columbia* had landed.

"No," said Vince, speaking from the ship. "That never happened."

There was nothing in the bag other than a crumpled piece of stationery. They held it up to the camera. There was something written in symbols unlike anything I'd seen before. "Show it to Yara," Henry said.

The AI replied that she could make nothing of it. The broadcast continued for another half hour while Korella's sun moved toward the western horizon. Henry and his team wandered around on the ground, looking for whatever else might be there. Nobody found anything. Eventually, as the sky grew dark, they returned to the lander and started back for the *Harbinger*. The network shut the broadcast down again.

I was in bed, halfway through the night, when Carmen woke me. "*There's something odd going on,*" she said.

"What's that?"

"Let me replay it for you."

They were all back in the *Harbinger*. Autumn was talking: "I know this sounds bizarre, but the place felt creepy."

"What do you mean?" Wilkinson asked.

"The whole time we were down there, I felt like something was watching us."

"That would have been Vince and Sam," said Jennifer.

I could hear Chuck breathing. "Autumn's got something," he said. "I felt it too."

Frustration wrinkled Henry's features. "Neither of you said anything while we were there."

"I thought it was my imagination. I was waiting for somebody else to react to it. Until Autumn did, I was ready to write it off," said Chuck.

Henry pressed an index finger against his cheek but said nothing more. Wilkinson smiled for his audience. "I can understand it," he said. "The place *is* a bit spooky."

$$) \;) \; \bullet \; (\; ($$

They spent almost a week adjusting orbits that allowed them to search for signs of inhabitants. They found nothing. And finally it was time to go home.

"Why," asked Vince, "is there a satellite here?"

"Why don't we take it back with us?" asked Jennifer.

"Yes," said Henry. "Good idea. It doesn't really seem to be doing anything. Can we fit it into the cargo bay?"

"It doesn't look very big," said Vince. "We should be able to do it. At least we wouldn't be going back completely empty-handed."

"We're entitled," said Sam, "after spending two months on this trip."

"But why?" asked Autumn. "What's the point of doing that?"

Henry delivered a tolerant smile. "We'll know that when we've had a chance to look at it."

"I don't think we should do it," said Autumn.

"She's right." Chuck looked as if he thought taking it on board was a terrible idea. "It was put there for a reason. Let's leave it alone, guys."

"The thing doesn't seem to have a propulsion system," said Sam, "so taking it on board probably wouldn't constitute a hazard."

"We sure it'll fit?" asked Henry.

"We can take it into the cargo hold. It'll be tight," said Yara. *"But yes, it will be okay."*

"Do it," said Henry.

For the next half hour I watched while they maneuvered in close, removed the lander from its cradle, which wasn't at all difficult when they shut down the artificial gravity system. Once they'd done that and cleared the area, they brought the satellite inside. It wasn't very large. When Jennifer stood behind it, we could still see her head. The panels were bigger than the lander but not by much.

The broadcast stayed live while they took the satellite apart and looked at the pieces. Eventually Henry told the viewing audience it was a significant discovery but it would need some work back home. "We'll turn it over to the engineers. Maybe they'll see something we missed."

They brought the lander back inside. "Well, Henry," Wilkinson said, "let's hope they find something."

Autumn was examining the satellite's solar panels. "I hope," she said, "we haven't created a problem for anybody."

6

The odds against our parents even meeting on a world crowded with almost four billion occupants are remote beyond reason. But given that unlikely event, the necessity for all of the genetic connections to come perfectly together forces us to recognize that our being born at all was virtually impossible. So maybe we should stop complaining about trivia.

—**Malkine Shulj,** *Faith: Why Belief Still Matters*

Delivered by Ulakans, 1436

I owned a couple of the Ulakan books. I needed some time to decide which of the others I wanted. Chad thought I'd have bought all of them, but I already owned more books than I'd be able to get to in a lifetime. When I finally made up my mind and gave the titles to Chad, he told me no charge, and that he would deliver them the following day.

I argued with him about the free books. "I almost ordered them from the Allegheny store downtown because I knew this would happen. But you'd see them at my place eventually, and that would be hard to explain. Look, if I can't pay you for them, I won't open the door when you get here."

"Then I think you should leave a couple of sandwiches outside."

We argued about it and finally settled on a compromise. I'd accept the books, and he'd let me take him to lunch during the weekend.

I ordered *Discovering Rimway*, *Why We Laugh*, *Living the Good Life*, *Empty Skies: Why We're Alone*, and *All the Time in the World*. I'd been surprised that there were no novels. Maybe they didn't do novels. When the Ulakans saw the sales numbers on their books, I suspected they might change their minds about declining any payment and be back with their versions of *The Decline and Fall*, *Marcus Aurelius*, *Seven Pillars of Wisdom*, and *Alone in a Great Wide World*.

Chad showed up the following evening at my cabin with the books. He put them on the couch and said he'd have liked to take me to Hogan's Bar & Grill, but he had a round of deliveries to make. Including a couple for Gabe. Then he pivoted and started for the door, pretending he was ready to leave before I opened anything. Chad loves to play games.

I took a quick look through the books while he paused, awaiting a reaction. In *Empty Skies* I noticed a quotation: "The surest sign of a weak mind is its ability to cling to an opinion regardless of the evidence."

"They've got that right," Chad said.

Living the Good Life opened with "the three elements essential to living well." They were "Think for yourself, respect your neighbor, and do no harm."

In the same book: "The most important decisions we make in a lifetime are choosing a mate and selecting a career. Unfortunately, the vast majority of us make these calls when we're too young to exercise good judgment."

"They sound more and more like us," I said.

He nodded. "I thought so too. It's something of a shock, coming from aliens. Especially from aliens that look the way they do. I haven't really had a chance to spend much time with them yet, Chase." He was referring to the books. "But I suspect what we're going to learn is that there are only so many ways to make a civilized society work. The species that can't figure it out probably will never get past a primitive existence."

"I wonder," I said, "if there's a species anywhere that needs three partners to produce an offspring."

"It'll never happen, love. Three to make one is too complicated. Look at the problems we have with just two." He said it with a straight face.

All the Time in the World offered a motif where our books normally place a dedication: "Enjoy the moment. Be aware of the value of time we spend with friends and family. The day will come when we would give anything to go back and relive those golden hours."

"It's possible," he said, "that there's another reason for the similarity between their literature and ours."

"And what's that?"

"We know they've been listening for a while. Maybe they just want to mislead us. Make us *think* they're gentle, decent creatures."

"Instead of?"

"Monsters."

"Chad, they have a quantum drive. They're obviously intelligent. They live in the same empty universe we do; there are probably billions of worlds out there with water and oxygen just waiting for them. Why would they want to pick a fight with another tech species?"

"I guess," he said. "Maybe it's just the way they look."

I lost myself in the Ulakan books during the next two weeks. They were gripping, hard to put down. Alex borrowed Discovering Rimway for several days. It was a detailed account of that historic mission. He was especially struck, he said, by the sheer determination of the ship's crew—it was not Ollie, Neo, and the others who had actually made the connection—and their sheer relief in finding someone else.

Meantime, Mary Everson, one of the Hochman anchors, conducted a sit-down talk with Quaid McCann. McCann looked tired and unhappy, seated in a worn terra-cotta-colored armchair. His left leg was crossed over his knee, while his jaw rested on one palm.

"It must be frustrating," Everson said. "You made one of the great discoveries ever and it's been taken away from you."

McCann frowned. "I can't entirely agree with that, Mary. The village was there. We saw it. We got pictures of it. The discovery was made not only by me, but by the research team. And even if the village never existed, there was a satellite out there. So there *were* aliens. At the moment we just can't explain any of it, but there *is* someone out there."

"Professor, I'm sure you're aware that there are a lot of people saying the whole thing's a hoax. To get more funding for DPSAR research."

"How do you explain the satellite?"

"It might have been manufactured and taken out on the *Harbinger*. Or by somebody else."

"That's ridiculous. The silliest explanation I've heard. Look, Mary, everybody who was on the *Columbia* saw the village. Vince Reddington saw it. He was on both flights. It's a long haul out to that place. Does anyone honestly think he'd have gone on the follow-up mission if he'd known it was all a lie? If you knew these people as well as I do, Vince and Sam and Jennifer and a couple of the others, you'd be aware that they would not go along with anything like that."

They sat a few seconds, staring at each other. Then Everson continued, "I can't imagine what kind of effect this must be having on you, Professor McCann. Can you tell us how you've reacted to it?"

"It's been painful. I won't deny that. But eventually the truth will come out."

"Have you any kind of explanation as to why whoever was there would have left? Could it have had to do with their sighting the *Columbia*? Did you guys do something out there that alerted them to your presence and scared them off?"

"I guess anything's possible, Mary. As far as I know, they were never aware of us. But we'll just have to wait until we get more information. The only thing I can say is that they were there. Why they left, or where they went, I have no idea."

"Is it possible the *Harbinger* just went to the wrong location?"

"I can't see how it could have. Eventually we'll figure it out.

But to answer your earlier question, Mary, yes, it hurts when my colleagues suspect there's even a possibility that we made this whole thing up. The town was there. I have no explanation for how they moved the buildings, especially the big ones. One of them was a block long. But they brought it off. And I would expect that instead of bogus accusations, we'd be talking about *how* they could have managed it."

The mail arrived as the interview ended. Two packages for Alex. He was sitting at his desk, staring out the window at sunlit trees. I don't know that I've ever seen him look so supremely satisfied. It was obvious he hadn't been watching the McCann interview. I stood in the doorway to his office with the packages, one of dental supplies and the other unmarked but apparently clothing. His monitor carried the display of the alien village, but he was concentrating on the trees. My first impression was that he'd come up with an explanation. But then his expression changed to one of annoyance. He needed a few moments to realize I was there. When he did, he waved me in.

"Good morning, Chase." He cleared a corner of the desk for the packages.

"You okay?" I asked as I set them down.

"Sure. Something wrong?"

"No. I'm good."

"Anything new on the Korella story?"

"No. Not that I know of."

"I think we got a pretty big break," Alex said.

"How's that?"

"We're looking at probably the most gripping historical mystery ever. It couldn't be better for us. At least, not after they found the backpack."

"Alex, I have no idea what you're talking about. Other than it sounds as if you're planning to go out there."

"You're reading my mind again, Chase. Yes, I'm interested in going out there. Assuming we can find out where the place is. You want to come?"

"To hunt relics? Is that why you're going?"

"It's as good a reason as I can think of."

"Chances are there won't be any more. Even if there are, we'd spend the better part of three months in the *Belle-Marie*. And the best we could hope for would be a few artifacts." His eyes narrowed. I knew that look. "You want to figure out how they moved the village."

"Well, that too."

"That too? Alex, what's this about?"

"If we can find some artifacts, they may tell us what happened to the village. If we succeed in doing that, I'll sleep well again at night. I think, though, that we won't have much luck tracking the village down. This doesn't feel like a puzzle that's going to be easy to solve. But that's okay. We're probably better off if it doesn't get solved."

"What do you mean?"

"Chase, it's all about artifacts. We're looking at one of the most mysterious events in human history. So if we can come up with some antiquities, they'll be pure gold to collectors. But probably less so if we can explain what happened to the village."

Alex is a good-looking guy, brown hair, dark brown eyes, clear features, slightly more than average height. In his longtime career managing artifacts for collectors and buyers, he's been a genius.

And he's also as good a boss as anyone could want. He doesn't hesitate to ask my opinion. He encourages me to talk even after he decides I'm on the wrong side of an issue. On this occasion, his tone suggested he wanted me to contribute something. I knew him well enough, though, to be aware his mind was made up. And he was right. If no one ever figured out what had happened to the village, any more remnants—backpacks or clocks or speakers or whatever—would be priceless. "One of the people who was on board the *Columbia*," he said, "called this morning. He had one of the ship's coffee cups. Thought it might be worth something." His eyebrows rose. "It is. Eventually, depending on what happens next, it might be worth a great deal."

"Pity," I said, "he didn't find a cup on the ground somewhere. Preferably with an alien symbol." We were in the process of selling one of those, left behind by the Ulakans ten days earlier. One of them had apparently been drinking from the cup when he came off the ship, took it into the Dellacondan Restaurant on Skydeck, and left it on a table. It had a symbol that matched one of those on the hull of the alien ship. The woman who'd salvaged it asked Alex whether it was worth keeping. It went to auction and the bidding had gone through the roof.

"I assume you didn't see the McCann interview?"

"No," he said. "How's he taking it?"

"He's rattled, but he'll survive. So when are we leaving?"

"We'll need some time. You game for it, Chase?"

I needed a minute to think about it. It didn't feel like an effort that had much chance of success. And my personal life had become especially enjoyable. I wasn't anxious to leave Chad to sit inside the *Belle-Marie* through what remained of the summer. "How optimistic are you?"

"Not very. If it were easy, we wouldn't be able to cash in on it."

"Is Gabe coming?"

"I haven't said anything to him yet. I wanted to check with you first to be sure you were on board."

Chad would have a heart attack. Still, I knew Alex thought of me as a valuable aide, and I didn't want that to change. And I trusted him. He was good at this stuff, and I suspected that if there was anything on the ground, we'd find it.

"Okay, Alex. I'll go."

"Excellent. And for the record: the goal of the mission is *strictly* to salvage artifacts. Nothing else."

"I'm not clear yet on the *real* reason we're going. What do we do if we find the villagers? We can't contact them."

"We'll figure out the details if it actually happens. In any case, there's a special circumstances provision to the no-contact mandate. I suspect we already have sufficient special circumstances. How else would you describe a first step toward understanding how they moved the village?"

)) ● ((

"I've been waiting for you." Gabe was relaxed in his recliner when we walked in. His notebook was open, lying beside him.

Alex grinned. "Am I really that predictable?"

"This one is perfectly designed for you. Nobody knows what's going on, and there's a good chance to walk away with a substantial paycheck."

"I can't imagine you'd be happy to stand by and let me do that."

"When are you planning to leave?"

"We have some work to do yet."

He looked at me. "I assume you'll be going too, Chase?"

"Yes," I said. "I wouldn't want to miss the next round."

His eyes settled on Alex. "How are you going to find out where the place is?"

"The follow-up mission has been there and got nothing. There's nobody there, so the first-contact rules don't exactly apply. It should be easy to pin down the location."

"Okay. I can see why you're interested. But I'm going to pass. This thing would just be too time-consuming."

"All right, Gabe. If you change your mind, let me know."

"Good luck with it. Nobody seems to have ever heard of Korella prior to the *Columbia* mission."

"The name was dredged up by the *Columbia*," Alex said. "Apparently on the day they discovered the village. That would have been when they realized they needed a name. McCann has an uncle Korella."

"I missed that," said Gabe.

"I checked his family tree." Alex grinned. "Of course it might be a coincidence."

"We're going to have to get somebody to talk to us," I said. "How about McCann?"

Alex shook his head. "I've already tried him. He says he has nothing to say. Cassell is due back in a couple of weeks. Maybe he'd be willing to tell us where the village is. Or somebody else on the *Harbinger*."

7

There is nothing so compelling as an event that defies explanation. Whether a scientific issue or the disappearance of a gold reserve from a sealed vault or a man murdered in a locked room high in a skyscraper, it does not matter. Everyone loves a mystery.

—**Maria Sumter, creator of fictional detective Maxwell Pelham, fifth millennium**

The media were out in force when the *Harbinger* docked. It was the middle of the afternoon in Andiquar. We'd known for a couple of days that the ship had surfaced and arrival was imminent. I watched on my office HV while they came in. The exit tube lit up. Sam, Jennifer, and Autumn were the first ones to come out onto the concourse. As a result of the constant media coverage, they seemed like longtime acquaintances. They tried to avoid the picture-taking and the questions, but in the end they gave in. The missing village had been disappointing, they said. And strange. Sam and Jennifer both threw up their hands and admitted they weren't sure they'd arrived at the right location. It looked the same as the pictures, but that was the only explanation they had that made any sense. Autumn shook her head and said she just didn't know what was going on.

I switched over to the Hochman Network, where Wilkinson was having a few final words with Henry Cassell in the passenger cabin. "So, Henry," he asked, "what happens now? Where do we go from here?"

The director's eyes closed momentarily. "We simply forget the whole thing, Lester. It's over."

"Would you encourage anyone else to go out there?"

"No. Absolutely not. It would be a total waste of time." He picked up a bag from one of the seats and looked toward the exit. "Time to go."

"Okay." Wilkinson was carrying nothing. It looked as if most of the luggage had been removed. "And thank you for allowing me to accompany you and your colleagues on this mission."

Henry responded with a smile that was almost pitiful. "I wish we could have had something more for you."

⟩⟩●⟨⟨

Alex waited a few days for the media coverage to go away. Then he called McCann. The automated response replied, "Professor McCann is not currently available. He will be informed of your call."

I was in Alex's office the following afternoon when Jacob told us McCann was on the circuit. "Put him through," Alex said. He signaled me to stay, but to retreat to the armchair beside the door, where I wouldn't be visible to McCann. Alex sat down behind his desk and McCann blinked on in the middle of the office. He was accompanied, off to one side, by an armchair, though he wasn't using it.

"Mr. Benedict?" he said.

Alex leaned forward. "Thanks for getting back to me, Professor. Please, take a seat."

"It's good to meet you, Mr. Benedict." He remained standing, ignoring Alex's invitation. "I assume you want to go hunting for artifacts?" McCann had obviously done his research.

"Yes, sir. If we can find any, they will eventually become historical treasures."

"I suspect you'll understand that I don't want anything more to do with that place."

"I'm sure what happened with the *Harbinger* has been frustrating for you, Professor. But you've made a major contribution to our knowledge of the Orion Nebula."

"And what was that, sir?"

"We know now that there *is* another civilization out there. Somewhere. And with the arrival of the Ulakans a few weeks ago, we don't feel nearly as alone as we used to."

"Yes, that was quite an experience, wasn't it? I would love to have had a chance to say hello to them. I don't suppose you had the chance to actually meet any of them?"

"No, I didn't, Professor."

"Call me Quaid."

"I'm Alex."

"Indeed. Before we go any further with this, I can see only one reason that would have prompted you to get in touch with me, Alex. And I have to tell you up front that I have no inclination to reveal the location of Korella IV. We have to maintain control over attempts at contact."

"I'm sorry to hear that, Quaid, but I understand."

McCann stood quietly for a moment. Finally he lowered himself into the chair. "It's essential that we not reveal the location of alien worlds."

"That place doesn't seem to be an alien world."

"Of course it is. Aliens were living there when we arrived."

"The evidence suggests they were not natives. You guys and the *Harbinger* both ran long searches and found no one else anywhere on the planet."

"Searching an entire world for small towns or villages isn't easy, Alex. It takes a lot of time. You of all people should be aware of that. And finding nothing doesn't mean they aren't there. But okay, you may be right. Maybe the world is deserted now. We just don't know. In any case, yes, we are aware that aliens have been there. The *Harbinger* brought back a satellite. So there's no question that they existed. We don't want our people going out to the place and taking it over. Once the location gets out, there'd be no way to protect it." He raised his left hand. "And to be frank, I don't know where the place is. If they'd needed me to help them, they'd still be drifting around looking. The reality is that even if I wanted to help, I wouldn't know how."

)) ● ((

"There's one other possibility," Alex said. "Robbi Jo Renfroe is an old friend of yours, isn't she?"

I wasn't surprised that he knew. I couldn't recall ever having mentioned our connection, but if Alex was persistent at anything, it was research. "Yes," I said. "We go back to early school days."

"I assume you don't want to ask her if she'd be willing to help."

"I don't like putting her on the spot."

"She's pretty much all we have left. You wouldn't have to put any pressure on her. Just let her know what we're planning and give her the opportunity to make an offer."

I hated going near her with the issue. If she broke ranks and gave us the Korella location, her career with DPSAR would be over. I'd been hoping Alex would make an effort to win over somebody from the Visitation Project, but he'd presumably already looked into that. The only ones who knew the details of the mission were very likely the pilots. Even Henry probably didn't know.

Alex read my reluctance. "If you have to pass on it, Chase," he said, "I understand."

I came close. If there'd been another option, I'd have backed off. But there wasn't, and I could sense the passion in his voice. He'd talked about money. But the money wasn't at the heart of this. He collected artifacts because they were a way to touch history. If we could come up with something on Korella, it would be the ultimate historical connection in his career.

)) ● ((

Robbi Jo lived in Parnau, about six hundred kilometers north of Andiquar, at the foot of the Konjour Mountains. I settled in behind my desk and called her. She picked up. "Hi, Chase. I've been meaning to get back to you. It was great to hear from you."

We had a bad connection; her image flickered, faded, and was gone. Then it came back at full clarity. She was seated in a chair, dressed for mountain climbing or maybe just camping, with gray leggings and a heavy pullover shirt. Two boots were on the floor in front of her. "Hello, Robbi Jo. How you doing? Hope all's well with you."

"I'm fine, thanks."

Robbi Jo had looked pretty good during her high school years, and she'd lost nothing. Her eyes gleamed. She was blond, with congenial features and an easy manner that indicated the relationship between us had not aged. Two windows provided a view of a sloping landscape. She wasn't alone. She made hand signals, and a moment later I heard a door close.

A golden retriever sat beside her chair, its jaw snuggled against her left leg. A full bookcase stood behind her. And beside the bookcase there was a framed portrait of a little girl standing on a porch. "I guess," she said, "we never did get together for that lunch we used to talk about."

"It's a pretty long ride, Robbi Jo. Does your family still live in Andiquar?"

"Yes. Actually, I've been down there a couple of times since I got back from the *Columbia*."

"What are you doing now?"

"I'm trying to decide whether I want to work for Spaceways." An interplanetary touring company. "By the way, I've been meaning to tell you, I've read a couple of your books, Chase. I've enjoyed the accounts of Alex's archeological adventures. You have a serious writing talent."

"Thank you," I said. "Would it be okay if I used that comment as a blurb on the next one?"

"Absolutely."

"Excellent. I write while you make history."

She laughed. "That was Quaid, not me. I got lucky. They needed a pilot."

"I thought you were going to become an astrophysicist."

"That was my original plan. But I couldn't see any point in

looking at stars through oversized telescopes when I could go out and poke them." Her eyes lit up and suddenly we were back on the basketball court. "I guess we both headed in the same direction."

"Looks like. I hope you've enjoyed the ride as much as I have. I should mention, by the way, that Alex doesn't think of himself as an archeologist."

She glanced at my bookcase and smiled when she saw the hardcover Ulakan volumes I'd received from Chad Barker. Three of them were in plain view. She turned back to me. "How *would* he describe himself?" she asked. "Alex."

"As an antiquarian."

"I'm surprised to hear that."

Her eyes brightened. "I have to tell you that I wish we'd had someone like you on board the *Columbia* to write a memoir of the flight."

"Thanks, Robbi Jo. I appreciate the compliment. Maybe next time?" That was supposed to be a joke. But she didn't smile. And she didn't take the bait. "We should have stayed in touch," I said.

Her bookcase was filled mostly with astronomy books. "That would have been a good idea. It's not too late, Chase."

"I'm in favor of that." She nodded, confirming the idea. "You must have enjoyed the experience, Robbi Jo. Finding aliens."

"Well, more or less. The aliens went missing. I have to admit the Ulakans would have been more fun."

"Did you get to meet them?"

"Not exactly. We tossed greetings back and forth. I was part of the crowd when they were leaving."

We talked about it for a few minutes before I tried again to move toward the *Harbinger* mission. "What do you think happened?"

"They must have gone to the wrong place. No way I can imagine they could have moved the town out of there. I felt sorry for Vince and the rest of those guys."

"It must have been a long, dreary ride home."

"Yeah. I'm sure it was."

"Do you know any of them? Other than Vince?"

"Just Henry."

"Have you talked to any of them since?"

"No. I'm maintaining a healthy distance." Her eyes left me. She was looking at something in her living room. Or wherever that was. "For a while I regretted not being with them. But the way it turned out—" She cleared her throat. "When we saw the village, the *Columbia* mission turned into one long celebration. I never would have believed the whole thing would crash and burn the way it did."

"I'm sorry," I said.

"Me too. The *Columbia* was the mission of a lifetime. Or at least it should have been. Now we have people saying the whole thing was a lie. That the village was never there."

"Robbi Jo, Alex would like to go out there, to Korella, and try to figure out what happened."

"I wish him luck." Her eyes locked on me. She knew what was coming.

"The problem is that we don't know where the place is."

"Why does he want to do that? Is he looking to enhance his reputation? Maybe help you get a bigger book deal?"

She'd changed from the young woman I remembered, who would not have backed anyone into a corner. I could have told her she was wrong, that Alex simply hoped to collect some artifacts. But that was not the answer that was likely to get her on board. "Robbi

Jo," I said, "he has no interest in making contact per se. He would just like to work out what happened. If he finds anyone, he'd keep his distance and do nothing more than come home and report the results." I managed what I hoped was an amicable smile.

She let me see that she hoped I was right. "I wish I could help," she said.

"You know where the place is, don't you?"

"Yes. I know. But everyone who was selected for the mission signed an agreement specifically barring us from revealing any location in the event we found someone. Or from doing anything that might assist anyone else who was on the hunt."

"Robbi Jo, I assume you know that Henry is saying they won't be running any future flights into the area."

"I know. Quaid has taken the same attitude."

"The whole point of the *Columbia*'s mission was to look for intelligent life."

"Not exactly, Chase. We were looking for worlds that could serve as bases or colonies for us. That was the stated purpose of the Visitation Project."

"The stated purpose isn't quite the same as the driving force behind the flights. They didn't want to stir up interest in getting people like Alex and me going out hunting for aliens."

She exhaled. "I suppose there's something to that."

"Why did they choose that particular group of stars in the Orion Nebula? They're too far to be of any practical use as colonies."

"Artificial radio signals have been picked up occasionally. A long time ago."

"How long?"

"Originally during the fifth millennium. And periodically since then. The most recent one goes back four centuries. But it's a long ride out there, especially in those eras. It would have taken a year or more."

"Okay. So the truth is out. We've been fascinated by the possibility of others all the way back to the early days of spaceflight. But the people in charge have always been nervous about what might happen if we actually found someone. But look how the Ulakans turned out."

"Yeah." She laughed. "Aliens finally show up—aliens other than the Mutes—and they're dedicated book readers."

"Right. Who saw that coming?"

She was staring again at the Ulakan volumes. "Have *you* read any of them?"

"I've read two. And they feel as if they've been written by us. How about you?"

"I read *Footprints in the Sands of Time*. It's about the significance of art and literature in civilized development."

"How is it?"

"It's excellent. Monteo says it's a classic. Right up there with *Looking Askance*." She obviously saw the title hadn't connected with me. "It's by Michael Leja," she said. "He was a third-millennium art historian."

"The name rings a bell. I don't know Monteo, though."

She smiled. "Monteo's strictly a critic. Lives on Dellaconda. Leja's book has been around almost since the beginning of western civilization. There are a lot of illustrations in it. In both books. The Ulakans have the same passion for art."

"I recall you used to do some painting."

"At one time I thought that was going to be my career. Didn't happen." She looked back at the painting beside the bookcase. "That's Tammy," she said. "Her mom's in the other room."

"It's beautiful."

"She is, isn't she?"

"I meant the painting. She is too."

"Thank you. I guess you know the Parkington is going to do one of the plays. One of the Ulakan plays."

"I hadn't heard that."

"They just announced it this morning."

"Robbi Jo, I can't help thinking how much all those generations probably missed because we and the Ulakans needed so long to find one another."

She sat quietly and pushed her tongue against her cheek. "Chase, I'm sorry. I wish there were a way for me to help you."

"If it were your call, you'd send out another mission, wouldn't you?"

She thought about it. "I would. But it's not my decision." She was staring past me again. "Sorry." She looked down at her link. "I've got to go. When we can find some time, Chase, let's get together." And she clicked off.

I wasn't quite ready to give up. I called Chad and bought hardcover copies of *Facing Reality* and *Why We Laugh*. The latter book described the importance of art and literature in the development of a civilized world. I provided Robbi Jo's address and asked him to ship them to her. "You want to attach a card?" he asked.

"Yes," I said. "'For my favorite artist.'"

"So how do we find the place?" I asked.

"I don't know." When Alex gets frustrated, he usually closes his eyes. This time he stared hard into mine. "We've touched base with the pilots, and with McCann and Cassell. Nobody's budging. And nobody else on either flight is likely to be able to find it." He sat at his desk, picked up his coffee, and took a long drink. We weren't getting any rain, but there was a lot of thunder and the wind was moving tree branches. "I guess we should just let it go for a while. Eventually somebody's mind might change."

"Okay." I shouldn't admit this, but I was almost relieved. "How is it, I wonder, that the Visitation Project was originally hoping to find someone, and then when they did, they were so quick to back away from it?"

"Because it went public. We aren't always rational, Chase. Searching for intelligent life was at the heart of what they were doing, but they didn't expect to find anything. And they even pretended they weren't looking for aliens. When it happened, it came as a shock. And they played it straight. But since the village disappeared, I guess it's become hard to walk away from the project."

He didn't broach the subject again for a few days. When I asked if he was still thinking about it, he let me see that he'd given up. "I took another crack at Reddington. But he won't budge."

"So it's over?"

"Yes. Though there's somebody else I want to talk with."

"Who's that?"

"The Mutes. They've been over to the Orion Nebula several times."

"That sounds like a long shot."

"I don't know. I don't think they have the same attitude toward aliens that we do. But let's find out. It's all we have. When you have a minute, see if you can set up a meeting with Torega."

Torega was a Mute with whom we'd done occasional business. He was a diplomat who was also a collector of artifacts from actions that had led to the war and the efforts to end it. We had obtained for him a draft copy of the Call to Victory, the challenge issued by the Mutes that had initiated the attack at Blenkoven and in effect blocked ongoing efforts to reach a settlement. We'd also gotten him the pen used by the Mute leader Andropoli to sign the agreement that brought peace. And there was an early version of "Finale," the famous poem written by Jora Modesta, expressing his appreciation that the war had ended.

So he owed us. I set up the appointment and, the following afternoon, accompanied Alex to the Kostyev House, in the center of Andiquar. The Kostyev House had been an embassy for the Dellacondans in an earlier time. Now it served primarily as the consulate for the Ashiyyur. For years, the Mutes had to tolerate angry demonstrators who thought they were monsters interested only in bringing down the Confederacy. The war that had been fought with them was long gone, but their fearsome appearance remained, as well as their ability to read minds. But happily, the sign-waving demonstrators were now gone too. That had happened when the Mutes came to the rescue of Salud Afar, helping get a shield in place to save that terrified world from a supernova.

We rode a tube up to the fourth floor and followed a carpeted corridor down to a set of windows that had not been there during my previous visit. They overlooked the courthouse. Long murals depicted men and women in modest cottages contemplating approaching storms, seated at crowded picnic tables, and looking out across broad rivers. Carved mahogany doors lined both sides of the corridor. Most were unmarked, save a legal firm and a tax adjuster and a couple showing only names. We paused in front of a set of double doors that appeared to be oak with a khaki color. A plaque indicated we'd arrived at the Ashiyyurean consulate.

Alex spoke his name. The doors opened and we entered. The Mute civilization was considerably older than ours, by thousands of years. And they were telepaths. Experts maintained they were more intelligent than humans, though it could be argued they hadn't always shown it. They could not speak, probably a result of their telepathic capabilities.

I'd been there on several earlier occasions. The furnishings had been upgraded since my previous visits. Before, the consulate had seemed simply mundane, not a place in which you'd want to spend much time. I don't remember details other than a sofa, chairs, and a desk, all looking as if they'd been acquired during a low-budget sale. There was a white door behind the desk. Worn books were piled on a table, supported by a pair of horse-head bookends. Two windows, shaded by green curtains, looked out over Bancroft Street.

There was a bookcase now. It held some of the volumes that had been here before, biographies of both humans and Mutes, a few histories of both species, and several books in the Ashiyyurean language. There was also a copy of Leisha Tanner's *Extracts from Tulisofala*. It's a book I've been wanting to read forever. Eventually I'll get to it. And I should mention that there was a copy of Alex's *A Talent for War*.

A light rain was falling. Alex settled into one of the chairs, while I stood looking at the books. And suddenly I got a sense that I was being watched, that we were no longer alone in the room. That shouldn't have come as a surprise. It had happened during my other visits. And I knew what was coming next: the white door opened.

I held my breath while a Mute entered the room. Their faces resemble ours except that they are less animated, with large arched diamond-shaped eyes and canines that suggest there is something of a vampire about them. It was a male. Almost a head taller than Alex. Its skin was like worn dark leather. I couldn't tell whether it was Torega.

"Hello, Alex," he said, speaking through a medallion that hung on a chain around his neck. Centered on it was a bird in flight that might have been an eagle. "It's good to see you again."

Alex got up and extended his hand. "Good to see you, Torega. It's been a long time."

"We've missed you, Alex." His eyes rotated toward me. "And you are Chase. Do I have that right?"

"Yes," I said.

"Forgive me. Humans all tend to look alike to us."

"It's okay," I said, trying to stop myself from thinking that all he had to do was look into my mind to find out who I was. "Good to see you again, sir."

"The pleasure is all mine, Chase." He indicated we should all sit. He took a place on the couch. "Alex," he said, "I haven't been able to help noticing that your archeological career has brought considerable success. My congratulations."

"I'm not really an archeologist, Torega. I'm just a retail guy. My uncle Gabriel is the archeologist."

"Oh. I don't think I ever actually understood that."

Said the guy to whom our minds lay open. Alex got the joke too and smiled. "I'm happy to clarify."

An associate brought in a round of drinks. Not alcoholic, more like tea with a taste of lemon. Torega tried it, showed his approval, and then addressed Alex: "So what can I do for you?"

Alex leaned back in his chair. "I'm aware that your people claim we are the only developed civilization you've ever encountered. Is that really true?"

"Probably not," he said, "although I've no way to know. Our people have been like yours. We understand how much damage high-tech visitors can do to a primitive society. And since there's really no way to control interstellar flights from our worlds, we've tried to deal with the issue by simply not releasing information about discoveries."

Alex nodded. "So if a couple of your people out wandering around find another civilization, how do you persuade them to keep it quiet?"

"How would DPSAR handle it?"

"We'd probably pay them. I can't see what else we could do."

"And there you have it, Alex. If they reveal anything, they lose the money and are given treatment to ensure it doesn't happen again."

"Treatment? What do you mean?"

"Their memory of the incident is wiped and replaced."

Alex took a long sip from the lemon tea. "I wouldn't have thought you guys could keep any secrets from each other."

"Of course we can. We don't live in each other's brains. Our natural inclination is to be completely open. But we can create blockage. It's not difficult. And I assume since the Confederacy, until last month, reported no evidence of newly discovered high-tech aliens, that you have a similar system in place."

Alex signaled me to respond. "You might be right," I said. "But I think we just do what we can to prevent others from using the information. Give it time and probably everybody will forget about it."

"You've had a wild ride recently. *Two* connections." Torega's eyes widened. "With the Ulakans and that odd business at Korella IV."

"That's why we've come," said Alex. "Obviously you know what happened on Korella IV, in the Orion Nebula. Is there any possibility that a group of your people got stranded out there on one of those worlds? And possibly got mistaken for another species?"

"There's always a possibility, Alex. Why do you ask?"

"One of the crew on the *Harbinger*, Autumn Ulbrich, reported feeling what she thought might be a telepathic connection. She described a sense of being watched. She thought it was someone in the forest." Alex had brought a copy of the report with him. He produced it and handed it to Torega. He looked at it and gave it back.

"It's certainly possible," he said. "We've seen no evidence of telepathy anywhere. Beyond ourselves. Hold on a moment." He gave the question to the AI. We waited a few seconds.

It responded, "*No record of any mission to or near the Orion Nebula losing any of its passengers over the last 847 years. To take it back further than that, I would need to make contact at home.*"

Torega's eyes narrowed. "That doesn't eliminate the possibility."

Alex smiled and said thanks. "Don't go to a lot of trouble. But if you hear anything different, Torega, please let us know."

The Mute's expression signaled that he would go to whatever trouble it took. "You know," he said, "I've no question that we sometimes underrate the fact that *you* have capabilities similar to ours. I would wager that humans are on the cusp of developing telepathic skills."

)) ● ((

When we got back to the country house, a note from Robbi Jo was waiting. "Thank you for the books, Chase," it said. "I'm looking forward to reading them."

Later that afternoon I heard Gabe and Alex in the conference room. Ellen Hargrove's Sonata no. 3 in A Major, the *Deep Sky* Sonata, was playing in the background. It was Alex's favorite piece of music, a classic composed four centuries ago. Alex had told me that it made the artificial world around him disappear and brought him to confront what really matters: beautiful women, irresistible rhythms, and the fact that time doesn't last forever. I'd seen him come seriously to life a few times when it was playing. This time he'd kept the volume down so I could hear Gabe speaking over it. "It just makes no sense," he was saying. "How could it have happened?"

I couldn't resist going in. "You guys need anything?" I asked.

They both declined. And Gabe let me see he had a question for me. "That small town on Korella: How could there be only one village on that whole planet? Can you think of any explanation for that at all?"

"I have no idea, Gabe."

He looked over at Alex, who simply shrugged and looked at the ceiling. "We're looking at a technologically advanced species on a world like ours. They have electricity and an artificial satellite and they all live in one village. Or at least they used to. This has to be a hoax. There's nothing else that makes sense. That makes riding out there absolutely pointless."

Alex's expression hardened. How many times had he heard that? "We don't really know enough yet to do anything other than come up with theories, Gabe. We need to wait until we have more information."

Gabriel settled back in his chair. "How you doing, Chase?"

"I couldn't be better."

A damp breeze blew in off the trees. Alex touched his link and the windows closed. "Look," he said, "everybody's interested in this. The village that moved. A few artifacts, if we can find them, would be invaluable."

The *Deep Sky* Sonata started winding down. Gabe frowned. "I don't know. I just don't like you and Chase going out there. It might be dangerous. "And I'm not sure that if whatever it is decides to move against you, hand weapons would be enough." Do we have any more information on the satellite? The one they brought home?"

The music stopped. "They haven't released anything of interest yet," said Alex. "The thing isn't much different from one we'd have built."

"Yes," Gabe said. "I suspect there isn't a great deal you can do to improve a satellite."

He pushed a chair in my direction. I sat down. "So what," I said, "are you suggesting? What do you recommend, Gabe?"

"There's a good chance these guys are considerably more advanced than we are. It looks as if they just move from world to world."

"I suspect," said Alex, "that they scare pretty easily. One ship goes out and sees them and they all clear out."

"I know," said Gabe. "That makes no sense either."

"I can't see that it matters whether they're dangerous. They're gone. That's what makes them interesting. That's all we'll be looking for." Alex smiled at me. "Chase, this could be the biggest payoff by far we've ever seen."

"You never really change, do you, Alex?" Gabe did not look happy. "You're leaving in a few days?"

"A week or two. If we can find out where the place is." Alex hesitated, and I understood suddenly that Gabe was waiting for another invitation. Alex delivered an uncomfortable smile. "You change your mind? You want to come with us?"

"Yeah." That produced a long pause. "If that's okay."

"We'd like to have you, Gabe. Of course."

"May I ask a question?"

"About the artifacts?"

"Yes. If I find any, Alex, will I have control of them?"

For a moment, we were back at the old point of contention. Gabe and the museums or Alex and Rainbow Enterprises. Alex nodded. "We've put that behind us. You keep yours, I'll keep mine. Okay?"

"Now," I said, "all we have to do is get there."

8

Scientific advance inevitably carries a price. Artificial intelligence cost countless jobs. Life extension keeps crooked politicians around longer. The internet provides voices to people who have nothing to contribute other than vitriol. Flying cars gave us drunks at 2,000 meters. And the FTL drive opened travel between the stars not only for us but for any deranged species that might be out there.

—Mary Gordon, physicist, multiple prize winner, 10,964 CE

I picked up a copy of *Skies on Fire* and got completely hooked by the plays. The dramas were enough to bring tears to my eyes. And the comedies literally broke me up. They frequently portrayed characters getting caught in hypocrisy and lies.

Meantime Alex touched base with Chuck Dumas, Sam Carmody, and Jennifer Hancock. They all said they had no idea where Korella was. Carmody added that it was in the middle of the Orion Nebula. That was more or less like revealing that it was in the sky somewhere. Jennifer suggested we try Autumn Ulbrich.

On the assumption that Autumn might be more responsive if the request came from a woman, I offered to make the effort. She'd been teaching math at Andromeda University for several years before getting involved in the *Harbinger* flight. She was also a participant in an amateur theater group in the area. The university is about thirty kilometers southwest of Andiquar. I got a break: She was conducting seminars at several of the local colleges. The next one was scheduled at Hamilton in Brock City. I got in touch with the administration and asked if they were accepting visitors for her presentation. They were not.

The entire Hamilton campus was located inside a single building. It was about nine stories high (though it was a streamlined design that didn't reveal individual stories) and stretched out over several blocks. An electronic sign provided directions to the seminar, which made it easy for me to determine which entrance and exit Autumn would use. I was waiting in the parking lot when she arrived. I had the timing on the presentation and was back when she came out through the exit. Several students and a couple of older people were with her. The group gathered for a few final comments and handshakes. Then they disbanded and Autumn headed for her vehicle.

The day was gray and chilly. I caught her eyes as I approached. She was wrapped in a dark brown jacket, carrying a notebook, and wearing a blue knitted woolen hat pulled down past her ears. We'd seen a good bit of her on the HV shows. She had hazel hair cut short and piercing dark eyes. She saw immediately that she had my attention, looked away, and picked up her pace.

I caught up with her as she reached her skimmer. Her expression indicated she'd had enough with media people or whoever the hell I was. She slipped into the vehicle. "Please, Ms. Ulbrich," I said. "Just give me a minute."

She had the link in her hand, but if she closed the door, it would have shut on my arm. "What do you want?" she asked.

"My name's Chase Kolpath. I represent Rainbow Enterprises." She shrugged. Never heard of the organization. "We want to find out what happened on Korella. As I'm sure you do."

She needed a moment but finally managed to exhale. "So where's this going?"

"We could use your help."

"In what way?"

"Whatever you can tell us."

"I assume you want to know where it is?"

"That would be good. Yes. We know you're not a pilot, but we thought you might be able to provide some information. Do you know how we could find it?"

"I do. And I feel much as you do. But I'm sorry. I can't say anything."

"Ms. Ulbrich, do you really want to see the disappearance go unresolved? I mean, my understanding is that's the reason the Visitation Project went out there in the first place. To find an alien civilization that had been sending radio signals for thousands of years."

"In fact, Ms. Kolpath, the project has been looking for worlds we can colonize."

"That's the cover story, isn't it?"

"No. That's actually why they were there."

"But you had a team trained specifically to manage first contact."

"Look, the truth is that we're not comfortable with what might be out there. We don't want to do anything that could draw unwanted attention to us. Yes, I'm a Xenocon, but it's only because when we encounter aliens, we want to have people who know how to respond. We're very lucky the universe is so big and so empty. Let's let it go at that. I'll concede that our tendency to hide our heads on this issue doesn't provide much of an image, but I think it's the smart thing to do. So to answer your question: yes, I know where Korella is, but I'm not going to help anyone looking for it. I'm sorry." There was a brief softening of her features. "I'm glad to have met you, Ms. Kolpath." She waited for me to withdraw my arm. Then the door closed.

I should have realized that we were talking with too many people to keep everything quiet. Two days after my conversation with Autumn—if you could call it that—I was just getting ready to go home when Jacob informed us that the story was appearing on the media.

ARCHEOLOGIST TO HUNT FOR LOST ALIENS
Alex Benedict Plans Follow-Up to Harbinger *Mission*

We watched for a few minutes. Jill Faulkner, one of the Golden Network's reporters, was talking: "We have no idea yet when they will be leaving," she said. "We don't even know who will be making the trip other than Benedict and presumably his pilot, Chase Kolpath. He hasn't responded to our call for an interview."

"They haven't called us," I said.

"They're on the circuit now," said Jacob.

Alex took it in his office. Two minutes later he was on the HV with Faulkner, stating that he had no comment and that he wasn't an archeologist.

"So you're not denying the story," she said.

"At the moment, we have no plans to go anywhere. Sorry, Jill, I'm on the run." He disconnected.

Faulkner rolled her eyes. "We'll stay on the story," she said.

I shut it down and heard Alex on the staircase. A moment later he walked into my office. "You see that?" he said.

"Yes."

"Actually, we've been talking with so many of them, I'm surprised it took this long for someone to catch up with us. We have to decide what we're going to do. And at this point I can't see anything other than walking away from the whole thing."

I had nothing to add, so I simply sat and let him see I was in full agreement.

)) ● ((

That evening I watched the media reports from my cabin. It wasn't the biggest story of the evening. That was the Gorman Webb scandal that had exploded when it was discovered that the governor had planted listening devices in an effort to get information on Manda Claver, who would be his political opponent in the upcoming election. Nevertheless, we were all over the networks. Interstellar was running images of Alex, while Lester Wilkinson predicted that he'd uncovered something. "Otherwise," he said, "there's no reason he'd be going." The Action Network was interviewing Jason Albright, who'd been on the *Columbia* mission. Jason was laughing while he maintained that it would be a complete waste of time. I was about to change channels when Carmen informed me that a skimmer was setting down outside.

I wasn't exactly dressed when they began knocking. "*Arcadia Network*," Carmen said. I thought about having Carmen inform them I was in a conference somewhere. But that wouldn't solve anything. I grabbed a robe and went into the living room while I thought about what to tell them. "Okay," I said, "let them in."

There were two of them. Both women. I didn't recognize either one, but I don't usually watch Arcadia. "Sorry to disturb you, Ms. Kolpath," said the older of the two. "I'm Edith Zoriah. This is Ellen Collins. We've been informed that your boss is going to be heading up a mission to Korella. Can you confirm that?"

"Last I heard, they're just talking about it."

"Okay. Be aware, by the way, that you're on camera. Do you know where we can locate Mr. Benedict? He seems to have gone out somewhere for a meeting."

I had no idea. And I should admit I hated appearing on HV in a blue knit robe.

)) ● ((

I wouldn't go so far as to say we'd ignited a firestorm, but we did find ourselves in the middle of a loud argument. The Golden, Hochman, Arcadia, and Coastal Networks interviewed guests who argued against voyages that might encounter aliens. Stay where we are, they said. Leave well enough alone. There are thousands of worlds out there available to us if we need them, but let's not go beyond familiar borders. They all favored exploration. But only in the local neighborhood. In areas that had always been quiet. There were some who disagreed. The noted physicist Juan Munson maintained that we had an obligation to do surveys as far out as we could. Not that we were necessarily looking for others, but that pursuing knowledge was what an intelligent civilization was all about. The Free Talk Network, which is a nonprofit corporation funded by listener contributions, admitted they just weren't sure where they stood on the issue.

Gabe and Alex did what they could to keep their heads down. Journalists were informed by Jacob that they simply had no comment at the moment. They had to cut back on their activities outside the country house. No restaurants, no attendance at conferences, and no visits to the beach. The latter wasn't a problem, since we were well past summer.

Gabe was in favor of announcing that the project had never been under serious consideration. But Alex was reluctant. Walk away from it, he maintained, and if we ever have a chance to pursue the damned thing, we'll look as if we just couldn't make up our minds.

$$)) \bullet (($$

The activity subsided. Henry showed up on *The Gene Kilpatrick Show*, which ran daily for two hours on the Free Talk Network, to say that he understood the passion to explore that we all have. But although he'd favored the effort most of his life, he'd decided that sometimes caution was the best approach. "To tell the truth," he said, "putting on a few years makes me happy that we never really found what I was looking for."

I had it on because they had announced he would be a guest. I routinely watched any show on which he was scheduled. Or McCann, who seemed to grow more despondent with every appearance. Free Talk was switching over to a fundraising segment when Jacob informed me I had a call. "From Robbi Jo Renfroe."

She appeared in an armchair with a book in her lap. I recognized the cover: it was an Ulakan volume, *Skies on Fire*. "Hi, Chase," she said. "I love the plays. Especially *Korval*." *Korval* was a comedy about a guy who enjoyed wielding power but was desperate that others would like him. He constantly embarrassed himself by going too far. "I hope," she continued, "that they stage that one. I kept thinking Mickey Denver would be perfect in the role. And I'd like to see *Battle Clouds* performed too." *Battle Clouds* was a musical about a weather analyst who consistently makes the wrong calls, wrecking sporting events, wedding ceremonies, and fundraising efforts. "The Ulakans seem to live their lives much the way we do."

"Some people," I said, "have suggested the whole thing is designed to mislead us about who they really are."

"You don't believe that, do you, Chase?"

"No. For one thing, the plays are too good. They're right on target. I don't see how a species that doesn't live more or less like us could create something that funny."

"I agree," she said. "When I first saw the titles, I was struck by the fact that there was a sacred book among them, *Faith: Why Belief Still Matters*. There's nothing specific, nothing biblical, no accounts of an active God, but they struggle with the meaning of existence in the face of a relatively short lifetime. They want to believe life has a purpose. I've no idea how long their life span is. They mention a couple hundred years, but I don't think anyone knows yet how long a year is for them. In any case, there's a desire for something beyond physics, a rationale that would offset a universe that seems designed to kill everybody."

By then I'd read most of the book myself and also been touched by the Ulakans' approach to death. "I don't guess any of us like the idea of drifting off into the dark," I said. "Anyhow, did you want to set up a lunch? Or did you maybe change your mind about the mission?"

"I'm thinking about it. But I got the impression you guys have called it off."

"Depends on which channel you're watching."

"Good."

Our eyes locked. "Robbi Jo, what do we have to do to get you on board?"

"I won't *tell* you where Korella is. But I'll *show* you."

"You want to go with us?"

"Yes."

"I don't think that will be a problem."

"Can you keep it quiet until we are out of here? The mission, that is."

$$)) ((($$

Alex was delighted. He informed Gabe but warned him to say nothing. I spent the evening with Chad and struggled throughout the entire two and a half hours to avoid telling him we were back on, and that it was largely because of the books he'd sent to Robbi Jo. She'd also purchased Living the Good Life from him. He mentioned that she'd been looking through the other Ulakan books. "I think she's going to pick up a few more," he said.

I smiled weakly and concentrated on keeping my mouth shut. The only thing I said was that I hoped she would enjoy them.

In the morning Robbi Jo arrived over the country house in her skimmer, descended into the parking area, and climbed out. Alex told me I should participate in the conversation unless Robbi Jo indicated she preferred I not be there. I'd have been surprised had anything like that happened. I took her into the conference room and got her a cup of coffee. Alex entered a few moments later and sat down with us around the table.

"Welcome aboard, Professor Renfroe," he said. "I understand you're an old friend of Chase."

"Please call me Robbi Jo. And yes, that's true. We've known each other a long time."

"Excellent. Well, we're certainly happy to have you join us. I understand you want to come along."

"That's correct, Mr. Benedict."

"I'm Alex." He pulled his chair closer to the table. "May I ask why you changed your mind?"

"I never agreed with the idea that Henry Cassell's been promoting. That since we don't know what's out there, we should stay home and hide under the bed. In fact, I'm pretty sure *he* doesn't believe it either. But it's the politically correct position these days. He's just not the guy I thought he was." She glanced in my direction and shrugged. "I said no to Chase before because I didn't want to get into trouble. This will mean the end of my career as a Xenocon, and maybe as an interstellar pilot. I don't know." She looked toward me. "Possibly you too, Chase. But we have an obligation to explore. I don't believe anybody's ever going to pose a threat to us. If they have intelligence enough to develop a higher level of tech than we have, they should be intelligent enough not to start stupid fights."

"Like we did with the Mutes?" I said.

"In the end it didn't amount to much."

"Okay." After all these years, I can read Alex pretty well. He still wasn't sure she'd be willing to give up her career and ride back out to Korella. "Did you enjoy your flight on the *Columbia*?"

"No. It was a long, dreary ride."

"And you want to go back there? Again? Why, Robbi Jo?"

She sat quietly for a minute, deciding how much she wanted to tell us. Finally she cleared her throat. "I've had a pretty fortunate life. Almost everything I've gone near has turned to gold. I used to walk around telling people I had no regrets. And they'd tell me only an idiot talks like that. But the truth is that I was getting everything I wanted out of life. I had a passion for astronomy, won a couple major awards, had a lot of good friends. I enjoy painting and I love teaching. And I was there when one of the biggest discoveries of the era was made." She leaned back in the sofa, crossed her arms, and stared at the portrait of the old warship *Corsarius* that hung on the wall. Or maybe she was just looking in that direction. "I've done some dumb stuff. Hurt a few people unnecessarily. Caused problems. We all have things in our lives that we'd change if we could. But for me everything's been pretty much minor league. The only thing I'd really like to get right is Korella. What happened to that village? I don't want that hanging over my head for the rest of my life. Quaid feels the same way. He'd give anything to be able to get an answer."

"I understand," said Alex, "you were once a student of McCann's. Is that correct?"

"He was one of my history professors at Andromeda University. He was the best teacher I ever had. He didn't just put out information and dates and whatnot. He used to change events, like with Rodney Blanchard." Blanchard was a ninth-millennium physicist who persuaded people on Rambuckle that they were poisoning the seas, and that there'd be a heavy price to pay. He almost got killed in a skimmer crash. He'd ask us what would have happened on Rambuckle if he hadn't survived? What would the world there

look like today? What would have happened if Blanchard had suc-
ceeded in his prime ambition, had carved a career for himself as a
musician and composer?"

Alex focused on Robbi Jo. "Okay. So we know what's happened since the *Columbia* mission. How do you feel about the
claim that the whole thing was made up? That the village never
really existed?"

She couldn't hide her annoyance. "I was there," she said. "I
saw the village."

"How do you explain what happened with the *Harbinger*?"

"I can't. I've no idea."

"Okay. Do you think we'll be able to come up with anything
different this time?"

"You probably won't. But there's a chance. Who knows?" Her
hands had knotted into fists. "Alex, this thing has been haunting
me. I still can't believe that place just vanished. There must be an
explanation. And this might be our last shot at getting it. At least
during my lifetime." She managed a smile. "So, if you're going to
do this, I'd like to go along."

Alex never took his eyes off her. "Of course."

"Thank you." She got out of her chair. "I appreciate it. By the
way, in case you're not aware, the area where we saw the village
gets cold. So we should all bring jackets."

He looked across at me. "Chase, you have any questions?"

"Only one. Robbi Jo, when you've time, get me a list of your
favorite movies."

We finished with a few details, and I saw her to the front door.
She got out onto the porch and stopped to watch a goose settle
onto a tree branch directly in front of us. It rested there a few moments, then spread its wings, and suddenly, with a cluster of others

that had been in a couple of trees and on the roof, it flapped into the air. We stared at them, watching them rise into the afternoon sky, flying in perfect harmony. Robbi Jo leaned forward onto the back of one of the chairs. "I wonder how they do that."

I had no idea. But wherever there are birds, whatever world on which they live, there are some that do the same group takeoff.

Looking back now, I don't think I ever believed until that meeting with Robbi Jo that we would actually make for Korella. So when Alex had checked with me initially about how I felt, I'd assured him it was no problem. He could count on me.

That had changed. We would need a few days to put the mission together. But we were going. No question now about it. I was thinking about Chad. And life in Andiquar. And two or three months sealed inside the *Belle-Marie*. I've never been able to hide anything from Alex. In his presence I feel much the same way I do when there's a Mute in the room.

"We don't know how long we're going to be out there," I told him. "I have a suggestion. It wouldn't be a bad idea to stop at Delmonte. It's not much out of the way, and we could top off the oxygen tanks. We might need it. Also, it's about halfway, and by then we could use a break. Get out of the yacht for a while."

"Okay," he said.

"We should bring bathing suits."

"Good enough." He hesitated. "Is something wrong?"

"No. Why do you ask?"

"You don't have to go, Chase," he said. "I understand. I can get someone else. Truth is, we'd be better off if you stayed here and took care of Rainbow. Robbi Jo can do the piloting."

I took a long pause before responding. "Let me think about it, Alex."

)) ❂ ((

Robbi Jo called me that evening. "I have a problem," she said.

"What's that?"

"I think you mentioned a boyfriend at one point?"

"I probably did. He's Chad Barker. The owner of the Collectors' Library in Salazar."

"I've been thinking what my life was like during the months before we left on the *Columbia*. I was explaining to everybody who was close to me how I was going to be gone for several months. It seemed like forever, because until we got to Korella we were just wandering around out there. But I had to tell my folks, my friends, a couple of guys. I didn't even know Chris that well yet."

"Chris is your boyfriend?"

"Yes. Chris Baxter. Now I'm doing it again. And I realized the kind of burden I've imposed on you and Gabe and Alex. I've asked you not to tell anyone about the mission. That was severely selfish, and I'm sorry. Tell Alex and Gabe to do what they want. You too. I suspect you'll be relieved to be able to let Chad—do I have that right?—let Chad know. And I'm assuming here that you haven't already told him and sworn him to secrecy. If you did, you won't have anything to worry about."

"Robbi Jo, it's okay. We can keep it quiet."

"Let it go. I'm going to tell Chris tonight. He's not good at keeping secrets."

9

The primary satisfaction to be derived from an accomplishment is not experienced until we recognize the goal has been achieved and raise a glass in its direction.

—**Aneille Kay, *Christopher Sim at War*, 1322**

I t took two days before the news showed up in the media. Longer than I'd expected.

Infomax 11/2/1436

We're hearing that at least one more alien-hunt mission is in the works. It's a pity that we aren't sensible enough to realize how fortunate we have been to be separated from other intelligent life-forms by a considerable distance. There is no more dangerous pastime than the one practiced by idiots with too much cash who have nothing more important to do than look for talking spiders and whatever else may be out there. We're still relatively young. It's only been about 14,000 years since we started paying attention to astronomy. There may be other high-tech species, and in fact probably are, hidden out among the stars.

If we come upon a civilization that's still in its early years, inventing plumbing or learning how to run a farm, no harm can be done, at least to us. And we've been developing science long enough now that we've developed a dangerous attitude that we will be the superiors in any confrontation. But we really have no idea what we might be facing. How advanced would a civilization be that is a million years past its pyramid phase? Or its quantum bomb development?

It's time we got a handle on this. No one should be allowed to own a private interstellar vehicle. I understand that the owners do not want to see the government coming for their yachts. If we can find a way to contain them within the Confederacy, that would be a workable solution. But until someone comes up with a way to make it happen, we are all at risk.

It's difficult to see that we have anything to gain by poking our heads into other star systems. But it's brutally clear that we have a lot to lose.

—Carl Comenides, editor

Arcadia ran a clip of a Quaid McCann interview on *Nightlight*. It had taken place two days after he'd gotten back from the *Columbia* flight, before it was discovered that the village they'd seen on Korella was no longer there. Most of the questions centered on how it felt to find a new civilization. McCann was absolutely ecstatic. I don't think I've ever seen an interview with a person who seemed more inclined to throw up his hands in pure joy.

Physicists, politicians, and show business celebrities were everywhere. Some were worried that we would discover and drift into the target sites of a dangerous adversary. More often, they were concerned that we would damage societies in their early stages of development. "Consider how we would have reacted if someone had descended from the sky into Europe during its medieval years," said Andy Kolaska, the lead star of *Judge and Jury*. "We just need to keep our hands off."

Veronica Walker had been spending time with Alex for about a year. She had chestnut hair, brown eyes, and, in Gabe's words, the smile of a Greek goddess. She'd first attracted Alex's attention when she'd outbid him for a Wally Candles lamp. That was hard to believe. She was a librarian, so she wasn't exactly wealthy. Alex was never short of cash, and he had a passion for Wally Candles artifacts. But it was obvious he'd wanted to do whatever it would take to make Veronica happy.

The day after the news broke, I was standing in the corridor, finishing a conversation with an accountant, when Alex walked in. He raised his hand, said hello without even glancing at us, and started up the stairs. That was utterly out of character for him.

He'd been at lunch with Veronica. When our visitor was gone, I went up to his office. He'd backed up against his desk and was staring out a side window. "You okay, Alex?" I asked.

"I'm all right." It was just loud enough for me to make it out.

I thought about pursuing it, but it wouldn't have been a good idea. So I held off and went back to my office. Later he came down to inform me that a client would be getting in touch. She claimed to have a viola that had once belonged to Archie Glazier during his years with the Twilighters. "Find out if she has proof of the claim, and how much she wants." He handed me a data sheet with her name and contact number. Then he turned to go. He was in a gloomy state, and he avoided making eye contact.

Alex is rarely anything other than his tranquil, complacent self. "Alex," I said, "what's going on?"

"I'm fine." He was headed for the door.

"What's wrong?"

He stopped. "Is it that obvious?"

"Problem with Veronica?"

He shrugged. "More or less."

"She wants you not to go?"

"That's part of it."

"What else?"

"I invited her to come with us."

"She passed?"

"Yes."

"I'm sorry."

"Me too."

"Why'd she do that?"

He needed to think about his reply. "She says she'd lose her job. And that she doesn't want to spend three months locked up in an interstellar." He lowered himself into the armchair near the window.

"We still going?"

"Yes. Of course."

"You're sure?"

He reached onto the side table and picked up a notepad. "I've work to do now, Chase."

Later he called me into the conference room. Gabe was seated at the table. "It's obvious," Alex was saying, "that whoever was there, on Korella, was not a product of that world. They came from somewhere else. Apparently they saw the *Columbia* and cleared out. But it's not likely they would have gone far." He waved me to a chair, and then continued, "Maybe they were riding all over the Milky Way. But whatever the reality is, we know they got out of there in a hurry. They were gone when the *Harbinger* showed up. So we should not limit our search to Korella."

"That sounds like a lot of travel," Gabe said.

"It will be."

"You don't sound," Gabe said, "as if we're just going there to dig up a few artifacts."

Alex nodded. "We're going there to see what happens. I can't think of a better way to phrase it."

Gabe needed a minute to think about it. "Cancel the mission, Alex," he said. "We aren't going to find anything, and it's not worth losing her." He obviously knew about Veronica.

A sad smile took over Alex's features. "It might be a bit late for that."

We began prepping the *Belle-Marie* for the flight. Belle, the ship's AI, operates out of my office when we aren't going anywhere. She said goodbye and moved electronically to Skydeck so she could direct the refueling, storing of supplies, and the rest of the getaway procedure. I spent the balance of the day out tracking down the ownership validity of a pair of artifacts, both of which were legitimate. When I got back to the country house in the late afternoon, Gabe and Alex were seated on the porch. It was chilly, so they'd closed the panels. They both looked half-asleep. "I didn't expect to see you back so soon, Chase," Alex said. "Everything okay?"

"I have some work to do. By the way, how are we going to handle business while we're gone? Are we turning everything over to Jacob?" We routinely did that when we left for a short period. But it wouldn't really work this time.

Gabe responded, "We're okay. Lou Banner's going to be here." Banner was a historian, and Gabe's longtime friend. "I should mention he'd like to interview you when you have time." He was talking to me.

"Sure." I looked toward Alex. "Would that be about you?"

"I think it would be about the whole process. I wish we could have kept this quiet."

I settled into a chair. "He'll probably have to wait until we get home."

"I suspect he'd prefer talking with you before we leave. For one thing, he needs to track down your responsibilities. Are you available tomorrow morning?"

"Okay, Gabe. How about nine o'clock?"

"Good enough."

Alex looked toward me. "We all set here?"

"I need to track a couple of items today." I was referring to artifacts that had just taken their place on the auction list.

"Anything interesting?"

"Not much. Mandy Estra's vase and a side table that's supposed to have belonged originally to Albert Kelfer." Mandy Estra had been the brilliant novelist from Point Edward who'd retired on Rimway, and Albert Kelfer was the guy who'd tried to betray the rebels during the Segorian Uprising a century ago. I looked back at Gabe. "What are *you* doing these days?"

"Just living the quiet life."

I spent the following morning with Banner. Alex was out of the building in the early afternoon when the postal skimmer arrived with a package from someone named Schriver at Skydeck. I signed for it and brought it inside. Packages from the space station weren't unusual in our business, but as far as I knew we weren't expecting anything, and I didn't know anyone named Schriver. I scanned it and saw five carefully wrapped coffee cups. Even material from the platform did not normally raise my eyebrows. But this did when I saw the inscription on the cups: *IVS COLUMBIA.* That, of course, was a reference to Interstellar Velloniko Searcher. The vehicle had been designed and jointly constructed by Velloniko and NASA. Several minutes later we received a second piece of mail, a document signed by Korby Estavos certifying that the cups sent from Skydeck on that date had been part of the original Korella IV mission.

Alex returned an hour later during a heavy rainstorm. I showed him the cups. Ordinarily he'd have gone upstairs to change and get some dry clothes, but he stopped long enough to open the package and unwrap one of them. "Excellent," he said. He held it close to a lamp and then turned and gave me a smile that suggested he'd just won a major prize.

"Should be worth a good bit," I said.

"Yes, indeed. Even if we can establish what really happened out there."

"Assuming what really happened wasn't a hoax." That was supposed to be a joke.

"I don't know," he said. "Even a hoax might work." He put the cup back in the package.

"Who's Korby Estavos?"

"He's the chief engineer at Velloniko."

"Did you have to pay much for these?"

"About eight times what they were worth when the mission left Skydeck. When I talked with Estavos, he looked as if he thought he was taking advantage of me." Alex was holding his drenched shirt out and squeezing water from it. "I paid more than the auction value, but not much. Their price has been going down the last few weeks. But if we can find anything at all, their value will rise considerably." He delivered a smile that suggested everything was going well. "Put them in storage."

"Let's hope we can get some alien artifacts."

He shrugged. "That would be good too. But even then I'd rather have these."

"You're kidding, right?"

"Chase, if we learn about an alien civilization, and establish contact with them, the alien artifacts will gain some value. But these will be the real prizes. *Anything* connected with McCann and the *Columbia* will go through the roof.

"When's the last time you saw anybody interested in a Mute transmitter? On the other hand, Captain Maybury's cap would bring enough money to set either of us up for life." Solia Maybury had been captain of the *LaGuardia*, which had made the first contact with the Ashiyyur.

It became obvious that everyone connected with the earlier flights was interested in what we were about to do. Including Henry Cassell. We didn't have much going on at the time. Business was slow. There were only a few items of serious interest on auction. I'd fallen asleep at my desk when Jacob broke in: "Alex is on the circuit with Professor Cassell. He wants you to participate in the conversation."

He connected me, and Alex informed him that I was there. Both men blinked on, Henry on a sofa nursing a drink, Alex behind his desk. "Going to take a break for a few weeks," Henry was saying, "just enjoy myself and spend some time with friends. Next week Joanna and I will be going to Paris."

"Paris?" Alex's eyes widened. "Marvelous. That should be a vacation to remember. You ever been there before?"

"My folks took me there when I was a teenager. I've been promising Joanna for years that we would do this. But I've always been too busy."

Alex nodded. "The perfect vacation for a historian. Henry, you're receiving Chase okay?"

"Yes. She just came on." He looked directly at me and smiled. "Hello, Chase. It's good to see you again."

"The pleasure is mine, sir."

"Chase will be accompanying us on the flight. In fact, she's the pilot." Alex set his elbows on the desk, joined his hands, and set his chin on them. "Henry, does your wife have a connection with it? With Paris?"

"She was born in northern Europe. After college, she started a career as a technician, which was what brought her out here. She tells me she always wanted to visit Paris, but life was moving too quickly and she never made it." He emptied his glass and looked down at it. "I've always wanted to go back myself. When I was a teenager, I didn't really appreciate the place."

He paused and I picked up the thread: "I've always been struck by the fact that cities like Paris, the historic cities, seem to survive forever. Rome, Athens, Belios, London, Beijing, Tokyo, Berlin, Amonda. They're all thousands of years old. And as far as I can tell, they look better than ever."

"That is certainly correct." Henry looked like the kind of guy who was inclined to volunteer to help any good cause that came his way. His green eyes focused on me. "Have you been to Earth, Chase?"

"A couple of years ago. With Alex."

He smiled. "We don't let go of the things we care about. New York's twice survived tidal waves. Beijing had to rebuild after a major earthquake. Of course I don't need to mention the Great London Fire. But the cities always come back looking even better. It's probably something in the DNA."

The wind was picking up. The tree branches outside began moving back and forth.

Alex glanced out at the trees. I couldn't see them, of course, the ones visible from his window, but I knew that was what had drawn his attention. "You know," he said, "speaking of ancient history, one of the things that always struck me was the conviction so many people had that the world was going to end soon. Of the fiction that has survived, there must be dozens of books that deal with an apocalypse. *The War of the Worlds, Cat's Cradle, On the Beach, A Canticle for Leibowitz, Childhood's End, Lost Angels, Downhill All the Way.* Incredible."

Henry frowned. "I never heard of that last one, Alex."

"I made that one up. But I'd be surprised if someone hasn't used the title. It's probably lost now."

They traded smiles, and Henry picked up the thread. "Actually, we survived in *The War of the Worlds*. The Martians got taken down by bugs."

"We almost always survive in those things," said Alex. "My point is that we seem to *enjoy* being scared."

Henry was clearly enjoying the conversation. "I hadn't really ever thought about the end of times. That's an issue that's gone now. We all assume the Confederacy will be here until the galaxy collapses. I mean, there are no end-of-the-world novels or movies anymore. There's no reasonable way it could happen." He was looking at Alex. "Other than an encounter with super-high-tech aliens. But maybe I should stop wasting your time. You must be wondering why I called."

"It's pretty obvious," said Alex. "You found out that we're going back to Korella IV."

"Yes." His cheerful expression faded. "I don't think it's a good idea."

"Why not?"

"Primarily because I doubt there's anything there to see. We looked all over the lake area, and we spent a lot of time orbiting the planet. If there really was a village, it's gone. I have no idea how or why, but it's gone. And other than the satellite, there's no indication of intelligent life anywhere. The entire planet is dark. It's a lot like Rimway: forests, oceans, mountain chains, except that there's nobody there. You're going to waste a lot of time and money. In the end, you'll have nothing to show for it."

"We've been hearing that all along, Henry. But I don't know anyone who has even the beginning of a reasonable explanation for what happened. Who was there when the *Columbia* arrived? Where did they go? How'd they manage it? Something's going on."

"That is clearly true. But the fact that something is going on doesn't mean we have a capability to find an explanation for it. Or that it even matters. And there's one more thing."

"What's that?"

"I'm sure you've heard about the weirdness experienced by a couple of the people who have set foot on the ground at Korella IV."

"Tell us about it."

"Nobody has seen anything. But there's a sense that something was watching us."

I broke in: "Did *you* experience that kind of feeling, Henry?"

"No. And ordinarily I wouldn't bring something like that up. But the two who did both swore by it. One of them, Autumn Ulbrich, thinks I might be inclined to dismiss anything that, as she put it, doesn't fit with my worldview. They were so adamant that I'll confess it rattled me. My natural tendency now is not to bring it up, but I've a responsibility to do so. Just in case."

)) ● ((

We got calls and mail taking us to task for the mission. Some claimed to be worried only about our well-being, but others were concerned about another alien war. Possibly with someone technologically far ahead of us. One piece of mail in particular argued that Alex, of all people, should be aware of the hazards involved in contact with other species. She was referring, of course, to his connection with Christopher Sim and the Ashiyyuran War. A fair number of our clients joined the chorus. Some threatened to break their ties with Rainbow Enterprises, and in fact a few did. The conversation with Henry Cassell did nothing to settle my own discomfort. The truth is, if I could have made the call, I'd have canceled. "You want to rethink this?" I asked Alex.

"No."

"It might cause serious harm to Rainbow."

"Chase, we only get one life. When there's something I very much want to do, I'm not going to let money get in the way. Or other people's reluctance. But if you want to bail out, I understand."

"Did you see the Infomax editorial by Comenides? About putting the entire human race at risk?"

"The only strategy to deal with that would be to send everyone back to Earth and turn off the lights." A grouper climbed into view at the window. It wagged its tail. "In any case, we'll make sure no one who's seriously dangerous will get any information from us. If we have to, we'll blow up the *Belle-Marie*."

)) ● ((

I'd been spending occasional evenings at that time with Chad. He was a full-time relaxed guy who was becoming an increasingly close part of my life. We were having dinner at Wentzel's when he asked when we'd be leaving for Korella. And when would we be getting back?

Chad enjoyed tennis, liked to read, and loved live theater. His idea of excitement was riding his bicycle along dusty hilltop roads shortly after dawn. He'd never been off-world, and as far as I could tell, had never been to any of Rimway's other continents. I suspected that if we didn't have antigravity, he would not have gone near an aircraft, either.

"We'll probably be leaving in a couple of days," I told him. "We have no idea how long this thing will take. It'll be at least two months. More like three or four, from what I'm hearing." His eyes blinked. I could see he was not happy.

"I'm sorry," I said. "I'll miss you."

He stared down at his plate. "I'll miss you, too, Chase." He shook his head. "Life is full of disappointments. Why are you doing this? There's nothing there."

"I don't have much to say about it, Chad. I'm his pilot. I can't back off."

"I understand." He sipped his coffee, put it back down, and looked across the restaurant. It was getting late. There were only a few people left. "You do stuff like this a lot."

"I guess. Flight time doesn't usually come anywhere near this one, though." It was the wrong thing to say, and I tried to make it look trivial. What's three or four months?

"I've got a question, Chase."

I could see it coming, though I hadn't expected it. He runs a bookstore. It's the passion of his life. "Any way you guys could take me along? Maybe I could help?"

"We don't have room, Chad. We already have four people."

"I thought your yacht could carry seven or eight."

"We can on a short flight. This time we can't get enough air and supplies on board for more than four. Especially since we don't know how long we're going to be out there."

"Okay." He was not happy.

I scooped up a spoonful of the gravy that had come with my meat loaf. It was delicious. "I understand it would be nice if we were together. But I've never heard you show any interest in interstellar flight before. This feels as if there's more to it than hanging out with me. Have I missed something?"

He gazed at the wall behind me as if I'd asked a dumb question. "Chase, you know what I do for a living?"

"You make classic hardcover books available to collectors. You

have a career a lot like the one Alex has, except you're special-
ized."

"You're probably not aware of this, but your tone suggests that I
don't do anything close to what Alex does. That my career is actually pretty insignificant."

"You're misreading me, Chad."

"I don't think so." He smiled at me. "And I suspect you know
it." He settled back in his seat as a waiter arrived to refill our
drinks. Wentzel's was a pricy restaurant overlooking the Melony. It
was one of the few places in the Andiquar area that employed serv-
ers rather than automating everything. "Look, Chase, that's not
a complaint. It's the way everybody thinks of me. Willie's an ex-
ecutive at Worldwide Broadcasting." That was William Conway,
with whom we occasionally shared dinners. "My sister Emma is a
singer with Deltacon. Walter's a prize-winning historian." Walter
was his brother. "Hell, you work for Alex Benedict. And Gabriel.
I've got a bookstore."

"Chad—"

"Let me finish, Chase. I'd like to do something with my life.
I don't mean I want to become famous. That would be nice, but
it's not what matters. What I'd like is to be part of something that's
meaningful. That makes history. If you guys are going to shake
hands with a bunch of aliens, I'd love to be there with you."

"I think Alex and I have already missed the boat on that one.
Look, Chad, I understand. But you're the owner of the Collectors'
Library. A treasure trove of classics. That's already a major contribution. Some of these books would probably not have survived if it
weren't for people like you. Most of the major literature from the
early millennia is gone forever. Think of the contribution you'd
make if you could find a complete copy of Shakespeare's plays. Or

even just *Romeo and Juliet*. That would be way beyond anything
Alex and I are going to do, even if we get lucky and stumble onto
some aliens. It's the problem with abandoning hardcover books
and putting everything on an electrical circuit. You're still in the
early years of your career. Give yourself some time."

He gave me a skeptical look. "You're the first beautiful woman
to talk to me like that."

I wanted to tell him that it wasn't the bookstore that stirred my
interest. But at the moment, that seemed like the wrong approach.
"Relax, Chad. You've already done considerably more with your
life than most of us manage."

Wentzel's musician had been on a break. She arrived back, sat
down at her piano, and began to play. She was across the room,
near a set of jasmine candles. She had a light touch, manipulating
the keys in a manner that held everyone's attention without inter-
rupting their conversations. It didn't hurt that she was an eyeful.
She'd begun with "Moonlight Interlude."

"She's good," Chad said.

"If you go over and let her know you own the Collectors' Library, she'll be impressed."

He smiled. "Not nearly as much as she would if I could tell her
I'm Alex Benedict's pilot."

"I'm serious. It's why *you* caught my attention." I delivered the
warmest smile I could manage. "You're a guy with a brain. That's
what draws women."

"You really want me to do that? Go talk to her?"

"No."

He reached across the table and took my hand. "Thank you."

Vince Reddington showed up the next night on one of the major shows, *Final Thoughts*. The host, Carol Brent, wondered if he'd been invited to join the *Belle-Marie* mission.

"No, Carol. I never heard anything from them."

"Would you go if they asked?"

"Not a chance."

Finally we were ready to leave. On the evening before departure, Alex took Gabe, Robbi Jo, and me to dinner at Molly's Top of the World. It's located on the summit of Mount Oskar, the highest mountain in the region. Alex, Gabe, and I descended into the parking area and climbed out of the skimmer. As he always did, Gabe walked slowly, allowing himself time to gaze at the surrounding view, other mountains north and west, and the Terran Canyon, through which the Melony River passed, though we couldn't see it from that angle. Andiquar lay to the east, between the mountains and the ocean. It was resplendent in light. But a few clouds were coming in, accompanied by distant rumbling. We'd just reached the entrance when Robbi Jo arrived.

Soft music drifted out of the dining room. A woman with dark black hair was playing a kora. The song was "Love in Time." Gabe had reserved a table near a window. We sat down, talked about how much we were looking forward to getting started. We kept our voices down, though, not wishing to attract attention. "Maybe," I said, "we'll get a surprise when we get there and the place will be all lit up."

"Not much chance of that," said Robbi Jo. She never lifted her eyes from the menu. "I never would have thought I'd be going back."

Gabe had made his decision and informed the AI of his order. Then he turned his attention to Robbi Jo. "You think anything will be different?"

"No. But I just can't bring myself to believe that they didn't miss something."

Lester Wilkinson had been asked several days earlier whether he'd been invited to go back with us and do some more shows. He hadn't been able to stop laughing. He probably said no a dozen times. Hadn't been invited. Wouldn't have gone if he was.

Alex changed the subject. He had attended a live performance the previous evening of *All In for Jeremy* at the Orpheum. "Hysterical show," he said.

Gabe was reading a history of the early efforts to settle Point Edward, probably the most remote world in the Confederacy. "Have you ever been there?" I asked him.

"Only once. Just to look around a bit."

"Did Mom make that trip?" I meant *my* mother, who for a while had served as pilot for Alex and Gabe. She'd never mentioned Point Edward to me.

"No," Gabe said. "That was before her time."

We ordered a round of drinks with our dinners. Gabe routinely eats light fare, on that night a salad and some broiled fish. Alex was dipping chicken strips into something. Robbi Jo and I both went with roast beef.

It was inevitable that the conversation would eventually focus on the lost village. It did, briefly, but it was old ground, and in the end we had nowhere new to go. I remember thinking that I should check the *Belle-Marie* library to make sure it was fully stocked. I'd asked Robbi Jo for some titles she thought she'd be interested in having on board, but I hadn't heard anything since. She told me I hadn't been in the office when she called with them, so she passed them on to Alex. Alex signaled that they'd gone on to Belle.

The woman with the kira took a short break while the restaurant substituted recordings of some of the same music. Twenty minutes after she came back, the thunder that had been rumbling in the distance turned to lightning. Rain began splattering the windows. We were just getting ready to leave, but Gabe suggested we wait it out. "Somebody once said, 'Never play with lightning.'"

"Probably a good idea." Alex and I traded smiles. "How about a round of desserts?" The evening had been on him, so sure, everybody was for it.

))◐((

When I got back to my cabin, I turned on the HV so there'd be some noise. I called Belle to check on Robbi Jo's books. They'd all been inserted. I told Carmen to make sure I was awake by nine. Normally I would be up well before that, but I didn't want to take a chance. My Skydeck shuttle was scheduled to leave at eleven forty-five.

I read for a while. It was going to be a difficult night sleeping. I didn't usually have that kind of problem before a flight. But this one had roused something inside me. I'm not sure what it was. It wasn't fear, or even nervousness, just unease.

Carmen caught my mood. *"You okay, Chase?"*

"Yes. I'm good."

"Excellent. Sleep well."

I was just finishing "The Adventure of the Dancing Men," one of the three original Sherlock Holmes stories that have survived. I shut down the screen. "You too, Carmen."

I turned out the lights, pulled the sheet up, and closed my eyes. And Carmen informed me I had a call from Chad.

Maybe he was what had been on my mind. "Okay. Put him through."

He sounded stressed. "You're still leaving tomorrow?"

"Yes, Chad."

"Be careful. I don't want anything to happen to you."

"Neither do I."

"Good." I heard him breathing for a moment. "There's something else I need to tell you." I was pretty sure I knew what was coming. "When you get back, it won't be long before you go out somewhere again. Where does it stop? I just can't live with this indefinitely."

"I understand, Chad."

"Okay." Another long silence. "Goodbye, Chase. Be safe."

10

Once more, farewell!
If e'er we meet hereafter, we shall meet
In happier climes, and on a safer shore.

—Joseph Addison, *Cato*, 1718 CE

Carmen wished me good luck as I headed for the door. "I'm sorry," she said, "you will be gone so long."

She wouldn't be alone, of course. She and Jacob conducted a running conversation. They played games, discussed philosophy, watched the news networks, and had gotten interested in *Herman*, an HV comedy series about an AI who tried, usually unsuccessfully, to keep his idiot boss out of trouble.

I got my bags out into the skimmer and took off. There were only a few clouds drifting through the sky. The Melony glittered in the sunlight, winding its way northwest past occasional hills. A few minutes later I descended into the parking area at the country house.

A small crowd of demonstrators stood outside the building, posing for cameras. They carried signs stating that the world would be a better place if we would simply stay home, demanding that we leave well enough alone. Lou Banner was apparently waiting for me. He fell in at my side and got me through the demonstrators. There were some boos and pushing and shoving as I walked up to the front door. The door opened before I reached it, and a couple of security guys came outside to give me a hand. Lou had to literally drag one protester out of the way before following me into the building. A couple of media guys, including Lester Wilkinson, were in the conference room interviewing Gabe. They turned some attention to me and I got some of the same old questions. Alex joined us a few minutes later and explained that we had to leave, that we had a shuttle to catch. Wilkinson took advantage of an opportunity to comment that we were probably wasting our time, but he hoped we'd find something that the earlier missions had missed. With the help of the security group, we moved the luggage out to the skimmer, said goodbye to Banner and the media guys. And got roundly booed some more by the demonstrators. Somebody threw some fresh fruit at us. Minutes later we were on our way to the Andiquar Spaceport.

Happily there were no more demonstrators when we arrived. Robbi Jo was there, waiting. Chris Baxter was with her. She introduced him, we all shook hands, and he wished us luck. "Be careful." He looked at me. "Bring her back, okay?" She'd already checked in. We followed suit, turned over our luggage, and sat down in the waiting area. Twenty minutes later we said goodbye to Chris, boarded the shuttle, and lifted into a bright sky.

We were all reasonably excited and happy to be underway finally. Alex seemed to have grown optimistic about our chances. Gabe, of course, was an eternal optimist. "Even if we don't find anything," he said, "we'll have established that whoever was there is gone. Off-world, that is. Not just moved to another lake."

I was seated with Robbi Jo. She was obviously experiencing mixed feelings. "I'll miss Chris," she said, "but it's good to be on the road again."

)) ● ((

Since we were going to be limited to the *Belle-Marie's* supplies once we left, we headed for the restaurant at the Starlight Hotel. I don't recall much about the meal other than that they had a good-looking young man playing "The Crimson Melody" on a Canova cello.

Robbi Jo was enjoying it. "He looks like one of the guys from DPSAR," she said.

"Maybe they're going to use him to try to get you away from us, said Chase."

She grinned. "I don't think they're that smart." The cellist finished and everybody applauded. "I should mention I play the cello too," she added. "Not like that guy, but I'm not terrible. Was in an orchestra years ago."

"College?"

"A few years later. At about the same time I was earning my license."

"Did you bring it with you?" Gabe asked. "The cello?"

"No. I had it on the *Columbia*. But I only played it a couple of times."

Gabe frowned. "Why?"

"You don't have much privacy on an interstellar. I didn't want to drive everyone crazy."

"It doesn't sound likely," Alex said, "that anything like that would have happened. I wish you'd brought it along."

"We might be able to pick one up at Skydeck," said Gabe. "I think we'd all like to hear you perform, Robbi Jo."

"Let's let it go," she said.

I told Robbi Jo and Gabe that, since four weeks one way is a long flight, Alex and I thought we might stop by Delmonte Station. It's slightly out of the way. We'd lose a few days. But it would give us a chance to go sit on a beach for a while, refill the fuel tanks, and hit a couple of the local restaurants.

Gabe thought it over. Robbi Jo delivered one of those light-up smiles. "It's a nice world," she said. "Chase has a point. I suspect we'd all be ready to go down and hang out for a day or so. I mean, there's no hurry-up on our getting to Korella."

"You've been there?" asked Gabe.

"Yes. Twice. I'd hate to miss a chance to stop by again."

Everybody signed on. Later, when I had a moment alone with her, I asked whether there was a guy there.

"No," she said. "Nothing like that. There's just a lot of sunlight and beach, and we're going to need it."

〉〉◉〈〈

Skydeck was relatively quiet. I suspect they'd taken measures to prevent demonstrators from causing trouble. The *Belle-Marie* was at the number five dock. Media people from probably every network were waiting for us. They took pictures as we approached, and one of them asked Alex whether he had a theory as to what had happened on Korella.

He smiled and said no. We pretty much had to push our way past them to enter the tube that connected with the dock. Alex led the way and Gabe took up the rear. He was still explaining to the correspondents that we hadn't come across any new information, that we were just taking advantage of the opportunity. One of them gave him a business card. "If you find anything, please call me. We'll pay the cost." She had that right. A call from Korella wouldn't be cheap.

We were all staring up at the dome that stores and maintains the interstellar vehicles operating out of Rimway. Some of the larger ones, the passenger ships, have their own individual stations in orbit around the planet. Any vehicles that were approaching launch time had been moved to one of the eight docks.

We passed through the tube and into the *Belle-Marie*'s passenger cabin. Our luggage hadn't arrived yet. Robbi Jo, Alex, and Gabe found seats while I went onto the bridge and said hello to Belle. Everything seemed in order. Robbi Jo, of course, had brought the location details for Korella with her. She turned the data over to Belle.

Twenty minutes later our gear arrived.

When we were all ready, I called comm ops. *"We can do departure in approximately eleven minutes, Chase,"* a male voice said. *"We've got one incoming."*

I sat down and ran a general check. Fuel okay. Air circulation normal. Generators good. And of course the lander was in place. We wouldn't want to get all the way out to Korella IV and discover we had no way to get to the ground. I'd set up the data information with Belle while she was still at the country house. But just to be safe I asked her for the details. She finished her response by posting the famous picture of the village.

I activated the allcomm and informed everyone that we would be leaving in a few minutes. "If you need to take care of anything, this would be a good time. When you're done, please belt down."

One of the entry ports was opening. It would have been easy to miss. We were still on the sunlit side of the planet. The dome was a light brown color, but it became difficult to see when the sun got behind it. Details consequently got lost. I told Belle to get us ready to go, and she started the engine.

We were picking up the conversation between comm ops and the incoming ship, which was the *Venerable*. Its owner obviously had a sense of humor. I checked to see who it was, but the name, McCarthy, was unfamiliar. Eventually the *Venerable* came in through the entry port. Its flight was by then controlled by the station. It crossed under the dome and angled toward one of the docks, well away from us. Then it slipped out of view.

"Belle-Marie, *this is comm ops*." A different voice this time. A female. *"You are clear to go."* There were no more incoming vehicles.

I alerted everybody. Belle informed me the engine was warm and ready.

I turned on the allcomm. "Everybody belted down?"

They needed a moment to decide. Then Gabe said, "We're good."

"Comm ops, take us out." They connected with our controls. The magnetics holding us in place shut down.

Comm ops doesn't often wish you good luck and a safe flight. But it happened that time. I relayed it to the passenger cabin as we passed through the port into a sky filled with stars. Robbi Jo said that was nice of them. The sun was well off to our port side, and there was no sign of the moon. *"They've turned our controls back to us*," said Belle. We started to accelerate but took it slowly. No need to burn extra fuel.

"Belle, set course for Delmonte."

She turned us slightly to starboard. *"Done, Chase."*

"Stay locked in," I told my passengers, though they were experienced with interstellars and knew the routine. Play it safe.

When we got to our jump velocity, about forty minutes later, I let them know. "We'll be going into Armstrong space in a couple of minutes. Don't eat or drink anything until we cross over."

"Whenever you're ready, Captain," said Belle.

"Hold a second." I opened the allcomm again. "You guys ready?"

Gabe answered, "We're good."

I looked out through the wraparound at the stars. Sol was visible well off to port. Then it disappeared, along with the rest of the visible universe. My stomach heaved for a moment, but whatever it was passed and I was okay. I switched over so I could hear what was going on in the passenger cabin. Everybody was okay. *"It should be thirteen days to Delmonte Station,"* said Belle.

Outside there was, of course, nothing. Just darkness. I got up and went back into the passenger cabin. They were all on their feet, stretching their arms, looking out the windows. It didn't seem to matter how many times people made the jump into the hyperworld; it always took some getting used to. A fair number of them got sick during the experience. In my early days with Alex, he had dizzy spells and simply hated it. He told me he'd have preferred to walk.

We retreated to our cabins to shower, unpack, and get some fresh clothes. When I went back to the main cabin, Alex and Robbi Jo were playing chess, and Gabe was seated with his notebook open on his lap. "What are you reading?" I asked.

"Elgin Walker's *Dark Years*. It's a discourse on how close we've come so often to eliminating ourselves: dictators who didn't give a damn, republican governments that dissolved into chaos, scientific clashes that led to the development of superweapons that we didn't know how to handle. That's the segment that really shocks me, that even scientists sometimes buy into the craziness."

"Fortunately," I said, "we're probably past that. I don't think there's been anything like that for a while."

"Chase, you forgetting about the war with the Mutes?"

"I wasn't aware that anything was threatened other than each other's fleets."

"That's not true. There were political leaders on both sides who pressed for attacks on cities. They thought it would scare the other side into submission."

"Gabe, they must have realized it would do nothing other than generate a counterattack of the same nature."

"Walker sees no evidence of that. Both sides knew of the possibility, but both had people arguing that the enemy would back down. In the end, he says, it all depends on who's in charge. That's why having the right leader is so critical."

"Sounds like one of the Ulakan books," said Alex.

I looked out at the darkness. Not *into* it. There is no sense of depth. It looked like a black cloth had been pressed down on the windows. No, not even that. It was as if the windows themselves were black. I've seen passengers try pointing lamps at the windows. Usually they get nothing. Occasionally, I've gotten a glimpse of one of the ship's wings. First-time travelers frequently ask to have the navigation lights turned on. They're not usually visible either.

But occasionally, yes, we'll get a brief glimpse of them. That's not supposed to happen, according to hyperspace theory, because there *is* no space. Don't ask me to explain that. I have no idea how that happens, and whenever I've asked a physicist, he claims I'm seeing light because I want to, not because it's really there. They like to talk about how our senses fool us.

Robbi Jo looked away from her chess game. She was on the opposite side of the aisle. "It *is* pretty gloomy out there, isn't it?"

Gabe frowned. "I wonder if anyone's tried taking a lander out into it? Or even putting on a pressure suit and climbing outside?"

"I've done that," I said.

"Really?" said Robbi Jo.

"Yes. It's been about twenty years. We developed a crack in the wraparound. Up on the bridge. I couldn't take a chance leaving it in place. If it broke while I was in there it would have been bye-bye baby."

"So what did you do?" said Gabe.

"We have replacement parts. I used a pressure suit, got a spare window out of storage, closed the hatch to the bridge, and replaced the wraparound. It was no big deal."

"But you didn't actually go outside?" asked Robbi Jo. "You did the repairs from the bridge?"

"That's correct."

"I never heard that story before," said Gabe. "Was Alex with you at the time?"

I'd drawn Alex's attention.

"No. This happened before I got involved piloting for Alex. It was a couple of weeks after I'd gotten my pilot's license."

We watched *The Road to Heaven* that evening. I'd seen it before, with Chad, at the University Theater. George Hassel is a nitwit who's consistently trying to help people who are having problems. He means well but he always goes too far. When a friend can't gather his courage to approach a woman with whom he's falling in love, George takes over, tells her everything, and of course scares her off. He creates so much pain that God sends in an archangel.

Gabe loved it. Robbi Jo understood why that made sense: the archangel was Gabriel.

We completed our second day in flight, our first *full* day, with a round of drinks and a toast to Gabe. (My drink, of course, since I was the pilot, was nonalcoholic.)

)) ● ((

I stayed mostly on the bridge and talked with Belle, as I normally do before retiring for the night. *"Do you guys,"* she asked, *"actually believe in angels?"*

"Never more," I said, "than at a time like this."

"I'm serious, Chase. Do you think they really exist?"

I hesitated. "Probably not. But I hope they do."

11

Solitude brings us into self-confrontation. It is how we discover who we are and whether we matter. It deprives us of any capability to do as we always do: to lie to ourselves.

—Madeleine Harkins, *Moonlight Talk***, 10,445 CE**

I was eating breakfast in the passenger cabin when Robbi Jo came in, carrying an open notebook. She ordered toast and grapes from the generator. The notebook had caught my attention. "What are you reading?"

"*Clarence Dingle's Brilliant Performance and Other Disasters.* It's by Horace Brandon. A collection of short stories."

"I don't know him."

"I wouldn't have either, probably, except that Chris introduced me to him. He discovered him when he was a kid. Brandon did

radio broadcasts in North America thirty years ago. Chris got connected through recordings that an uncle had and became a fan.
He's one of the funniest guys I've ever read. Or heard. He does a
lot of material about growing up. How when he was a teen, he was
scared to ask one of the girls in his class for a date. Anytime he got
near her, he froze. Then one day he saw an ad in a kids' magazine
for an electronic hypnotizer that would chase away all fears. A
young teen boy's dream come true, I guess. Anyhow, it didn't work."

"I like the title. Is he still broadcasting?"

"No. He was lost on an interstellar flight years ago. The
thing broke down and left him stranded. By the time they found
him . . ." She held out her hands.

"Sorry to hear it."

"I've been thinking a bit lately about the real reasons we
should probably not be doing things like this."

"You mean looking for aliens?"

"Yes. And, Chase, I'm not talking about having them follow us
home and blow up Rimway. The real dangers are more likely to
rise out of ways in which we are seriously different. In which they
are better than us."

"What, for example?"

"How about if they're substantially smarter we are?"

"That may already have happened."

"You're talking about the Ulakans?"

"Yes, Robbi Jo. We got a quick demonstration when they
started beating everybody at chess. It's not so easy to pick that up
from books. But I'd be interested in getting a better look at their
technology. Or maybe we run into a species with a life span of a
thousand years. Or who are virtually immortal. I don't know about
you, but I'd find that annoying."

"It would cause some jealousy."

"Or we could find aliens who look like us, only a lot better. A race of people who all look like Gary Landis and Jean Raymond." Movie stars.

Robbi Jo smiled. "Maybe if we encountered anything like that, we'd learn how mature we are."

"You think that would be our reaction?"

"I can't imagine a race that could produce a guy who looks better than Chris. Or a woman who'd leave you and me behind." She couldn't resist laughing. "I guess we wouldn't need to worry about finding anyone more modest than we are. But seriously, suppose we found a species that had simply been around a lot longer than we have, and who have solved all the scientific issues? And they are inclined to hand everything over to us?"

"That would be a problem?" I asked.

"What happens to us when we solve all the issues about how the universe works? When there's no progress left to be made?" A bell dinged. Her breakfast was ready. She took it from the server and stared at it for a moment.

"You've got a point," I said.

We'd planned to start physical workouts after our first overnight on the *Belle-Marie*, but we just didn't get around to it. Too busy eating breakfast and taking naps, I guess. We got started on the third morning. The workout room is in the after part of the yacht. Space is limited. There's not much you can do back there other than push-ups and touch toes and ride the stationary bike. I went back with Robbi Jo and we did a forty-minute routine. Then we turned it over to the guys, got showers, and changed clothes.

Robbi Jo's notebook was open on her lap when I returned to the passenger cabin. "It's by Richard Myers, Chase. He's a physicist, just published *Interstellar Christmas.*" The subtitle was *Why Holy Days Matter, Even If God Is Not There.* "I'm interested," she said, "to see why holy days matter.

"His explanation is that families and friends celebrate them together and are thereby united by them. They remind us that enjoying each other's company is critical to living a good life. That we have a lot to be grateful for, and we should stop complaining. We have to face the reality that our years in the world are short, and time passes quickly, so it's critical to make the hours we have count. How, he asks, did people in earlier millennia manage to enjoy themselves? Prior to the twentieth century, relatively few humans made it to fifty years of age. Even as recently as the ninth millennium, there weren't many who lived past the age of two hundred.

"Technically," she added, "we don't call them holy days anymore. They're all holidays now. I mean, that's so long ago hardly anybody is even familiar with the term. But the heart of it all is still there, Chase. Love thy neighbor. Appreciate the world around us. Do no harm."

"I can't argue with that. I'm glad, Robbi Jo, to have had you in my life."

)) ● ((

Over the next few days, we moved away from the films and the HV shows. Gabe was a frequent contributor to *Archeology Today* and the *Deep Ground Journal.* He spent most of his time working on an article for one or the other of them. Alex and Robbi Jo played a lot of chess. They invited me to participate, but I couldn't compete with either. My chess was pretty much limited to Belle with her skill level tuned down. I went back to the books that occupied most of my free time at home.

I read some of the stories in the *Dingle* collection, read *Heaven's Awake*, which lays out a new theory for the origin of the Big Bang, and *Love on the Corner*, which was advertised as a romantic novel but is really an attack on women.

Gradually we moved in on Delmonte.

12

We tend to think of our home as a physical structure in which we live, a place that provides a shield against rain and cold weather. It is, rather, a collection of memories, experiences, and passions that we carry around in our souls. No matter how far we travel, they are always with us. They are who we are.

—**Edward Cantor,** *A Portable Life*, **1419**

We were a few minutes away from making our jump out into normal space. It was an hour after midnight on the *Belle-Marie*. Everybody was up and belted into their seats. They were running a Lou Prescott comedy. No one seemed much interested in it. They'd probably have to watch the end of it on the other side, assuming they cared enough to stay awake for it. Robbi Jo leaned over and said how glad she was that we were close to Delmonte. "We could use a little excitement." I looked around at the black slats that, almost two weeks earlier, had been windows. "I know coming here will cost us some time," she said, "but it'll be worth it."

I went back onto the bridge and took my seat while Belle started a slow countdown. Alex and I have been doing this for years. Stopping at deep-space stations to renew supplies or simply take a break. I'm pretty sure Gabe has too. But I doubt any of us before had been looking forward to it with so much anticipation. My heartbeat was picking up. Belle always did a countdown, but I didn't recall ever being so locked in on it. She got down to three and then said, "*Uh-oh.*"

That wasn't good. "What's wrong, Belle?"

"*We've got a red light.*" I watched it appear on the control board. "*The system isn't letting us return to normal space.*"

"Why not?"

"*No information yet.*"

There wouldn't be. The Korba drive has a built-in safety feature. When we begin the process of leaving Armstrong space and returning to the normal universe, the system is enabled. A group of particles containing scanners are released. After a minute, they are recovered, if possible, and if there's a problem, they inform us of its nature. If, for example, there's an asteroid approaching. Or maybe we're headed directly for a moon. There could be an even more serious issue. Maybe if we actually surfaced, we would be inside a planet. That wouldn't be good, of course, and in addition we would probably not be able to retrieve any of the particles. But it wouldn't matter. If they don't come back, it signals the danger is extreme, so the system prevents us from completing the jump. I got on the allcomm and let everybody know what was happening. "No danger," I added. "Just a minor delay until we get clear of it."

The system would wait three minutes until we were in a different location and would then send out another set of particles. Until it got a positive reading indicating that the outside world was safe, we would continue moving through Armstrong space.

The red light blinked off. A few seconds later it was back. *"Still have a problem,"* said Belle.

The passenger cabin was quiet. I knew they were all looking at windows, waiting for the stars to emerge. Meanwhile we went through the red-light process a couple more times. Whatever the problem was, it was big.

Eventually Alex's voice came through the allcomm: *"Chase, everything okay?"*

"The drive doesn't want us to leave."

"Why not?"

"We don't know yet. There's no problem, though. We just wait it out until we get clearance."

"Okay. Maybe we should just leave the neighborhood altogether."

"Belle," I said, "can you make that happen?"

"Too late, Chase. We just got clearance and have begun our exit."

My inclination was to stop it. I could have tried, but the effort might have done some damage, maybe even leaving us forever in that dark quantum world. The only rational course was to let the *Belle-Marie* continue. "No need to worry," I told the allcomm. "We're okay." We probably were, but I'll admit I breathed a bit easier when the stars appeared.

We have a scanner aft, which provides a view to the rear. I activated it and found myself looking into a sun. *"We are safe,"* said Belle. *"I do not have specifics, but we are not experiencing extreme heat*." I dimmed the view and put the image on-screen in the passenger cabin. "Take a look, guys."

"You mean," Alex said, "we were inside that thing?"

"No," I said, "we were never inside it. Armstrong space is a different reality."

"I know that. But that's where we would have surfaced?"

"No way to be certain, Alex. More likely we were just too close to it."

Robbi Jo was taking a deep breath. "I've never experienced anything like that before."

I couldn't help smiling. "I think you guys were talking about how we needed a little excitement."

)) ● ((

We were two days out from Delmonte Station. Mostly we just sat around watching movies, playing games, and reading. Robbi Jo joined me on the bridge toward the end of the first day. "I've always enjoyed this place," she said.

I was glad to hear it. Beaches and sunlight and a bar were just what I needed. "Sounds good. Was it like this on the *Columbia*?"

"You mean tedious?"

"Pretty much. You guys were gone for—what, five months?"

"Close to six. But we had more people on board. Seven. And we weren't riding in a yacht. We're kind of squeezed in here. And I should add that we were stopping at every K-class dwarf star we got near. They constitute about eight percent of the stellar population and are most likely, according to theory, to have life in their planetary systems. They're stable, and they put out minimum amounts of radiation."

"Any regrets about doing this?"

"None whatever, Chase. I've had times that were more exciting. But this has a lot of potential. And we have Delmonte coming up. They have nice beaches. You're going to enjoy that."

Delmonte was a perfect terrestrial world: wide oceans, a big moon, beautiful vegetation, and large birds flapping wings in all directions. Also, it was in the center of the Goldilocks Zone. It's covered with forests, and, I'm happy to say, our footprint is not large. There are only two cities. Other than those, you'd have a hard time finding any sign of humans.

We were about 4,000 kilometers out when I handed control of the ship over to the space station. They asked about the purpose of our visit and I told them we were tourists, that we wanted to look around on the ground, that if it was okay we would use our lander, and that we would like them to take a look at the *Belle-Marie* and provide whatever service it might need. Especially fuel and oxygen.

They brought us into the dock. We almost cheered when I opened the exit hatch and we looked out into the tube that would take us to the concourse. The station was considerably smaller than it would have been had it serviced one of the Confederate worlds. Out here there just wasn't much going on. Probably a few techs coming and going, and some imports, and a few vacationers.

We saw only one restaurant. Gorvin's Café. It was empty except for us and a couple of the techs, but it didn't matter. It felt like a crowd. They joined us, asked where we were going, and told us how much they enjoyed having company.

They were both guys and both got interested when Robbi Jo revealed she'd been there before. One of them asked whether she was planning on staying awhile. When she let them know we'd be leaving the next day, the disappointment was clear. One of them even asked whether we were *all* leaving.

Gorvin's made good spaghetti and meatballs, and they had an automated piano that played whatever we asked. We invited it to play its own favorites, so it went mostly with colonial music, songs like "Lost in Your Arms" and "It's a Long Walk to Arideo." Arideo, of course, is one of the two cities on the ground.

After we'd finished, we returned to the *Belle-Marie* and boarded the lander. Arideo was the closer of the two cities. Robbi Jo on her previous trip had visited Corsela, which was on the other side of the planet, but she had no preference, so we made for Arideo.

)) ● ((

Describing it as a city is a bit of a reach. The population is approximately 32,000. It occupies ground on the eastern side of an ocean. There's a wide beach lined by a six-kilometer-long boardwalk. It was midafternoon, and half the population must have been on the beach. There were several piers, which were home to amusement rides, a casino, and a theater. One of the piers supported a roller coaster that, midway through the ride, entered a tube and plunged into the ocean. There were also various shops, restaurants, clothing stores, and a game center.

We descended into a parking area just off the beach, climbed out into a warm breeze, and strolled onto the boardwalk. It was beautiful. The air smelled of roses, birds were singing in trees, and kids were chasing each other into and out of the surf. "Looks as if life here," said Alex, "is just a long vacation."

Gabe smiled. "Doesn't sound much different from the Confederacy."

It was probably our clothes, or maybe our accents, but we drew a fair amount of attention, waves and smiles from passing people.

There was a small paneled building on the beach, with males and females going in and out on opposite sides. Obviously washrooms and changing stations.

"Let's do it," said Alex. Thirty minutes later we were hanging out on the beach.

)) ● ((

Seashells were scattered across the sand. Insects with golden wings fluttered past. The sun was still high in the western sky. We took pictures of each other. Half a dozen of them decorate the walls of my office as I write this. Most have the sea in the background. And no one is ever alone. Robbi Jo and Gabe are in one, laughing and waving, Robbi Jo and me in another, showing off bathing suits. Something not visible in the picture was the attention we were drawing from passing guys. Doesn't matter where you run into them, guys are always the same. We got a passerby to take a picture of the four of us. And I have one with Alex. And another with Gabe and Alex peering into the sky, apparently looking for the *Belle-Marie*.

Alex was obviously enjoying himself. The beaches at home were always loud and crowded. "I wish we had a tent," he said. "I wouldn't mind spending the night out here."

"It's probably going to get cold when the sun goes down," I said.

"I think," said Gabe, "we could live with it."

We swam for a while and eventually came out of the water, dried ourselves off, and spent time just sitting in the sunlight. Alex stretched out and looked up at some clouds. "Pity this place isn't closer," he said. "I love it out here."

Robbi Jo smiled. "If it were closer, it wouldn't be so empty."

〉 〉 ● ((

I guess we all love beaches. We still had an hour of sunlight left. It had been a while since I'd wandered around at the edge of an ocean, where I could smell its flavor, and feel the sand between my toes.

Eventually it was time to go. We got dressed and went for a stroll on the boardwalk. I picked up a shirt with an *Arideo or Die* imprint. We stopped at a rec center and played a game that put us on a sailboat and required us to outmaneuver a creature very much like a whale. Gabe and Robbi Jo got swallowed. We rode the roller coaster into the ocean. That wasn't so difficult. The real challenge in the ride came when it turned upside down.

We stopped by a café for dinner and later visited a bar, where we danced the night away, with each other and with some of the patrons. When we came out, we were looking up at a half moon. I felt completely at home. I would have loved to have Chad at my side to share it with me.

13

If anything differentiates us from each other, it is the degree to which we exercise independent thought. The mind provides us, to a degree, with control over events. It allows us to rise above group meditation to arrive at truth. At reality. It prompts us to make the decisions that offer a life worth living. Or simply, in a complex situation, to do the right thing. All that is needed is to focus, stay clear of herd responses, and plunge ahead.

—**Kory Tyler,** *Musings,* **1412**

We spent the night in the Bannister Hotel. It was a pleasure to stretch out in a full-size bed. I could hear Robbi Jo running the shower as I sank into a deep sleep. I recall waking once with a sense that there'd been a flash of light at the windows, lightning maybe, or possibly an aircraft passing overhead. I thought about going over and looking out at the boardwalk, but I was too comfortable and having trouble opening my eyes.

I don't remember anything after that until I was looking at sunlight filtering through the windows. Robbi Jo was getting dressed. I showered and met her down in the lobby. Alex was there, and Gabe was on his way. We ate in the hotel, checked out, and made for the lander. I suggested we stop there again on the way home from Korella. Alex changed the subject, but he didn't indicate any opposition.

We said goodbye to Arideo and talked about what a good time we'd had. We needed almost an hour to get to the space station, where we refueled the lander, thanked the techs, said hello to Belle, and launched. We turned toward Korella and slipped back into Armstrong space. *"Time to destination,"* Belle said, *"sixteen days, four hours, eleven minutes."* That was, of course, the time during which we would be submerged. After we surfaced, we would probably add a few more days. Everybody was in the passenger cabin when I entered. They were looking at the beach photos and generally having a good time. The windows naturally had all gone black again, but nobody seemed to care.

There were more pictures: Gabe standing at the edge of the water with his arms spread as if he owned the sea. Alex entering the lander on the ground. And Robbi Jo and I posing for a couple of guys outside the hotel. At the time I hadn't realized I was doing it.

A lot of those would eventually show up in Alex's office. His walls are covered with framed photos. The *Corsarius* rests in a central position between two windows. And a photo of ten-year-old Alex visiting Earth's Moonbase with Gabe. And of Alex and Veronica on the boardwalk in Atlantic City. There were more than a dozen pictures of the boss and his associates, usually taking part in expeditions to recover antiquities or celebrating their successes.

We'd gotten rid of the gloominess that had hung over us the first two weeks. The flight had abruptly morphed into a vacation, and even if our visit to Arideo had been limited to a single overnight, nonetheless it had happened. And we could probably look forward to more on the way home. "We'll remember yesterday," Gabe said, "and wish we could come back here, the four of us together, and do all this again." He looked at the black window beside his seat. "And I'm not just talking about the boardwalk and the beach. I had a teacher at one time who told us if we were bored talking about nouns and verbs, we should take a moment and realize that one day in the future we would love to be able to return to that classroom and live again through that moment. Be with friends and family whenever we can." He raised his glass of wine. "She was right about that. Here's to us, the Arideo Four."

We spent the evening trading memories, listening to Robbi Jo describe her reaction when they found the village on Korella IV, and occasionally justifying our probably pointless mission by talking about the regrets all of us had for things lost because we hadn't been willing to try.

After we'd enjoyed dinner, I suggested a musical that had won some awards the previous year. But the enthusiasm wasn't there, and it became clear we didn't want to sit and watch a film. The evening was too energetic. "Pity," said Gabe, "that we didn't bring Robbi Jo's cello."

I turned in her direction. "When we get home, we should throw a party. And hand the entertainment over to you."

"I don't think that would be a good idea," she said. But she was delivering some false modesty. It was going to happen.

)) ● ((

We actually enjoyed the next sixteen days. It became somehow a much shorter mission than the first half of the flight. The conversations became increasingly personal, and we spent a lot of time laughing at ourselves. We watched Mr. Peters Goes to Breckinridge, one of my all-time favorite movies. It's an Edwardian comedy in which an idiot politician is dispatched to the Confederate capital to clean up corruption. He gets the job done, but not without causing chaos. It stars Hank Shekel, one of the funniest people in Dalrymple, which has been turning out what they like to call pretty good comedies for the better part of a century.

We didn't pay as much attention to the black windows, or to the sense that we were not moving. We ate our meals together more than we had before, and we agreed that if we didn't find anything when we got to Korella, it would be no big deal. At least, everybody agreed, we'd have made the effort.

We weren't reading as much anymore. During the first two weeks I'd finished two classical novels by Richard Wright and was well into a third one, The World Is Still There, which deals with people reacting to the death of a child. But I put it aside shortly after we left Delmonte and still hadn't finished it. I wouldn't go so far as to say that the days passed quickly, but there was no longer a sense that we weren't moving, weren't really going anywhere. Gabe had a birthday and we threw a four-person party. The following day we put on pressure suits, went down to the cargo bay, and opened the outer hatch. You're not supposed to do that in Armstrong space, theoretically because we don't know anything about it other than it gets twisted sometimes. I'll admit that leaning outside into that blackness gave me an unsettling feeling, but we were all laughing as we did it. Robbi Jo commented that sometimes it's a good idea to behave like a kid.

)) ● ((

We arrived on schedule a few billion kilometers from Korella, the star, and raised a round of drinks for everybody. Robbi Jo couldn't participate because she had taken over as pilot during the celebration so, as she put it, I could enjoy myself. When it was all done we jumped into the system, emerging near a planet that was located three hundred million kilometers outside the habitable zone, away from the sun.

"I suspect it's cold," Robbi Jo said. "That's not it."

There were two worlds in the zone. The closer one was a little larger than Rimway, in exactly the right place for pleasant temperatures. "That's the one," said Robbi Jo.

"Looks perfect for life," said Alex. "How long will it take to get there?"

Robbi Jo passed the question to Belle. *"Approximately five days,"* she said. *"Or we can get there with a jump in a few minutes. After we recharge. By the way, we have an asteroid coming up from the rear, off to starboard."*

Gabe looked behind us, out his window. "Oh Lord," he said, "we've got the force fields activated, right?"

It wasn't much bigger than we were, a smooth chunk of rock, long and narrow, tumbling through the night. It was coming fast, only a few kilometers behind us. "Nothing to worry about," Robbi Jo said through the allcomm.

"I've never seen one come this close," Gabe said.

Robbi Jo was on the bridge. The rest of us were in the passenger cabin. "It's fairly rare," I said.

Robbi Jo banked slightly to starboard.

"Robbi Jo," said Gabe. "We aren't playing any games here, are we?"

"Negative," she said. "I thought you'd enjoy a close-up. Belle, pull into a parallel path with the asteroid. Maintain distance of a hundred meters."

Gabe looked over at Alex, who was wearing a smile that he had to find annoying. "I wish she wouldn't do this," Gabe said.

Alex continued smiling. "You need to get out of the house more."

I reached over and put a hand on Gabe's arm. "Have a little faith."

Robbi Jo told Belle to release the controls. We were all watching the rock. It was a jangled gray mess, lumpy and battered from collisions. Belle took a reading and told us it was made of silicon and oxygen, iron, nickel, gold, and other elements. Mostly standard stuff. We were now able to see it was probably bigger than we were. Robbi Jo angled us slightly closer. It was still on the starboard side, running on a parallel course. "Can we get a picture?" Alex asked.

A brief pause. Then: "Done," said Robbi Jo.

The rock bounced off the force field. We felt the impact, as if a sudden burst of wind had hit us.

"I never really thought about this before," said Gabe, "but does the force field have limits? Does it matter how big the asteroid is? Or how fast it's coming?"

"Oh, yes," I said. "Sure. For example, we wouldn't want to collide head-on with a moon."

"But if we got too close, the force field would do what?"

"It would move *us*."

"You ever get hit by one? By a rock?"

"Sure. You can't really navigate out here without running into stuff occasionally. But I'm not aware of any ship in our era that's ever been damaged by a collision."

We watched it gradually begin to decrease in size.

We recharged the drive unit, took aim at the target world, and submerged. We arrived a hundred thousand kilometers away a few minutes later. Belle immediately turned the scope on it and put the results on-screen for everybody. The first thing that caught my eye was that there was no sign of an ocean.

"And nothing green," said Alex. He'd joined Robbi Jo on the bridge.

A large moon hung in the sky. Like most moons, it was strictly rock and craters.

Alex was still looking at the planetary surface. "Anybody want to go down and look around?" It was endless hills and deserts and plains and mountain chains. But no sign anywhere of a tree. "Is this really where we want to go?"

Robbi Jo sat beside him, sucking her lip. Finally she said, "It's the other world, Sorry. It's hard to tell terrestrial planets apart at these ranges. This is starting to remind me of happy days on the *Columbia*."

We sat through another recharge, put away two more meals, took aim at the second world in the habitable zone, and submerged again. When we surfaced a few minutes later, we were two days out. "That's it," Robbi Jo said. "Korella IV."

The time spent approaching was leisurely. Gabe finished an article that would later appear in *Archeology Today*. Alex and Robbi Jo watched a few movies. I joined them for a couple.

The mood in the *Belle-Marie* during that mission had never been more resplendent. Belle kept the telescope focused on the planet as we drew closer. Everybody else was looking for signs of villages. I was watching for satellites.

14

Artifacts matter because they allow us to reach back through time, touch the players, and watch the events that have formed the world in which we live.

—Eleanor Atkins, *As Time Goes By*, 8114 CE

Korella IV had a large moon. We got close to it on the way in. It showed no sign of having ever experienced visitors. As we cruised past, we saw nothing other than craters and ridges. If there's anything in the cosmos that always looks the same, other than stars, it's moons.

Planets, on the other hand, are a different ball game. They range from giant gas spheres to worlds that resemble vacation hideaways, filled with forests and plains and mountains, all surrounded by vast oceans. This one was typical. Large cumulus clouds drifted through its skies. It literally sparkled in the sunlight.

"Okay," said Alex, "let's talk about how we do this." Gabe nodded. They'd already obviously discussed the details. "Everybody assumed that when the village disappeared, the inhabitants went elsewhere on the planet. I know the other expeditions looked around, but we're talking about a *planet*. This area looks as if it has a lot of space that would work if you wanted to set up the same place. Even more if you wanted to conceal your location. And if they *really* didn't want company, which appears to have been the case, all they had to do was keep the lights off. It's also possible they came from another world. If that was the case, they might have simply gone back home. Or they might have headed out to another place. So before we do anything else, let's try to make sure they're not just sitting on the ground somewhere. We start by taking a close look at the original location, in case they've come back or left something that might be of use." Or left some artifacts. He seemed to have forgotten why we were out there.

Belle put together an orbital design that would allow us to conduct a wide search around the planet. We entered orbit several hours later. The lake where the village had been found was located on a long continent that reached from the south pole past the equator and ended about thirty degrees below the north pole. The lake was near the ocean, on the east coast, about two hundred kilometers north of the equator. With Robbi Jo on board, it was easy to find. Our approach wasn't going to allow us to get a good look without burning a lot of fuel, so Belle had taken that into consideration. Consequently we did not reach the original site until our third pass.

Robbi Jo joined me on the bridge as we approached. "Well," she said, "I have to admit it would be something of a shock if they were back."

We were coming in up the coastline, traveling north. The continent where the village had been located lay directly ahead. There were mountains to the south and islands scattered everywhere. We came in over wide forest and beaches. Robbi Jo was leaning forward, looking out ahead slightly to starboard. "There's the lake," she said. "That didn't take long."

We took pictures as we passed overhead and compared them with the images of the village and of the area that had been taken by the *Columbia*. The lake was about fifteen kilometers from the ocean into which it drained. It was more or less rectangular, several kilometers wide. A river flowed into it from the northwest.

The plain on which the village had stood was on the south side of the lake. Robbi Jo pointed to a fallen tree at the edge of the forest and to a downed tree in the *Columbia* pictures. It was clearly the same tree. No question: this was where the village had been.

So had they moved to a new location on the planet? "Maybe," said Gabe, "we should concentrate on the night side. Just look for lights."

"That would burn a ton of fuel," Robbi Jo said. So we stayed with the standard orbit. We'd still have our time over the night side and there was, after all, no reason to hurry. What was more important was to make adjustments after each orbit to continue moving over new ground. Our first pass took us over two more continents, countless mountain ranges, a couple of deserts, and lots of islands. We saw nothing that suggested occupants.

We moved over plains and jungles, surveyed islands, and checked mountaintops for signs of activity. We watched for vehicles, satellites, and antennas. Tents. Roads. Anything. We paid special attention to areas that could have served as boating facilities. We looked down on grasslands and flew through the night, hoping to see lights somewhere on the ground. We stood individual watches, each of us doing six hours daily. Usually there were two or three of us moving around at any given time. I recall everyone being asleep or at least off reading somewhere one night, but even then I had Belle for company.

We continued in that vein for several days, looking out windows and at several monitors that carried telescopic images. We listened for radio transmissions. But we saw no lights, and no indication anywhere of a village, although it would have been easy to hide one in the shadow of a forest. There were no boats anywhere, nothing that could have been a road. There were trails, but they were easily attributable to large animals.

Finally Gabe confronted Alex. Robbi Jo was in her cabin. I was on the bridge. "There's nobody down there," he said, keeping his voice low, probably in the hope I wouldn't hear him. "Are we really going to keep doing this? Or are we going to do what we originally talked about and try to find some artifacts?"

"I know," Alex said. "I guess we've had enough."

We returned to the lake and entered a stationary orbit. Gabe continued to watch through his window. "This is really weird," he said. "The guys on the *Harbinger* must have been seriously shocked when this was all they found." He was talking to Robbi Jo, but he never looked away from the outside view.

"They just thought they were at the wrong place," she said. "Or at least that was what they reported. What else could they think? Nothing was there." She closed her eyes.

Alex was seated across the aisle from him. He was also half out of his seat, his eyes fixed on the ground. "It might have been a hologram," he said.

"Why would there be a hologram here?" I asked. "Who would they have been trying to fool? It makes no sense."

"Neither does any other explanation." Alex took a deep breath. "How could they have moved the courthouse? And all the rest of those buildings?"

Robbi Jo laughed. "I think they have pretty good tech."

The cabin went quiet. "You guys were looking," I said, "at a world that seemed empty. Nobody here. Then you find the village. I think my heart would have stopped."

"It *was* a jolt. We'd probably have missed it altogether if not for the lights."

)) (((

"They had electric lights, is that correct?" Gabe asked.

Robbi Jo sighed. She'd obviously had to answer that question too many times. "Yes. They had streetlights and lights in the houses."

"That was at night?" Gabe was beginning to sound desperate.

"Yes."

"You also saw the place in daylight?"

"That's correct."

"Did you see anything that suggested electrical wiring? Any posts?"

"Lampposts, yes."

"And nothing else? Nothing that looked like a power source?"

"No, nothing."

"Good enough," Alex said. "I guess we've done enough sitting around. Let's go down and see what we have."

)) (((

I came down off the bridge while the others were climbing out of their seats. We left the cabin and entered the cargo area. "Chase," Alex said, "you stay with the ship, okay?"

"Sure."

"Nice not to have to wear air tanks," said Robbi Jo. "This should actually be fun."

We all went down to the cargo bay. The lander was, of course, positioned on a cradle. The launch door is on the starboard side. Gabe opened one of the cabinets and extracted three instruments that resembled portable computers on three-legged stands. He activated the screens. "These are roentgen trackers," he said. "They will allow us to see anything that's buried in the ground. As long as it's not too deep. Be careful where you point it, though. Don't get your hands or any part of your body—or anyone else's body—in front of it." He picked one up and showed us how to turn it on. Then he opened the lid. A blue button was fitted beside a small lever on the back of the device. "Touch this"—he pointed at the button—"and it will put a picture of what's below the ground on the screen. If you want to go deeper, push the lever. Okay? As far as I've been able to determine, the *Harbinger* wasn't carrying any of these."

"They were looking for aliens," said Robbi Jo. "I doubt they had any interest in artifacts."

Gabe took a minute to distribute the roentgen trackers, and then watched while Robbi Jo tested hers by looking through the deck. Alex, of course, was already familiar with the device. The trackers came complete with plastic bags.

Gabe took down two shovels that were clipped to the bulkhead. "Good," I said. "You don't want to forget those." He carried them into the lander and secured them. I added a round of meals. The plan was to go down and stay as long as they had daylight.

"Guns powered up?" asked Alex. He and Robbi Jo were wearing blasters. Gabe had a cutter. They checked their weapons, nodded, and were ready to go.

Robbi Jo focused on me. "Chase," she said, "you can go down if you want. I don't mind sitting up here to guard the *Belle-Marie*."

"It's okay. I've got it. I'll go down tomorrow after you guys make sure it's safe."

15

Like the dew on the mountain,
Like the foam on the river,
Like the bubble on the fountain,
Thou art gone, and forever.

—Sir Walter Scott, *The Lady of the Lake,* **1810 CE**

Alex took them down. They descended through a sky filled with sunlit clouds and touched down near the lake. The hatch opened and Alex led the way out, carrying both shovels. Robbi Jo followed. Gabe stepped quietly down onto the ground and stood surveying the area. They leaned the shovels against the side of the lander. All three wore imagers, so I was getting pictures and sounds.

It hadn't been so obvious from the pictures, but the village had been wedged between the forest and the lake. There was a wide variety of trees and shrubbery. Some looked familiar, like the quaila and bork trees back home, except that the coloring was different, somehow more intense. Others would have drawn attention, some with huge flat leaves, others with branches that seemed ridiculously long. Vines dangled everywhere, and there appeared to be a range of fruit. Robbi Jo provided close-ups at the edge of the forest, and I was struck by the sheer size of the flowers. Some towered over Gabe and Alex.

We'd studied the *Columbia* photos at length. There'd been roughly sixty buildings spread around the field, of which probably all but five were houses or cabins. The town itself would have taken about twelve minutes to walk through, from the trees to the edge of the lake. "The grass is thin," said Gabe.

It was. In fact, we could almost have drawn an outline of where the village had been from where the grass had either turned brown or was missing altogether. "Something else," said Gabe. "They seem to have had electrical power, but there should be a sign of it somewhere. Post lights or something." They were looking across a barren field. "I don't see anything."

Eventually they spread across what they began to call the village area, Alex toward the lake, Robbi Jo into the central section where the larger buildings had been, and Gabe along the edge of the forest. The tracker bags were slung over their shoulders. It was only a few minutes before all three were using the instruments to look belowground. Occasionally, I got a glimpse of the tracker screens. They were not seeing anything.

"If that place was real," said Alex, "they don't seem to have put much energy into basements or plumbing."

"Somebody was here," said Gabe. "Look." He pointed at the

ground. I couldn't make anything out at first. Just grass and soil. But Gabe explained: "It's compacted. There was a building here. And over there." He pointed off to his left. In fact, the ground was compacted throughout the area. "The ground's been pressed down here." He went down on one knee and ran his fingertips across the grass. "This is the edge of it." He got up and followed it for about fifteen steps, turned left, and eventually traced a rectangle. "It was a building."

Robbi Jo responded, "We got plumbing?"

"Not that I can see." They'd all begun walking around with their trackers pointed at the ground. There were not only no pipes, but it looked as if there never had been any.

"How do you manage a house with no plumbing?" said Alex.

"That's the way they were in early days," said Gabe.

They moved in all directions and found evidence of other buildings. They eventually arrived where the courthouse had been. Again they found the rims pushed out of the ground, formed by something heavy. And a lot larger than the other buildings. They found holes, deep holes, in the ground. "If there were some pipes around here," Gabe said, "I'd guess it was a water tank."

They spread out again but found no other evidence of support material that one would have expected for houses. There was no plumbing, no basements, no foundations.

I had a question for Alex. I'd have preferred asking it privately, but with everyone linked in, I didn't have that option. So I went ahead with it: "A couple of people on the *Harbinger* mentioned getting a feeling that they were being watched. Anybody feel anything like that now?"

Alex looked at his partners. They all shook their heads. "Nothing here," he said.

The response was so quick that I suspected it was a question they'd been expecting. "It was probably just their imagination."

They were each using the same technique with the tracker. You started high, near the surface, and descended into the ground until you saw something or simply turned it off.

After a few minutes Alex raised a fist. "Got something. It's close to the surface. Looks like a battery." He put a rock down as a marker, returned to the lander, and got one of the shovels. Gabe and Robbi Jo joined him and dug it up. It *was* apparently a battery, about the size and design of one for a flashlight. "A little bigger," Gabe said. "It looks so much, though, like one of ours. Maybe it was left here by the *Harbinger*." He held it up in the sunlight. "Don't recognize the language, though. Or the symbols."

"It does look like a perfect fit for some of our equipment. Seems odd," Robbi Jo said, "for an alien device."

Gabe nodded. "I suspect there are only so many ways to make a battery."

They saw nothing else and eventually spread back out around the area. The western sky had begun getting dark. Thunder rumbled in the distance. "Heads up," I said. "You'll probably be getting rained on soon."

A couple of minutes later, Robbi Jo had something. "It's not very big. Looks like a spatula, something you might use to flip a pancake." She extracted it from the soil, wiped it clean, and held it where we could all see it. Then she laid it off to one side, reactivated her tracker, and aimed it near the place where the spatula had been. "Well," she said, obviously disappointed. "Doesn't look as if anything else is there."

They spread across new ground, carrying the shovels, and working for another half hour with no results. Clouds came out of the west and it started to rain. Gabe muttered something I couldn't make out and started back toward the lander. Robbi Jo followed him a few moments later. Alex, carrying the remaining shovel, was examining the ground, gazing down at the compact marks the buildings had left. He aimed his tracker at the soil. And suddenly he put the tracker down and began using the shovel to rake the ground. Then he leaned over and picked up a piece of black cloth.

"You got something?" I asked.

"Yes. Looks like a cloak."

Gabe almost leaped out of the lander. He picked up the other shovel and hurried back to help Alex. But there was nothing else. Just the piece of black cloth. And it *did* look like a cloak. He held it up so we could all see it.

"It might have been left," I said, "by somebody in the *Harbinger*. Or maybe someone in another ship. I'm beginning to think maybe this place has had a few visitors that never got any coverage."

"It's possible," said Alex.

The rain was getting harder. The three of them hurried back toward the lander. I couldn't help noticing the cloak would have been a good fit for me.

The rain subsided after about twenty minutes. Then they went out again and did another search. The sun was sinking into the trees when Gabe found a cup. It was dark brown with something that looked like a light blue diamond etched on the front. It had a handle. And it was large.

Okay. We had a cup and a cloak. The cloak didn't have a label. So we had at least one, and maybe two artifacts.

Alex and the others retreated to the lander and returned to the *Belle-Marie*.

Gabe turned the cloak over to me. I loved its soft, velvety texture. "Alex," I said, "you have any objection if I cut this down a little so I can wear it?"

His eyes brightened. "You planning a superhero career?"

In the morning Robbi Jo again offered to stay on board so that I could go down in the lander. Alex and Gabe made the same offer, but since artifacts were their business, and the official reason we'd come, I accepted Robbi Jo's graciousness and explained what she should do if things went seriously wrong on the ground. If, for example, a tornado showed up, picked up the lander, and dumped it into the lake. "You really think I need help with that?" she asked.

"So what would you do?"

"I can't imagine a tornado could actually sneak up on us, but I'd tell Belle to seal the hatch and let it sit at the bottom of the lake until it's gone. And I'll hope you guys aren't gone with it."

"Sounds good."

"Be careful down there. I have no interest in going home alone. And I suggest you stay out of the woods." It was a joke, of course, but in a strange place, you just never know. That was the moment she brought up the subject we'd all maybe been avoiding. "I've got a feeling something's been watching us." She looked at Gabe and Alex. Had either of them noticed it? Obviously not. Both their brows wrinkled and they shook their heads. "It felt real," she added.

"Why didn't you say something yesterday?" Alex asked.

"I was waiting for one of you guys to mention it. Something that would maybe confirm it wasn't just my imagination." Her eyes settled on me. "*You* didn't notice anything, did you?"

"No."

"What was it like?" Gabe asked.

"It was just pure emotion. As if somebody was watching me. Toward the end of the day, I spent a lot of time keeping my eyes on the forest."

"But," said Alex, "you never saw anything?"

"No. Nothing other than a few critters."

"That's a fairly common experience," said Gabe, "when you're in an area that's completely empty. I've seen it happen to other people, and to be honest, I've had the feeling myself on occasion. Psychologists claim that it's our subconscious trying to get rid of the solitude." He grinned. "That it's trying to do us a favor."

"Did it feel like the Mutes?" Alex asked.

"Yes," she said. "That's exactly what it felt like. I kept telling myself it was my imagination, and it probably was. But I thought you should know."

I tucked a cutter into my belt and we boarded the lander. Gabe had picked up a sack somewhere. Robbi Jo left the cargo area and closed the door behind her. We took our seats and depressurized. The cargo door opened and the cradle took us outside. A few minutes later we settled onto the plain facing the forest, just a short distance south of the village area. We opened up, picked up our trackers, and climbed out of the lander. I'll admit that I was a little on edge, less concerned about hunting for coffee cups than I was about what Robbi Jo had found so unsettling. I'm not saying that I thought we were being watched. But it was hard to think about anything else.

Gabe lifted the shovels out to Alex, and we split up around the area. Alex went out near the lake, I went west, and Gabe to the east. We'd been at it only a few minutes when Gabe found a vase.

It was large, dark brown with two handles, apparently made of ceramics. Two curved silver lines passed through each other. Other than that, there was no decoration. We took a long look at it. Then Gabe put it inside the lander.

A while later I saw something in the ground a few inches down. An electronic mechanism. I dug it up and wiped it off. It would have fit easily on one of my bookshelves. And it had a cord with an insertion device. It was rusted and looked as if it had been buried a while. Gabe joined me. "Certainly been in the ground the better part of a year," he said. "So if we've been worrying that the other stuff we've found might have been left here by us, we can exclude this."

Robbi Jo spoke from the *Belle-Marie*: "Why don't you guys say something to it? Maybe somebody will answer."

It had a stud. Probably an activator. "Hello, electronic mechanism," I said. "Anybody there?"

I'm not sure how I'd have reacted if it had actually responded.

We spent the next few hours wandering around, using the trackers to search the ground, but saw nothing else. Clouds gathered overhead and the sky grew murky. The wind picked up and eventually rain began to fall again. We retreated back into the lander.

Alex took a long look at the electronic mechanism and said he had no idea what it was for. "No markings on it anywhere. It'll be worthless as an artifact." He was obviously frustrated. The original design for the mission was beginning to look as if it had hit a wall. "I'd love to see something that's unquestionably alien."

Gabe shrugged. "We've got the battery."

"Good luck on that," I said.

The rain picked up. Thunder rumbled overhead and we saw lightning. I was thinking maybe we should go back to the *Belle-Marie*, but I didn't want to be the one to suggest it. Finally Gabe and Alex decided they'd had enough of the weather. Gabe's first act was to pick up the vase. He stared at it with mounting frustration. It looked very much like a human product. "It would help," said Alex, "if there were something in the design that made it clear the thing is alien."

Gabe nodded. "I'd love to have an alien vase on my desk. This just looks like something we could have picked up at Shapiro's." Shapiro's is a kitchen store located a block from the main courthouse.

Eventually Gabe suggested we call it a day. "We've covered enough of this place that we could probably finish tomorrow."

Alex looked out the window. "I think the rain's getting weaker."

It stopped. The sun reappeared and we went back out and resumed our search. The ground was muddy. We slushed around some more.

And up near the lake, I found a gun. In this case, at least, there'd be no question about its source. Nobody had ever seen anything like it. We couldn't figure out what it fired. Not bullets. It was electrical. "Maybe a laser," said Gabe. It had a few unfamiliar symbols above the trigger. I was tempted to pull the trigger, but we couldn't be sure that it wouldn't explode.

I was holding it while Alex and Gabe were coming over to look. And something stirred behind my eyes. *Something is watching me.* I didn't mention it to them because I knew they'd conclude the feeling had been brought on by the weapon. Or by Robbi Jo's admission that morning. And of course I understood that might be exactly what was happening.

I stood quietly with them while they examined it. They both paid close attention to the symbols. And the trigger guard. "Small," said Alex. "Not for one of us."

Gabe agreed. "Maybe we've got something." He put it into his bag.

Then I heard Robbi Jo's voice. "Chase, you okay?"

It occurred to me that she'd gotten her first good look at me, at my face, as Gabe and Alex approached wearing their imagers. Her question drew their attention. "I'm fine," I said.

I almost asked what had brought up the question. But I knew, and now my partners were studying me with quizzical expressions. "Something wrong, Chase?" asked Alex.

"I'm getting cold," I said.

He nodded. "Yeah. Me too. Why don't you go back to the lander for a while? Turn the heat on?"

I held up both hands. "I'm all right. Just give me a second to get myself together." I raised the zipper on my jacket, put my tracker on the sand, and shoved my hands into my pockets.

Alex insisted. "Go back inside and warm up." I did, finally. I took the gun with me. I knew that Robbi Jo would have liked to talk with me privately, but there was no way to do that. The air had been actually chilly, and I was glad to feel the rush of warm air out of the vent.

I lowered myself into a chair. I was tired. More than I'd realized. I'd spent a few hours walking around and digging, so that was no surprise. But I wondered whether the gravity level was a bit higher than at home. In any case, I was glad to get off my feet.

Alex and Gabe were conducting their search on opposite sides of the lander. Alex was close to the lake; Gabe was halfway between the edge of the town and the forest. Neither showed any sign of thinking something was watching them.

That feeling had not gone away. I kept looking up and down the line of trees, convinced somebody was there, and somehow equally sure my imagination had run away with me. Finally I couldn't stall any longer. The forest looked increasingly threatening. "Guys," I said, "there's something in there. Be careful. Especially you, Gabe. It's in the trees." I felt like a crazy person saying that. But it was a mental penetration similar to the one I always got when Mutes were in the room.

"I'm getting it too," said Alex.

Gabe cleared his throat. "It's the solitude," he said. "Places like this always have that kind of effect. I've never heard of anyone being attacked. We just need to calm down. I don't know about you guys, but I'm exhausted. Maybe we should quit for the night and go back upstairs."

"There doesn't seem to be anything here," Alex said. He was standing near the edge of the lake. "I'm ready to quit if you are, Gabe."

The night Gabe had referred to was on the *Belle-Marie*, where midnight was about two hours away. The sun was on the edge of the horizon.

The length of a day on Korella IV was about an hour and a half more than our standard length. I'm referring to the daylight period. Korella's rotation took about three hours longer than Rimway's. "Something else we should think about," Alex said. "If we go back up now, we're going to spend a lot of time trying to figure out what's going on in the forest. Why don't we take a walk in the woods before we leave and try to get it settled?"

They didn't want me going along with them, but I didn't want to be sitting alone in the lander. So, in the end, they said okay, I could go with them.

)) ☾ ● ☾ (

Ten minutes later the trackers were back in the lander and we were standing on the edge of the forest, looking up at the trees. The world was quiet, and everything seemed back to normal, which made it hard to avoid the sense that it had all been our imaginations. Robbi Jo reminded us it was getting dark and suggested we should stay out of the woods.

"Just relax," said Gabe. "Robbi Jo, we'll be careful." And we started toward the trees. Gabe led the way. The trees were tall, with big trunks and swirls of branches filled with leaves and assorted fruit and vegetation. The ground was covered with various types of shrubbery, illuminated in patches by whatever red-gold sunlight could filter through the branches.

A gentle wind blew through the early evening, carrying with it aromas of cypress and evergreen and, as we moved on, of pine oils and musk. I noticed a lemony fragrance as well.

"It's beautiful in here," Alex said. We walked from one tree to the next, sometimes squeezing past bushes. Gabe couldn't stop staring up at the vines and branches. "This is the kind of place I've always liked to vacation in. Other than it's a trifle crowded." A joke.

"And remote," said Robbi Jo.

Something like an oversized beaver came out of the underbrush and walked casually across the ground in front of us, barely bothering to look our way. A jumble of something like grapes was growing out of one of the bushes. The beaver bit down on one of the grapes, tore it loose, and chewed on it. It continued chewing and paid no attention to us as we walked by. "That's odd," said Alex.

"I guess he knows the local predators. We're strangers."

Robbi Jo again: "He looks like a big pet."

Moments later we heard wings fluttering behind us. A large bird with blue coloring descended almost beside the beaver, took another of the grapes, chewed on it for a few moments, and leaped onto a higher branch. The beaver glanced at it and helped himself to another grape.

Alex looked up at the bird. "Anybody still feeling threatened?"

Gabe was wearing a broad smile. "Not me."

Nor was I. The sense that I was being watched was still lingering, but that was all. I no longer felt in danger. "You had it right, Gabe. I guess we just didn't like feeling so alone."

We didn't go very deep into the forest. Probably not more than fifteen minutes. There was no trail or path to follow. We came across a shallow brook, but there was no bridge or crossing. We could have waded across, but we had no rationale for anything like that. Eventually we turned around and started back. We didn't have anything to help us keep track of directions, so we didn't want to get too deeply into the woods. Alex commented that getting lost would have been easy.

We saw a few more animals on the way back. A couple of birds, one that was red and another brown and white. The latter one was big and spent much of its time drinking out of a brook. There was also something that looked like a teddy bear that simply sat on a rock and watched us pass.

"I wish *we* had animals that friendly," said Alex. I was thinking the same thing.

Eventually we went back to the lander, got on board, and returned to the *Belle-Marie*.

When we got up in the morning, it was still a couple of hours before dawn on the ground. We sat it out, waiting for sunrise. Robbi Jo was enjoying some peanuts when she said she'd like to go down on the next trip. "No problem," said Alex. "I'll stay with the ship."

That was a surprise. Digging up the area where the village had been was the whole point of the mission. I knew it wasn't easy for Alex to wait in the *Belle-Marie* while the rest of us looked for artifacts, but I suspected he'd lost whatever concerns he might have had that there was anything dangerous on the ground. And he understood that Robbi Jo had also endured the long flight from Rimway, and consequently deserved to participate fully in the hunt.

We launched shortly after dawn and descended through bright skies. We landed in the same location, again facing the forest, and stepped out into a cold day. The mental disturbances had dissipated. The world was still, and quiet, except for the rumbling of the surf. Nevertheless we decided to stay together. We chose an area that no one had looked at previously. We spread out over it so nobody was in danger of getting in the way of someone else's tracker. It was fortunate we took that precaution, because Gabe lost his balance and went down with the tracker turned on. The penetration ray swept across the area, but fortunately we were all able to stay clear. He was about to throw himself on top of the thing until he realized we were not in danger. Alex issued a warning about being careful and asked if everybody was all right.

Finally we got to work. I kept looking over at the trees. But the world seemed perfectly normal.

We'd been there a couple of hours when we saw clouds coming out of the west. I was still watching them approach when Robbi

Jo announced that she had something. She grabbed one of the shovels and began digging.

"What is it?" Gabe asked.

"Looks like a glove. It's close to the surface." A final thrust with the shovel and she bent down, cleared away a handful of earth, and held it up for us to see. It *was* a glove, black, bigger than would have fit any of us. The material, she said, felt like the same as that of the cloak. And it had six fingers.

"Wonderful," said Alex. "Be careful with it. Gabe, where's your bag?"

"Don't worry. We'll take care of it." Gabe was trying not to let his annoyance show. He tended not to appreciate unnecessary advice from his nephew.

Robbi Jo was still examining it. "I guess," she said, "we have proof now that the village really was here and there really were aliens." She was smirking.

"I don't think," I said, "we ever really doubted it."

"Oh, come on, Chase. Half the people on the planet never really believed the story. They were always looking for another explanation. Honestly, I didn't think you guys actually expected to do anything other than discover this whole business was a misunderstanding of some kind."

"Robbi Jo, you think we came all the way out here even though we never bought the story? Alex wanted nothing more than to discover something. And we've done that."

It was beginning to rain again. We got some thunder and lightning and climbed back into the lander. I was concerned about who was going to claim the glove. I'd have suggested we all shut down our comm links with Alex until we got it figured out, but there was no way to do that without annoying the boss. "I suspect," said Gabe, his eyes focused on his imager, "we've acquired a pretty valuable artifact."

"We need to find something else," I said.

"Why's that?" asked Robbi Jo.

Gabe replied, "Because Alex and I have an agreement that if we found something like this, it would belong to whichever of us found it."

Robbi Jo looked suddenly uncomfortable. "I'm not sure, but I have the impression *I* found it."

Gabe was still climbing into his seat. "That's why we need another artifact. Something Alex and I can get into a debate over."

"That's a thought," I said. "Maybe Robbi Jo and I should stay in here when the rain stops. Give you a chance to come up with something."

He didn't appreciate my attempt at humor. "Let's let it go," he said.

"It's okay," Alex said. "We'll figure out a way to manage this."

Robbi Jo was not happy with the direction the conversation was taking. "Listen," she said, "you guys supplied the transportation. You decide where the glove goes. But pick a place where people will be able to see it. Okay?"

"You don't care about the money?" I said.

"I wouldn't go that far, Chase. Museums buy artifacts, don't they?"

"They do," said Gabe.

"All right. You make the arrangements. I'll settle for a quarter of any payout we get."

Alex broke in: "Listen, guys, I have no problem with what you do with the glove. Without Robbi Jo, we wouldn't have gotten here. As far as I'm concerned, the decision is hers. Whatever she wants to do is okay. That all right with you, Gabe?"

"Good enough, Alex."

)) ● ((

The intensity of the storm increased. Rain poured down on the lander. "This looks as if it's going to last a while," said Gabe.

"You could come back up here," said Alex.

"It's okay. The rain's a bit heavy right now. Let's wait it out. Maybe when this thing lightens up a bit, we can find something else." A lightning bolt crackled down into the forest.

"That the kind of lightening up you were talking about?" I asked.

"That looked close," said Alex.

Gabe nodded. "Right next door. I don't think we want to go anywhere until this calms down a bit."

"I agree with that," I said. "We're also getting some heavy winds."

"Okay." Alex sounded worried. "Just stay safe."

Neither seemed inclined to raise any fuss over the artifact issue. I'd expected the old debate about museums and collectors to break out again, even though they'd backed off and turned the glove over to Robbi Jo. Maybe they'd both grown tired of the old animosity. I thought about saying something along those lines, but I figured that it wouldn't be a good idea.

Robbi Jo leaned over and planted a kiss on Gabe's cheek.

We settled in to wait out the storm. Gabe opened his notebook and began reading. Robbi Jo and I simply sat and talked about how happy we were to be along on what was beginning to look like a historic trip. "Even if we don't get any further than the glove and the cloak," one of us said. I don't recall which, but we both felt the same way.

Alex had closed his link. When the storm began finally to ease off, we reconnected with him and picked up the impassioned rhythms of the *Deep Sky* Sonata. We listened for a few moments, reported on the rain, and disconnected again. Gradually the rain went away and sunlight began to break through the clouds. We activated our imagers, hooked them back on our jackets, collected our trackers, and headed outside. The air was damp but the storm had passed and was on its way out to sea.

We ignored the mud and headed for the area in which Robbi Jo had found the glove. When we got there, we spread out. I pointed the tracker at the ground and turned it on. The music was still coming in from the *Belle-Marie*. "You okay, Alex?" I said. I knew he couldn't be happy alone up there while we were doing the stuff he loved.

"I'm fine. The weather looks better."

"It's perfect." I was looking at the tracker images. Nothing was showing.

"Good luck," he said. "Let me know if you find anything."

We looked all through the area, but none of us got any hits. Finally we moved to another location. Gabe was talking to Alex: "We'll be finishing up soon. If we want to cover all the ground here, we'll need a few more hours tomorrow. I'll take over the bridge so you can come down here. Then I guess we can go home."

"I'm sorry, Gabe."

"For what?"

"Talking you into this. It's turning into a waste of time."

"Alex, we got the glove. And the cloak. Anyhow, you didn't talk me into this. I was on board for my own reasons."

"I'm glad to hear it. Thanks, Gabe."

I was beginning to feel depressed. Maybe it was the tone of the ongoing conversation. Maybe it was the empty plain we were looking at. But I was becoming aware again of a presence. Somebody was out there. In the forest. It had to be in the forest.

And then a strange cry formed in my head, not something heard but only a distant whisper: *Help me.*

16

Of all man's works of art, a cathedral is greatest. A vast
and majestic tree is greater than that.

—H. W. Beecher, *Proverbs from Plymouth Pulpit*, 1870 CE

Help me.

I was standing behind Gabe. He was staring at the trees. As was I. "You hear that?" Gabe demanded. He sounded rattled. That didn't happen often.

I was frozen in place, the tracker open in my arms.

"What?" said Robbi Jo. "What are you guys talking about?"

"What's going on?" Alex's voice.

I'm not proud of this, but my first reaction was to retreat toward the lander. It came back, a voice in my head. *Please.*

"I hear it, too," Gabe said. He was looking in all directions.

There was nothing out there other than forest, the plain, and behind us, the lake.

"Somebody's trying to talk to us," I said.

"Okay." Alex sounded frustrated. "That's enough. You guys get out of there now. Get back to the lander and leave."

Help me.

It had become more distinctive. And somehow more desperate. We put down the trackers. It was still not really a voice, but a presence somewhere inside my head. As if I was talking to myself. We drew our weapons.

"It's not a sound," said Gabe.

"Telepathy?" I asked.

"Yes. There's a forest on Point Edward. You go near it and the trees talk to you. They say hello and thank you for stopping by."

Biologists had been studying the issue for centuries. We'd known for a long time that flocks of birds communicated as they flew or left a tree. They turn in a given direction and do it together, not following a leader but traveling as a unified group. Plants do something similar. I've read some explanations for how it happens, but I couldn't understand any of them.

"Get out of there," said Alex.

Robbi Jo's teeth were clenched. I felt the way I always did when a Mute was in the area.

"Alex, we need you to keep quiet. Please." He started toward the trees.

"Gabe," said Alex, "don't go in there. If—" It was as far as he got before Robbi Jo shut down her link.

Gabe told him again to be quiet, and then turned his off as well. I cut the volume on mine. Alex, of course, could still *see* what was happening. He repeated the command before settling into some coarse comments. It was unusual to hear anything like that from him.

I was using my hand to shield my eyes from the sun. "So what do we do now?" asked Robbi Jo. The cries, and the angst flowing from them, were getting more desperate. She moved up beside Gabe and put a hand on his shoulder. "Where are you?" she asked in a loud voice.

There was no response. We stood there looking at one another. Then it came again: *Please help me.*

"I'm going in," Gabe said. "You guys wait. I'll get back to you when I figure this out. In any case, I won't be more than a few minutes. If you don't hear from me, if we lose touch, leave the area. Go back to the *Belle-Marie.*"

Robbi Jo touched my arm. "*You* go back to the lander, Chase. I'll stay with him."

"I can't do that."

"Why not?"

"Just let it go, okay?"

Gabe was tired of all the talk and was already walking into the trees. Robbi Jo and I fell in behind him. Alex was still grumbling. "We'll be all right," I told him as quietly as I could. We kept going. The sunlight faded, shut off by the vast tangle of branches. "Anybody have any idea where it's coming from?" I asked.

"Inside my head," said Gabe. "You guys hearing the same thing I am? Pleas for help?"

We were. The ground was uneven and covered with roots and bushes. Vines of multiple sizes hung down on all sides of us. "Watch where you walk," Robbi Jo said.

We scared some birds as we passed under the trees. They leaped out of the upper branches, squawking and flapping. Oddly, though, they didn't fly away from us. One even landed on a mound of earth a few steps away. It was the size of a vulture, and it drew its wings together and watched as we got closer.

"I think," said Gabe, "he wants somebody to pat him on his head."

Robbi Jo managed a smile. First one I'd seen from anybody for a while. "I'll leave that for you, Gabe."

I was still feeling fear and desperation. Maybe it was mine, maybe it was flowing in from whatever source had gotten into our heads. We began picking up sounds, grunts and cracking branches in front of us. Eventually we could see movement and suddenly we were facing something that looked like a leopard. I grabbed my cutter. The leopard was standing on two legs. The other two appendages appeared to be arms. It was pulling on a branch. It saw us, but nothing changed other than that its jaws opened. It showed us a set of fangs, although there was no indication it was considering us for dinner. It yanked the branch clear of the tree, lost its balance, and almost fell. We all had our weapons drawn. Alex's voice reached a level that allowed us all to hear him swearing again. "Get out of there, damn it!"

Nobody was moving.

The leopard regained its balance, stared for a moment, and then disappeared into the bushes.

In what I thought at the time was probably the dumbest action of my life, I followed it. And saw that the tree to which the branch had been attached had collapsed, maybe struck by the lightning we'd seen earlier. It had broken free of its roots and fallen against another tree, into a fork formed by two of the branches.

And there was another leopard. It was halfway up the fallen trunk, trying to rip away more parts. Gabe and Robbi Jo were beside me. It stopped to look at us. Then it joined the other animal on the ground. Both simply stood quietly, not taking their eyes from us.

My emotions were churning. They weren't just fear, as I'd have expected during an encounter with leopards. And again I couldn't tell whether they were actually mine or imported. But they began to calm down. The two leopards backed away. And I felt a wave of relief. As if someone had just come to my rescue. "I think," said Gabe, "we're getting a lot of this from the tree."

Robbi Jo's eyes widened. "That's crazy."

"The leopards were trying to help," he said.

I tried to wave everything off. "That's crazier."

The desperation never went away. It was not as if I was listening to someone who was terrified. And frantic. It was me. A terrible weight was bearing down on my shoulders and neck. I screamed and went to my knees. Gabe and Robbi Jo also went down. Then it was gone. The pain was. But not the desperation.

"No way they can move it," said Gabe.

"Neither can we." Robbi Jo stared up at the broken trunk. It was much too heavy.

"We should get out of here." I was still concentrating on the leopards and my cutter, which, despite their lack of ferocity, I still had pointed at them.

"I know this sounds crazy," said Gabe, "but it's the tree that's asking for help. And the critters are trying to do something for it."

"That's nuts," Robbi Jo said. "Rescue a tree?"

"Anybody else have a cutter?" I asked.

"Wait a minute." Robbi Jo was looking at me as if I'd lost my mind. "Guys, it's a *tree.*"

Gabe reached out, put a hand on her shoulder. "Plants are

aware of their surroundings. And they talk to one another. We've known that forever."

"Yes," she said. "With chemicals. But it's all more or less automatic. I don't think anybody's ever shown they're conscious."

"Let's debate this later," he said. "Right now, let's just go with the flow."

I turned the cutter away from the leopards, took the deepest breath of my life, and walked in their direction. Alex was telling me to stop. The leopards were watching. I'd had enough of Alex, so I shut the link down. I needed the leopards to move and was about to wave my arm and ask them to get out of the way when they did exactly that, walking off to one side.

The fallen trunk was a bit more than a half meter thick. I got close to it and took an angle that would endanger no one. Then I activated the weapon and cut through the lower part of the dead trunk. We got lucky and it broke free and fell to the ground, away from the damaged tree. But its top half was still wedged among the upper branches.

"That's a good start," said Gabe, "but I still don't see how we can get it clear."

"You're right. It's too heavy."

The leopards climbed into the lower branches and tried to pull it away. It was just too big. Even if they were strong enough to make it happen, they might have pulled it over on themselves. "Wait," I said. The leopards turned, and incredibly, as if they understood me, they backed away.

The fallen trunk had several branches. I'm not big on climbing trees, but I got up as high as I could and used the cutter to sever every branch I could reach. It lessened the weight. But it was still too heavy to lift it clear. "We could use the lander," I said.

Gabe frowned. "You think that would work?"

"It might."

"Why?" asked Robbi Jo. "I don't think we should put the lander at risk. I mean, this thing is a *tree*." She sighed. "Well, it's apparently something more than a tree, but we don't want to get stuck down here."

I had been feeling less desperate and less scared, but suddenly my growing optimism vaporized into near despair. Robbi Jo and Gabe were looking in all directions, feeling the same warped emotions. "I didn't mean to offend," Robbi Jo said. She was speaking to the trees. "Who's out there?" she asked. "Who are you?"

We'd not really had a direct answer to any question. And it didn't happen that time either. What we got was a vision of the forest, of birds that might have been finches flying just above the trees, of the trees themselves, of small, furry animals munching on low-hanging fruit. And again: "*Please.*" It was purely internal, exactly the kind of effect you get from the Mutes.

The message was clear enough: get the dead trunk away. I looked around at the vines. "We may have gotten a break. I'll drop some lines down from the lander. You guys tie them around the trunk, and I should be able to drag it clear."

Gabe was nodding, but he looked skeptical. "You really think the lander can do that?"

"I'll let you know."

Gabe was looking at a sky clouded with branches.

I walked back out of the forest and headed for the lander. I was halfway there when my link buzzed. I turned it on. "Hi, Alex."

"Chase, stop. Don't do this. I don't want to lose you guys. Nothing would be worth that. In case you've missed it, it's a *tree*."

Gabe had already told him about the voice in our heads. There was no way I could add anything to that. So I let it go for a while and just said we had no choice. Alex has always been a stable, rational individual. But that day everything changed. The world had lost all trace of sanity. "Wreck the lander," he said, "and you're all dead. Do not do this, Chase."

"Alex, I'm sorry. I haven't got time to talk about it right now."

"That sounds like an epitaph for your tombstone. If you continue with this, and you are lucky enough to survive, you'll be looking for a new job."

I thought he might tell Belle to lift off. To get the lander away from me. "Sorry, Alex," I said. "Gotta go."

He started to say something, but I shut him down again.

I held my breath as I crossed the last few meters. But the lander didn't move. There were three cables inside. I should mention that the lander has skids, not wheels. But I couldn't tie the cables to the skids. The trunk was too heavy and would simply tear the bottom out of the vehicle. So I looped them around the hull, front, center, and rear, and tied each of them together.

I still wasn't sure Belle, at Alex's direction, wouldn't seize the lander. He could have done that even after I was in the pilot's seat. But it didn't happen. I took a deep breath and began to ascend. I've probably given the impression that the antigravity device allows me to simply lift off. It helps, but primarily by preventing the lander from falling out of the sky. To gain altitude, as you probably know, we need to get air under the wings. So my principal concern during that takeoff was to avoid having one of the lines get tangled with something on the ground. I turned away from the forest and headed over flat ground toward the lake. When I got enough altitude to ensure I'd be safely above the trees, I swung back and flew toward the forest.

The lander was equipped with two small rockets to allow maneuvering in space. And it uses a jet engine for atmospheric acceleration. I kept the jet at minimum thrust, and, trailing my two lines, I circled around until I located the fallen tree. When it was just a short distance in front of me, I shut down the jet. That left me drifting forward while maintaining altitude. Gabe called and told me to stay straight.

I knew Alex was listening when I responded, so I limited myself to saying I got it.

"Keep coming," Gabe said. "Just a bit lower."

There was an imager in the underside of the hull, which allowed me to see what was below the lander. Gabe, Robbi Jo, the injured tree, and the broken trunk came into view. Exactly what I needed. I blinked on the forward jet, which stopped me in place, directly overhead. Then I began to descend.

"Perfect," Gabe said.

I became aware of a telepathic—if that's really what it was—communication that was taking place. Back of my head again. I was injured. And afraid.

"You got the lines, Gabe?"

"Yes. Hold in place for a minute." I watched him and Robbi Jo climb onto the top section of the tree, which we'd used the cutter to separate from the lower trunk. They looped the cables around the section of trunk still tangled between the branches. One of the leopard bipeds showed up off to one side. But I saw no threatening gestures. Not sure what I could have done had things gone wrong then. It took considerably more than a minute, but finally Gabe was back: "Okay, Chase, we've got both of them secured."

"You talking about the lines?"

"Yes."

"There are *three* of them." I looked at the screen. I could see the tops of the cables, but I couldn't follow them down through the trees.

"One of them must be caught somewhere. Chase, give us a minute. Robbi Jo is signaling that she sees the third line. We'll take care of it."

I waited. Robbi Jo had gotten lost in the trees. It took a while, but finally he came back. "It got tangled in the branches. In fact, they all did. Good thing you didn't try to take off. You should be okay now."

"Good."

"Hold on a second." Gabe was on the fallen trunk, trying to get down. Robbi Jo reappeared on the ground a few meters below him. She helped him off, and they both backed well away from the area. Then Gabe came through again: "Whenever you're ready, Chase."

I set the jets for minimum acceleration and started them. Two of the three lines straightened. I moved forward and began to ascend. But progress slowed and stopped. I increased power and heard creaking somewhere.

Gabe called. "We've got it. Give us a second." Then, a minute later: "You're good."

I added power to the jets.

"It's moving."

The creaking got louder. And we were stuck again. "You need more juice, Chase."

"Belle," I said, "you following this?"

"*I am.*"

"You have a suggestion?"

"*I have insufficient data. An increase of power is needed to break the dead tree loose. But you are risking the vehicle.*"

I thought about junking the whole idea.

"We need a cutter," said Gabe.

I got out of my seat, pulled mine out of my belt, opened the hatch, got their attention, and dropped it into an open area.

"Got it," said Robbi Jo. "Hold on a minute."

It took longer than a minute. But finally Gabe said, "Try it now."

I increased the power again. Somewhere something broke and we jumped a short distance. "You got it," said Gabe. "The trunk's clear."

"Nice going, kid," said Robbi Jo. "Give us another minute or two so we can cut the lines."

I felt the release, reduced the jet to minimum thrust, and moved out over the trees. Below, the trunk lay still tangled with branches, but clear of the damaged tree. Two minutes later I set down, climbed out of the lander, and cut the cables that were wrapped around the hull.

Another call came in from Alex. "Thank God," he said. "You got lucky. But that doesn't mean I've changed my mind."

Then Gabe again: "Beautiful, Chase."

I closed my eyes and reached out for the voice that had been impacting me for the previous hour. It was gone. There was only a sense of relief and satisfaction mixed with regret. I wasn't happy about facing Alex. And I couldn't help thinking what it would have felt like had things gone badly.

Robbi Jo and Gabe came out of the forest a few minutes later, climbed into the lander with me and congratulated me, either for moving the trunk or for not damaging the lander. Alex, reconnected, said, "Well done." I could hear relief in his voice, but also a chill.

17

The physical gift is far less significant than the motive of the giver.

—Reverend Agathe Lawless, *Sunset Musings*, 1312

Books are to be call'd for, and supplied, on the assumption that the process of reading is not a half-sleep, but, in the highest sense, an exercise, a gymnast's struggle; that the reader is to do something for himself.

—Walt Whitman, *Democratic Vistas*, 1870 CE

"We ready to go back up?" I asked.

"Hold on." They hadn't closed the hatch. Robbi Jo leaned outside and looked back toward the trees. "Hello," she said. It wasn't the first time she'd asked the question. There was still some frustration in her voice. She wanted a reply.

She didn't get one, though. "You owe us," she said. "Who are you?"

A lonely wind blew across the field.

"You getting anything?" Alex asked.

We stared at one another and shook our heads.

Then something caught Gabe's attention. "Look." There was movement near a couple of the bushes. And one of the biped leopards walked out. It held something in its arms. A *book*. Suddenly we were back on Skydeck with the Ulakans. It was coming toward us, holding it out as if it was ours. While we watched, the second leopard appeared, but just stood without moving.

We stayed inside the lander. We'd done enough reckless stuff. It walked up to the door and laid the book on the ground. Then it joined its partner and both disappeared into the trees.

Robbi Jo was about to go out, but Gabe said, "No. Absolutely not." He opened the door, climbed down the ladder, and picked up the book. He took a quick glance, returned inside, and closed the hatch. Then we all looked at it. And I aimed my imager at it so Alex could see it.

It was a large volume, hardcover, printed in an alien language completely different from the one we'd seen on the Ulakan volumes. It was an astronomy book, with a shredded plastic cover depicting two galaxies that were probably orbiting each other. It was filled with photos of stars and gas clouds and planets. And diagrams. "Pity," Robbi Jo said, "it's loaded with text and captions and we'll probably never be able to read any of it."

Some pages contained columns of symbols. Others featured maps with disks and triangles of various sizes and designs. One single drawing spread across two pages showed a portrait of a planetary system. A sun occupied the center, with seven planets. The planets were reproduced in color and with some details, three with rings, and three others had orbiting stations.

There were also photos of aliens in space suits. Helmets covered their heads, but we could see they were the same species that had occupied the village. One photo depicted someone looking across a desert landscape. Unfortunately, the camera was behind him and only his outline was visible. He was wearing a hat, so we still had no view of the top of his head. Robbi Jo turned pages while the rest of us watched. There were numerous pictures of stars, one of a supernova in a distant galaxy, and one of a pair of spiral galaxies. She turned a few more pages and stopped again. "It's the Whirlpool galaxy," she said. There were others with which she was familiar.

There was also a drawing of a sky with eight stars. We assumed they were stars, although they were ordered like an arrowhead. One star was at the tip of the arrow, two were angled out on each side, and three more lined up almost directly behind the point. The names of the stars—again that was what we assumed—were listed at the bottom of the page. And there was a caption, of course. I sat there thinking how much I'd have enjoyed being able to read it.

Robbi Jo stopped at a page with an explosion. "I know what *that* is," said Gabe. "The Big Bang."

Robbi Jo agreed. She looked out one of the windows. "I was hoping they'd stick around. The leopards. I wish somebody here would talk to us." She closed her eyes momentarily. "You think it's okay for us to take this?"

A large white bird, mostly wings and beak, leaped out of the trees, circled the area, and disappeared back into the woods. "Looked like an egret," Gabe said.

I heard Alex take a deep breath. "It's a gift. They're saying thanks."

"For saving the tree?" I asked.

Gabe seemed completely taken over by events. "We've known for a long time that plants and animals could do this," he said, "but I never expected to experience it at this level." He went back to the hatch and reopened it. "Hello," he yelled. "Who are you? Can we help you in any way?" A steady wind was blowing out of the northeast, off across the lake. Gabe waited, shook his head, sighed, and finally came back in and closed the door. "Let's go, Chase," he said.

A few minutes later we were on our way.

$$)) \textbf{(} \textbf{(} (($$

When we got back to the *Belle-Marie*, Alex shook hands with each of us, told us he'd been worried that we wouldn't make it back, and asked me specifically whether the lander had taken any damage. "No," I said. "Far as I can tell, it's fine." Other than that, he said nothing further to me. There was a stiffness in his attitude that I'd never been aware of before.

Robbi Jo couldn't resist commenting that it was a pity the book was in a language that probably no one would ever be able to read. "It would be nice to have access to it. I'd love to be able to read it."

"It seems to have become the season," said Gabe, "for alien books."

Alex was still paging through it, after more than an hour. "Actually," he said, "this one will more than pay for the cost of the flight. There are a lot of collectors back home who will desperately want this." He lifted another page and studied a photo of a ringed world. "It's in pretty good condition."

"I assume," I said, "it was left by the villagers."

Alex agreed. "I can't imagine where else it could have come from. Certainly not one of the trees."

"Why would they have done that?" said Robbi Jo. "Left it here?"

"Don't know. If we can find them, we'll ask."

From the *Belle-Marie* we trained the telescope on the section of forest where the downed tree had been. There was nothing we hadn't already seen. Alex reached for the book. Gabe gave it to him and sat down. I got up and went onto the bridge. A few minutes later Alex followed me. He closed the hatch behind him—not a good sign—and sat down. "Chase," he said, "we need to talk."

"Okay."

"We're in uncharted territory here. So far there's been no indication of hostility, but we just don't know what's going on."

"I agree with that, Alex."

He sat down in the right-hand seat. "I want you to stay with the company."

"Okay. Thank you."

"But when I tell you to do something, I expect you to comply. All right? Is that understood?"

"I know that. But there was no way I could back off what I was trying to do."

"Why?"

"Because somebody was in serious trouble. All we had was the lander."

"Somebody? You mean the *tree*?"

"I know it sounds silly."

"It *is* silly."

"We were getting cries for help, Alex."

"I was listening the entire time. I didn't hear anything."

"We weren't exactly hearing something. Not anything audible. But we were getting telepathic screams. Somebody pleading for help."

"To rescue a tree?"

"That was what we found. You saw the leopards?"

"Yes. You're talking about the things that were trying to drag off the downed trunk?"

"That's right."

"And you concluded it was the tree that was calling for help?"

"I'm sorry, Alex. You had to be there to understand. I know what this sounds like, but if you'd been on the ground with us, I'm pretty sure you'd have reacted the same way."

"I've *been* down there."

"Not when the lightning hit."

"Okay. You're right. I don't get this. I never really bought into it. Telepathy from Mutes I can manage. But not from a tree. Still, okay. Obviously something happened. Gabe and Robbi Jo have the same story. Let's put that aside for now. Get some dinner and some sleep. Tomorrow we'll try to get it settled. If somebody's really talking to us, we'll find out who it is. Meantime, though, I need to be certain that in a crisis, you will do what you're told."

"Alex, we've been associated for a long time. There may be an occasion, like this one, where I have information that you don't. When I'll need you to trust me. If you can't agree to do that, I would, with great reluctance, have no choice but to leave."

"All right. Let's just relax for a bit. Maybe whoever's in the forest thinks we have some sort of connection with the villagers?" He started to get up but then settled back into the chair. "There's something else. I guess I lost my temper while all that was going on. I'm sorry about that."

"It's okay. I understand."

"I don't think you do, Chase." He looked out at the sky. "I don't want anything to happen to you. I don't want to lose you." He turned back and his eyes locked on me. "Not ever."

18

What's the point of being alive if you're a tree?
—**Reverend Agathe Lawless**, *Sunset Musings*, **1312**

If the decision had been left to me, I'd have simply packed up and gone home. I think Robbi Jo felt the same way. But Alex apparently spent much of the night with the book. In the morning, when I made for the bridge, he was in the passenger cabin. It was open on his lap. "You find anything?" I asked.

"Well, it has a lot of pictures. Andromeda, star clouds, all kinds of stuff. I can't decide whether this is a book for cosmologists or for high school kids. It *did* belong, though, to the villagers."

"How can you be sure?"

"The numerical system is duodecimal, base twelve."

"So we're back to something with twelve fingers."

"That's correct."

"How can you tell?"

He started digging through the pages. "Here." He found what he was looking for and turned the book so I could see: somebody looking through a telescope. The telescope was big, and the viewer was small. The photo had a long caption. There was also a side panel. "It's a list of places and their distances. It's pretty easy to tell which symbols are numbers. They have thirty-two items listed. One set of symbols on the left, twenty-three different ones. Those would compose most of the alphabet. A completely different set on the right, totaling only twelve."

"That's consistent with the rest of the book?"

He was losing patience with me. "I didn't go through the entire book. But yes. I found a few more letters. Wherever I was able to make out numbers, there were no new ones. And they always match up at twelve, not ten."

"Good morning," said Robbi Jo. I hadn't heard her come up behind us. She leaned over, looking down at the book. Alex leaned back out of her way. When she sat down, he handed it to her and she began paging through it, looking for something. When she found it, she held the book so we could both see it. There was a picture of a sun. Someone had drawn a red circle around it. It wasn't part of the print, but rather had been done by a reader. She frowned as she pointed at it. "You have any idea what this is?"

"No," said Alex. "Does it mean anything to you?"

"No. But I'd bet it's their sun."

"It might be the one here," I said.

"Belle says it isn't."

"Okay. I assume you asked Belle if she could identify it?"

"The colors are different. This one is class K. The one with the circle is class G." She returned the book.

"Okay," Alex said. "We'll look into it later." He closed the book and got out of the chair. "So where do we go from here?"

Robbi Jo smiled. "We need to go back down and find out who we were talking to."

"We tried that yesterday," I said. "You have any ideas for a better approach?"

Alex and Robbi Jo looked at each other. "There has to be a better way," said Alex.

"Hello, Tree," I said. "How are you doing today?" Now they were both looking at *me*. "Why do we care about it?"

"A tree with telepathic abilities? It's still hard to believe. Anyway, whatever it is, it probably knows what happened to the villagers."

)) ● ((

I went up onto the bridge. The truth was, I didn't like having something getting into my head. But Gabe said how it was his turn on the bridge and he didn't want me stuck in the ship for another day. "Anyway," he added, "I've had enough ghosts for one flight."

I wasn't sure I wanted to go back down. But I couldn't see a way to back out of it without embarrassing myself. We went down two hours after sunrise. Gabe's trackers were still in the lander, but it seemed unlikely we'd have any further use for them. I brought the lander in only a short walk from the trees, the same place where we'd been the previous day. I felt the mental intrusion starting before we even got to the ground. That was scary. I wasn't sure it, whatever it was, couldn't take the vehicle away from me. "Holy cats," Alex said, as I shut the engine down. "There really *is* something here." I wondered whether his insistence on returning to the forest had resulted from a conviction that we would find nothing and we'd all have to admit our imaginations had been running wild.

Alex opened the hatch and looked out. "It's quiet."

"No leopards?" said Robbi Jo.

"There's something out there that looks like a turtle."

"Really?" Robbi Jo went over beside him. "I love turtles." She almost squealed when she saw it. It was chewing on the grass.

"Anybody getting any mental vibrations?" asked Alex.

"That's all we'd need," said Robbi Jo. "A conversation with a turtle."

I was thinking that at least they weren't unhappy we were back. If they were, we'd probably know it.

Robbi Jo led the way out. I was waiting for her to try turning everything into a joke by pretending another signal was coming in. But it was all too serious. She stepped off the ladder and looked around.

Alex started down behind her but stopped halfway down the ladder, looked at the hull, and then frowned at me. "What happened here?" he asked.

I'd noticed that my cutter had left a mark while I was slicing vines. No serious damage, but a line about two meters long was visible. I explained what had happened. Alex listened and nodded. "Good foresight," he said. "Sounds as if you did it exactly the right way. Hope the tree appreciates it." He was snickering.

I followed him down. Our links were switched on so Gabe could be part of the conversation. He told us to be cautious, that there were too many unknowns. The talking tree, of course, was at the top of those. We started walking toward the forest. "Take us exactly where you were yesterday," Alex said.

Another egret came out of the branches and flew past us, its silver wings gleaming in the sunlight. Robbi Jo took the lead. A few minutes later we were standing in front of the damaged tree. The broken trunk lay off to one side. Alex glanced around, as if expecting to see someone, and then concentrated on the tree. "I feel like an idiot," he said. Then he went silent. Branches rose and sank in the wind. A small critter came out of the bushes and looked up at us. A few birds fluttered past. And suddenly I felt a wave of gratitude flowing through me, a sense that a vast weight had been lifted from my shoulders.

Alex tried to conceal his surprise. He closed his eyes. I almost expected him to say, *You're welcome*.

Red-gold sunlight was shining through the branches. Then we heard Gabe's voice: "Are you getting a response?"

"Yes," Alex said. "It's hard to believe. But something *is* here."

My eyes were getting wet.

"Hello," Alex said. "You still there?"

The overhead branches were waving gently in a soft breeze. Alex closed his eyes again. I'm not sure how to describe what happened after that. A series of images, old memories, flickered through my head. Not *my* memories, but someone else's. And I know how that sounds. I was looking down from the sky. Trees passed beneath me, and the world grew dark. A thousand stars appeared overhead. Then I was floating over the alien village. Its lights were on. And moments later it was gone and I was looking up at Alex and Gabe, who were standing looking past me, over my head, as if I were not there. And Gabe, of course, was in the *Belle-Marie*, not on the ground.

It went on for a while. Then I heard a whisper—or *thought* I did. I couldn't make out what it said until it spoke again: *I am here*.

It was almost audible. Daylight returned and I was back on the ground, Robbi Jo standing beside me, one arm on my shoulder, holding me steady. Gabe was gone.

"You hear that, Alex?" she said. If he responded, I didn't pick it up. She turned to me and asked if I was okay.

A garbled attempt at conversation followed, with Alex speaking aloud, and a voice in our heads responding. The actual exchange was difficult. But the voice seemed to be acquiring the language, and we were getting more than emotions. "You can hear me?" Alex asked.

Yes, I can understand you.

"Who are you? Can you give me a name?"

What is a name?

"It tells us who you are. Distinguishes you from others."

There are no others. There is only me.

My head was starting to hurt. Alex was staring up at the tree.

It spoke again: *I am not a tree.* I thought I detected laughter somewhere. I was getting seriously spooked.

"Then what are you? Where are you?"

I am all around you. I am the collective forest life.

I could see Alex wasn't buying it. But he apparently decided to play along and get to the reason we'd gone out there. "We appreciate the book you gave us. May I ask where you got it?"

There were visitors, briefly, not long ago. The seasons have gone through a substantial part of their cycle since they left. The book belonged to them. You know about them, obviously. You have been searching at the place where they lived. I thought you and they were the same. But it appears that was a misjudgment.

"That is correct. We are not related to them. But we are interested in who they were. Are there others like them anywhere here?"

None that I have ever seen.

"How long were they here?"

Less than a season. They stayed only a short time and then, at a sunrise, they were gone.

"They'd built a village, a town, at the edge of the forest. It disappeared also. Do you have any idea how they managed that? To make it go away?"

I do not. They were gone, and the structures were all gone with them. The village was not large. But even so, I've never understood how they could have taken it down without my being aware of it.

"Do you have any idea why they left?"

For a long time it was silent. Then: *I cannot be certain. But yes, I probably know why.*

A small furry animal that looked like a baby bear came out of the underbrush, walking on two legs, and took up a position staring at Alex. It had large round eyes.

"Why would that be?" Alex asked. His right hand had hold of his blaster.

They suffered a severe level of discomfort while they were here.

"And have you any idea what caused the discomfort?"

Yes.

"And that was—?"

The same issue you and your friends have had. Unfortunately, I cannot shut down our communications. We are in continual touch with each other. I cannot stop thinking, and when I did it seemed to disturb our visitors, both them and you. My mere presence upset them until they could deal with it no longer. I tried to stay out of their heads, but I simply could not manage it. Eventually they could not take any more.

"Where did they go? Do you know?"

I do not. They did not wish to leave. There was a sense of desperation. But when I deliberately contacted them, it only made conditions worse.

"And they just disappeared?"

They left one night after sunset. I was turned down as I usually am during the late hours. I knew they were planning to leave, but I did not think they would simply vanish.

"I have another question for you."

Yes?

"Are you alone on this world? Or are there others like you?"

If you mean are there other collective beings, yes. There are others.

I couldn't resist jumping in. "All the living creatures in given areas form a single being? Do I have that right?"

Not all. Some simply do not have the awareness.

"But trees do?"

Sometimes.

"How do predators fit in?"

What's a predator?

Part of the linguistic technique with the creature was to form images in my mind at least as much as words. So I conjured up the image of the hawk that had taken off with my pet kitten when I was a kid. It had never gone away.

The presence in my head recoiled. *Such things exist?*

"Of course."

And Robbi Jo asked the obvious question: "How do the creatures here survive? What do they feed on?"

Suddenly I was looking at images of hanging fruit and vegetables. An evolutionary system in which major life-forms were in direct mental contact with each other. The baby bear had sat down just a few meters away. I couldn't resist walking over to it and petting the back of its neck. It made no effort to escape or attack but just bent its head forward and purred.

"You have no idea where they went?" Alex asked. "Your visitors?"

I do not.

"But you spent time in their heads, right? You must have known a good bit about them."

I know they came here to find refuge. I never understood from what. I know they were pleased to be here. In the beginning. And the truth is, I was happy to have them. But I couldn't avoid joining them, and they knew it.

"You couldn't stop?"

I should have tried to break contact with them, and possibly I did. I'm not sure. They knew I was here, but they didn't know who I was, or why I was interested in them. I couldn't stop, and they couldn't make the adjustment as you have. So finally they fled. The sun came up on that last dark day and they were gone.

"I'm sorry," said Alex.

Are you actively seeking them?

"We were hoping to find them."

Good. If you do find them, please inform them that I am sorry about what happened. For a long moment, the branches began moving in a sudden wind gust. *They were mostly children. I tried to stay out of their way, but it was simply not possible. It would have been like your trying not to think. The truth is that I frightened them. They did not understand me. Even the older ones, the adults, were disquieted by my presence. I would have preferred to shut down, but I just could not manage it. That's why they left.*

"I'm sorry to hear it. But you meant no harm. That is what

matters." Alex paused. I saw a brief image of their children, laughing and playing like human kids. Then they were all gone.

"You want to find them because intelligence is so rare in the universe. Do I have that right?"

"Yes. But if we've lost *them*, we've found *you*. Life-forms like yours are extremely rare."

I hope you are not planning to run off as well.

"Unfortunately, we won't be staying. But I suspect now that we know you're here, others will come to study how you developed. If you don't mind our revealing your presence."

If they would be as generous as you have been, I would be pleased to see them.

)) ● ((

We had just begun walking away when Robbi Jo said, "We need a name for this."

I'd been thinking the same thing. "How about 'Collective'? 'Collie' for short."

Alex looked at me with an expression that suggested would I please get serious. "I mean it," Robbi Jo said. "If you don't like 'Collie,' how about 'Larry'?"

"*Larry?*" Alex was getting annoyed. I was backing away from the baby bear when I stumbled over a root. Robbi Jo grabbed me and we both went down.

"You guys okay?" Alex came over to help.

Gabe was also asking if we were okay. I'd come down on my head and I could feel a swelling already starting around my left eye. Otherwise I was fine. Robbi Jo was bending over me, looking at my face. "How's your vision?" she asked.

My lid was hanging slightly. "I'm good."

She didn't look pleased. "You're going to get a black eye, kid."

"We'll have something in the ship to treat it," I said.

"You know what that might be?"

"No. But Belle will know."

"Good. So where are we with Larry?"

"I guess," said Alex, "we can call this whatever we like. I mean, they don't know what a name is. I certainly didn't see that coming."

"What's that?" I asked.

"A hive mind that includes trees." Alex was wearing a large smile. "You know, we came out here to try to figure out what happened to the villagers. Where they went. That was going to be the big story if we could come up with an explanation. But if this one is legitimate, if we've actually got a section of forest out here that's alive, and functioning like an intelligent being . . . Damn, that doesn't happen often. The Ashiyyur constituted a major shock when we realized what they were capable of. But they're nowhere close to this thing."

"Careful," I said.

"About what?"

"Calling Larry a 'thing.' Keep in mind that they can pick up everything you say. Or think. We might want to be a little careful about the labels we pin on them."

"You're right, Chase. I guess I better get my act together."

Robbi Jo smiled. "Maybe they'll arrange for one of the leopards to come out and talk to us instead of having us stand there and talk to a tree."

We said goodbye to Larry and returned to the lander. Robbi Jo opened the hatch.

We looked back at the trees. Maybe we expected to see the baby bear come out and wave. But nothing was moving.

Alex took a close look at my eye. "We'd better get you back to the *Belle-Marie* before it gets any worse." We climbed inside. "How about," he said, "if I sit in the pilot seat? If there's an emergency—"

"I'm all right, Alex. But you can sit there if you want to."

"Maybe Robbi Jo would like to take over?"

"Sure," she said. "I've got it."

Gabe rejoined the conversation. "Do we still want to track down the aliens? You guys are right: we have a much bigger story now."

Alex replied, "Why not? We've come this far. If they got scared off by Larry, they probably wouldn't have bothered to go far."

Gabe continued, "Even if that's true, Alex, and they're nearby, searching a planet for a village is a fairly big deal. But okay. We should probably do what we came for."

A flock of birds showed up and fluttered by in a wide arc. There were more than a hundred of them. They were small birds, with blue bodies and white wings, and they flew in formation. As we watched, they circled us a couple of times and settled on the lander, all of them, squeezing in together. A couple lost their balance and slipped off, but then came back and found a place. Robbi Jo started the engine and was about to lift off when, in a single instant, they rose into the air and flew back toward the trees.

19

The most compelling advantage to be gained from our knowledge of history is that we should be able to avoid making the same mistakes a second time. But another lesson to be learned is not to expect similar events to repeat themselves.

—**Tiel Chadwick**, *Memoirs*, 1309

Unfortunately, while the book the leopard had given us was filled with astronomical pictures, there was no photo of the editor. But of course, after our encounter with Larry, that seemed of trifling significance.

Gabe was on the link as we closed in on the *Belle-Marie*. "I think," he said, "we should find out whether the collective is a one-shot, or whether living forests really exist elsewhere on this world." We were still struggling with the name. Nobody liked "Larry." "That's going to be the first question we hear when we get home. Maybe, for that matter, it'll give us a sense of whether they've been telling us the truth."

"About whether they're a collective?" I said. "Why would they lie?"

"I don't know." I could almost see Gabe up there shaking his head. "I have no idea."

Robbi Jo was seated to my left, in the pilot's seat.

Behind us, Alex was tapping his fingertips on the arm of his chair. "It's not a bad idea," he said. "Though I'm not entirely sure how we could confirm it."

Gabe was waiting with a cozaline medication for the left side of my face, which had swollen to immense proportions by the time we reached the *Belle-Marie*. It didn't get rid of the swelling, nor would my left eyelid open, but it eased the discomfort. "You get an application every six hours," he said. "I'll set the timer."

Everybody sat back and relaxed. We had dinner, crossed an ocean, chased a sunrise, and found ourselves over a block of land that would have been ranked somewhere between a giant island and a small continent. "Ideal place to check," said Gabe. "Let's go down and take a look."

I didn't think they would let me go to ground again, and to be honest I was glad for the opportunity to take a pass. Robbi Jo said she was tired, so the guys went.

The landmass was mostly forest. There were a few hills, a mountain range, several rivers, and three large lakes. We set the *Belle-Marie* for a stationary orbit. They landed just off the edge of a forest on an open field north of one of the lakes. Alex checked in, reported no unusual circumstances.

They activated their imagers so we could follow them. The surrounding forest wasn't quite as dense as the one where the village had been. They climbed out of the lander and stood there in bright sunlight, looking around and waiting for the feeling that they were being watched.

"You getting anything?" Robbi Jo asked.

"Nothing yet," said Alex.

"It took a good while before any of us started hearing Larry," she said.

They waited a few minutes and seemed simultaneously relieved and disturbed that nothing was coming through. They started toward the forest. They talked more than they usually would have in this type of situation. Maybe they were hoping, if there was a collective, to get a quick response from it. They reached the trees, found a trail, and followed it into the woods. Gabe periodically said hello to the trees. After about a half hour they came back to the lander. "We're not getting anything," Gabe said.

They climbed back inside, lifted off, and flew south across a mountain range. On the far side they descended near a river onto an open patch in the forest surrounded by hills. We stayed with them in the *Belle-Marie*. The river glittered in the sunlight, its banks filled with an array of multicolored blossoms. Birds circled the area, and one was floating in the water. "You guys would like this place," Gabe said. "The aromas are—" He sighed. "Don't know how to describe them, but everything's off the charts here."

"He's not exaggerating," said Alex. "If you were planning on retiring, this would be the place. Except that it's back."

"What's back?" Robbi Jo said. "The watcher?"

"Yes. There's another one here." Alex looked around at the trees but obviously saw nothing. "Hello, out there," he said. "We know you're here."

Robbi Jo took a deep breath. We were both on the bridge. "Chase, I wonder if we automatically try to block off this kind of hive mind? That would explain why it took us so long to pick them up."

"I suspect that was maybe the same problem I was having: I didn't want to recognize that something had penetrated my head until there was no way to back off the reality."

Alex and Gabe stood close to each other, a few steps from the lander. We could hear the wind glowing around them. Finally Alex said, "I guess we've answered the question. Larry's not alone."

"What do we do now, Alex?" said Gabe. "You want to go for a walk in the woods?"

"That's probably not a good idea. Let's play it safe. Get back in the lander and clear out."

But they didn't move.

"You still getting vibes?" I asked.

"Yes, Chase. Somebody's interested in us."

I'd enjoyed our experience with the collective, after we managed the rescue. But nevertheless, this wasn't a world I would have picked to live on. Robbi Jo let me see she was in full agreement. We were using the telescope to scan the area. It looked like an ordinary forest. On the ground, Alex was calling out again to the presence, but apparently still not getting a reply. Then they started walking toward the trees. So much for playing it safe.

Belle's lamp came on. "*Got activity,*" she said. She enlarged an area near the edge of the field, where the shrubbery was spread out. Some of it was moving, but we couldn't see what was causing it.

"Maybe just the wind," Robbi Jo said. She leaned over her link. "Movement at the edge of the woods, guys, off to your right."

They needed a minute. Then Gabe responded, "We can't see anything either, other than some vegetation swaying in the wind."

Alex continued talking to the collective: "You there? Anybody listening?"

I was glad to see them both unbuckle their blasters.

The movement stopped.

"Maybe it was just the wind," I said.

Gabe replied, "Don't have any wind at the moment."

Belle broke in: "*Shrubbery is moving again.*"

Something was emerging from the bushes. It was hard to make out because it was the same color as the vegetation. But gradually we saw what appeared to be a large round head, and as more of it became visible, we realized we were looking at a huge snake. Or maybe a dragon. It had several pairs of legs, and the head possessed eyes and a mouth large enough to swallow either Gabe or Alex.

"That thing is seriously large," Robbi Jo said. "Get the hell back to the lander."

Alex raised his left hand as if signaling no need to worry. "We see it."

"It's headed in your direction," I said.

"Don't worry about it," said Alex. "It's not a problem."

"What are you talking about? That thing could have either of you guys for lunch."

"Relax, Chase." Gabe was standing in front of Alex's imager. He smiled and waved.

Robbi Jo broke in: "That thing does not look like something you want to fool around with. Get back in the lander and get the hell out of there."

"We're okay," said Alex.

"What gives you that stupid idea?" I said.

"It feels right."

"It *feels* right? Can you see that thing?"

"Take my word for it, Chase. No need to panic."

"It's okay," said Gabe. "We're good."

Robbi Jo's hand gripped the chair arm.

The creature was completely out of the underbrush, walking calmly toward Alex and Gabe. I never thought of a snake walking before. Or wearing an expression. The thing looked hungry. "Alex," I said, "please. Get out of there. Now."

"Calm down, Chase. Everything's okay."

Gabe seemed to have entered a hypnotic state. He was just standing, facing the approaching creature, his blaster in his right hand, pointed at the ground.

Robbi Jo had lost whatever composure she'd had. "Something's happened to them. We have any way to intervene?"

If we took the *Belle-Marie* down, we'd never get back into orbit. Even if I could, there was no way we'd get there in time. The creature was headed for Gabe, mouth open, drool spilling out onto the grass. "Gabe," I said, "shoot it. Stop that damn thing."

"It's okay," Gabe said, sounding as if he was looking at a squirrel. "Don't worry."

We had one chance. "Belle."

"*Yes, Chase?*" Even the AI sounded in a state of shock.

"Play the *Deep Sky* Sonata. And make it loud."

"*Why?*" she asked.

"Just do it."

She turned it on, not at the beginning, with its solemn, gradually building melodies, but with the rousing harmonic intensity that comes almost midway, with the complete reversal of the original theme. We couldn't see Alex. The telescope was trained on Gabe and the walking snake, which was only a few steps away from him. I was holding my breath, terrified.

We were getting the adagio in G major, which broke into its hurricane rendition. Gabe staggered. I thought he was going to fall, but he caught himself and struggled to raise the weapon. While he did, the creature's head exploded and the thing collapsed. We heard Alex: "Gabe, get away from it. Get clear."

Gabe was still not going anywhere.

Alex fired a second round at the animal, but it was pointless. The thing was dead, sprawled across the ground. He hurried over to Gabe. "You okay?"

"Yeah. Why'd you do that? I thought it was friendly." He sank to his knees.

"I picked up a sense that you looked tasty. Come on, let's get out of here." He helped Gabe back onto his feet. Then they turned and started for the lander.

A half-dozen birds came out of the trees. They looked like hawks, circled the open field, and began to zero in on the lander. Or really on Gabe and Alex as they hurried back to the vehicle. The hatch opened. They were both holding their blasters, but Gabe was muttering in a confused manner. Alex stopped, turned, and fired the weapon. One of the hawks blew apart. He helped Gabe onto the ladder and took out another hawk. The others sailed overhead and retreated toward the trees.

Moments later they were both inside, breathing more easily. Alex closed the hatch. He looked into the imager that Gabe wore on his shirt. Which is to say, he looked directly at Robbi Jo and me. And probably at Belle's lights. "Thanks, guys," he said. "And Chase, anytime you want to ignore me and go in a different direction, feel free."

"So much for my assumption," said Gabe as we gathered in the passenger cabin, "that any collective intelligence was likely to be friendly. Like Larry. This place is going to provide a challenge for anybody who wants to figure out what's going on here."

"Maybe we need to keep in mind," said Robbi Jo, "that it's apparently another group intelligence. Larry's group were friendly little birds, baby bears, trees, and two-legged leopards with no claws. Remember how shocked they were when we started talking about predators?"

Alex settled into the chair behind mine. He reached up and put a hand on my shoulder. "We're fortunate you guys were here. Thanks. We got seriously lucky this time."

Gabe sat, breathing. "I guess we know why the villagers decided to leave."

"You think they knew about other collectives?" asked Robbi Jo.

Gabe still looked a bit out of it. "Maybe not in detail. But I'd bet they suspected the one they'd experienced wasn't alone. Even if they was, who'd want to live with them in the area? I can't believe what happened down there. I was staring that monster in the face, but I was completely immersed in a warm, friendly sense that everything was okay, and that the creature would do no harm. I literally couldn't fire the weapon. I don't even think I wanted to."

"You kept behaving," said Robbi Jo, "as if that monster was a friendly kitten. These group minds are more dangerous than we thought. This one apparently took you over. Both of you."

"I'd never have believed," said Gabe, "that was possible." He put a hand on Alex's shoulder. "You have a hell of a staff, kid."

Later, Alex joined me on the bridge. "It was you, I assume, who thought of using the sonata."

"Yes."

"That was brilliant. Thank you."

"I'm glad it worked. I couldn't think of anything else that had even a chance."

"I should apologize for jumping on you about using the lander to save the tree."

"It's okay, Alex."

"I want you to know that you'll always have a place with Rainbow, as long as you want it. And I trust your judgment completely to do what's best."

"So what do we do now? Check out the nearby worlds?"

"That sounds like a plan."

"Okay. Since we have no idea where they could be, we might want to refuel."

"How do we do that?" Gabe asked. He'd come onto the bridge and was standing behind me. The flights Gabe took were mostly just around Confederate worlds. So I wasn't surprised that he didn't know much about long-range missions.

"We use a gas giant," I said.

"How do you mean?"

"They're fueling stations, Gabe. We go in and skim the atmosphere. It's loaded with hydrogen and helium."

"Sounds good. Are there any in this system?"

"Yes. There are two or three of them here."

Gabe excused himself and went back into the passenger cabin. "Chase," said Alex, "something else I should tell you. Other than what you did for us today, I want you to know that you've been a critical part of my life for a long time. Please be careful out there."

We'd had a brief fling years before. Alex mentioned it in his memoir, A *Talent for War*. But we'd both eventually realized that there was no serious romantic chemistry between us. That hadn't changed, but I understood what he was saying. That he hoped we would be in each other's lives forever.

"My feelings exactly, Alex." We leaned over and did the best hug we could manage sitting in our chairs. "I'm just grateful the sonata worked."

"Me too," he said.

20

Silently, one by one, in the infinite meadows of heaven,
Blossomed the lovely stars, the forget-me-nots of the angels.
—Henry Wadsworth Longfellow, *Evangeline*, **1847 CE**

When you're proceeding into the atmosphere of a gas giant, you don't want to do anything too quickly. There are occasional rocks and ice, magnetic fields, serious lightning, and extreme winds. And of course, once inside the atmosphere, you don't have much vision.

Compared with stars, gas giants aren't very big. And, since you're not blinded by light, you normally get a good look at the atmosphere before you make entry. You're looking down onto a collection of clouds that seem to continue forever. There's no sense of a horizon the way there is when you stand on a Rimway hill and watch the sun set. I wasn't sure about the exact size of the one we'd picked for our refueling stop, but Belle estimated its diameter at about 130,000 kilometers.

There was a large storm adrift in the atmosphere. It was probably one of those thousand-year monsters, but there was no way to know. They're common on Jovian worlds. "You'll want to keep away from that," said Gabe, who was with me on the bridge. He's usually on his game, but occasionally he can be Master of the Obvious.

There was a ring system, with something like thirty moons. They glittered in the sunlight. One of the moons looked as if it had vegetation. That was possible because we weren't that far out from the sun. Temperatures there would have been cold but probably not frigid.

As we approached on that first night, we watched a movie after dinner. It was a comedy, but nobody laughed much. Afterward I got back onto the bridge. Gabe joined me again. The gray mist spread out below us in every direction. "You ever do this before?" he asked.

"A few times."

"We're just going to skim the surface, right?"

"We'll go down into the atmosphere, but not too deep, Gabe. The farther down we go, the more quickly we fill the tanks. And the only issue we have to be concerned with is turbulence. There's no real danger here, as long as we don't do anything stupid."

"You mean there are no rocks or anything in there we might crash into?"

"We'll have the scanners on. And of course the force fields. If any junk gets in there, the gravity takes it down pretty quickly. We should be fine."

A gas giant doesn't rotate the way a solid world does. The equator spins slightly faster than the polar regions. This one's equator was moving at about 40,000 kilometers per hour. We were midway up over the northern hemisphere. We'd left the storm far behind us.

The fuel level had gotten low. Not dangerously so, but taking care of it was the right call. We weren't burning much during the approach. Just riding in. Half a dozen of the moons were visible, as of course were the rings, which were thin but bright.

Finally I told everyone to buckle in. Then we began decelerating again. When I had it down to about forty kilometers per hour, equivalent to barely moving, I lowered the collectors. "Everybody hang on," I said. "It'll get a little bumpy." And we dipped into the atmosphere.

We were riding through an endless cloud. I had virtually no visibility. Belle used the scanner to search the area ahead for anything that might be a problem. "There's nothing alive here anywhere, is there?" Gabe asked.

"No. Scientists say conditions in these places just don't allow life to get started." I was watching the fuel tanks begin to fill. "Though I suspect they'd say something similar about trees."

He pushed back in his seat. "I hate moving when I can't see what's in front of us."

"I know. I've never been comfortable with this either. But when we travel this far, we haven't much in the way of an alternative."

The wind began to pick up. A gust hit us on the port side, almost turning us over. We leveled off and I got on the allcomm to assure Alex and Robbi Jo that everything was okay.

"How long's this going to take?" Gabe asked. When I asked what was wrong, he clapped his hands together. "Nothing, really. I'm okay. I guess it's just a sense that the laws of physics aren't as reliable as they used to be. Too much strange stuff going on."

I understood. I suspected my view of the cosmos would never be the same either. Not because of our immediate environment, but because of Alex and Gabe welcoming the snake. "We'll need about another twenty minutes to fill up," I said. "Maybe we should think about getting a bigger vehicle. On this kind of flight, a yacht just doesn't cut it."

We continued to rock and roll, but there was nothing we couldn't get through. Twenty-five minutes passed before Belle said it was okay to pull out. *"The tanks are full."*

$$)) \text{ ● } (($$

We came out of the gas back into a sky full of stars, moons, and rings. Next was to visit nearby systems and take a look at terrestrial worlds. We submerged for an hour and surfaced well outside the Korella system. Our assumption was that the Korella visitors, when they left, would have chosen another class-K star. Belle had already conducted a spectranalysis of everything within a dozen light-years. She'd found six nearby.

The immediate problem was that we were in unknown territory, so we couldn't be certain about the distances the six stars were from us and from each other. But there was a process. Belle recorded the angular position of each. Then we submerged again, stayed about twenty minutes, and returned to normal space. The angular positions of the stars had changed, and Belle was able to calculate ranges. The closest one was six light-years away.

"Okay," said Alex. "Let's start with that one."

"*Not a good idea*," said Belle. "*It works well if we find what we're looking for immediately. But if we don't and then go to the next closest one, and continue until we have visited all six, which could happen, we will travel considerably farther than if we plan the flight to accommodate all six from the beginning."*

She was right, and Alex told her to set up a route that would take us to all six through the shortest distance.

Gabe asked Robbi Jo whether the *Columbia* had already looked at them during its Visitation mission. "I'm embarrassed to say this," she said, "but I don't know. I might recognize them when we get there. But Vince was doing the piloting. I was just pretty much looking out windows. And there are a ton of stars in the area."

"No problem," Gabe said. "Belle, I assume you have the alternate route set up?"

"Give me another minute."

"Closest one is probably best," said Gabe. "That's the one they would have been most likely to select."

Alex leaned out of his chair. "Of course. But what are the odds that it has a Goldilocks world? They'd probably have to go deeper to find one."

Belle produced a plan that would take us first to a star that was nine light-years away. "About eleven hours," I said.

Alex held up both hands. "Let's go."

☽ ☽ ● ☾ ☾

Two planets were orbiting in the habitable zone. The nearer one was nothing more than an oversized rock. We visited the other one, which had forests, jungles, oceans, and a wide array of animals.

Belle reported no radio signals. We spent three days looking for lights or any other sign of occupants. But there was nothing.

The second star had no planets. The third had nothing in the zone except a gas giant. The fourth star was the one nearest to

Korella, the one that could have been our first visit. Again, two planets orbited in the zone. One was not much more than a desert. The other was filled with giant lizards. Not a place you would want to go for a walk.

Neither of the other destinations gave us anything. There were five worlds in the two habitable zones, but they were all piles of rock and sand with occasional meteor craters. There was no indication there'd ever been so much as an insect on any of them. "What do we do now?" asked Robbi Jo. "Look for more class-K stars?"

"I think it's over," said Gabe.

Alex wasn't ready to quit. "We've invested too much to just walk away."

Gabe was at the end of his patience. "They could be on a relatively nearby star and we could still spend years out here without finding them."

I waited for Alex and Gabe to make the call. It took a while before, finally, Gabe agreed to spend another two weeks. "After that," he said, "we clear out. Okay?"

"Okay."

"So where," I asked, "do we go next?"

"I've been doing some research," said Alex.

"Okay."

"Do you know why K-class stars are more likely to produce living worlds?"

"They're stable and they don't put out much radiation."

"And they live a long time."

"Okay."

"If we were looking for a place to set up a colony, we probably wouldn't care much whether the star lives a hundred million years or a billion, would we?"

"I guess not."

"Chase, the villagers wouldn't care much what class the star was, as long as it wasn't near the end of its life." He looked out through the wraparound. Stars were everywhere. "Two of them are closer to Korella than any of the ones we looked at."

)) ● ((

We designated them Alpha and Beta. Alpha was a half hour away. We arrived there, well inside the system, and got a quick reading from Belle. "Two worlds in the zone," she said. "One looks to be strictly gas. But I wouldn't describe it as a giant. The other looks green. No sign of oceans, though. Not on this side, anyhow."

"Okay," I said. "Any radio transmissions?"

"*Negative.*"

Alex was seated beside me. "Let's go take a look," he said.

)) ● ((

It had a moon, and we could make out vegetation. No oceans, apparently, but there was plenty of water.

As we got closer and watched the world rotate, we became certain that there were no oceans. Lakes were scattered everywhere, though, many connected by tangled rivers. The world was decidedly green. My first impression was that it was a happy combination of sunlight, water, and vegetation. "Paradise," said Robbi Jo. "If they came here to look, it's hard to believe they wouldn't have moved in. Assuming they don't have giant snakes with mental abilities."

And Belle spotted a satellite. "*Probably artificial,*" she said.

Gradually it slipped behind the planet.

"Let's use the drive," Alex said. "Take us to the dark side. Let's see if there are any lights."

When we surfaced, we were looking down on unbroken darkness.

"Nothing there," said Gabe.

"Where's the satellite?" asked Alex.

"It should be visible in a few minutes," Belle said. *"Or if you want, we can change course and accelerate the process."*

"That's okay," said Alex. "Just take us closer."

An hour later we slipped into orbit. We needed another twenty minutes before the satellite showed up. It was coming in our direction. Belle turned the scope on it. I'd swung around in my seat to talk with Robbi Jo, who'd come onto the bridge. "What the hell?" said Gabe. And Alex, back in the cabin, said, "No, no, no. That's not possible. Belle, you've screwed up somewhere."

Robbi Jo's eyes left me to focus on the monitor. They went immediately wide.

21

Savages do not leave footprints in the sands of time.
—**Margo Wakefield,** *Aliens: Why Fear Is Pointless*, **6111 CE**

The satellite was mostly a rock. But two rows of houses stood on it. They were separated by a walkway. There were fences, sheds, a swing hanging at an odd angle, and a streetlight. All afloat in the sky. The streetlight wasn't on. I saw no sign of any occupants, fortunately, because the construct was sloped down at about thirty degrees, so that anyone coming out of a house would have tumbled across the lawn and ultimately fallen off the edge. Which was why the swing hung at an angle.

We all froze. Finally Robbi Jo broke the silence. "Belle," she said, "could you replace it with a picture of the Korella village?" The satellite blinked off and we were looking at the village by the lakeside. The street was visible near the center of the town. It was identical. Swing, streetlight, nine houses on one side, eight on the other. "I guess we found them," she said.

"The buildings are the same style," said Alex. They were. There was a country aspect to them. They were mostly made of stone. And I know how that sounds. A couple might have been wood. There were no chimneys, but there were lots of windows. All the houses had porches. Village in the sky.

"How the hell," I asked, "did they do this? *Why* did they do it?"

Gabe threw up his hands. "I have no idea what's going on here."

"I hope," I said, "that we aren't going to put a couple of us on that rock and start knocking on doors."

"So," said Robbi Jo, "how do they pick up sections of their village and just move them around? How do you put a street on the outside of a satellite?"

"That's a good question." Alex took a deep breath. "Let's get a closer look."

🌒 🌑 🌘

I think we'd all suspected that it was a hologram. But we sent the lander over. I turned on its spotlight and watched the beam move across the front of one of the houses. It looked solid, but there was no way to be certain.

We switched our attention back to the ground. Did anybody see any lights anywhere? Anything at all? We moved across the sky, through sunlight and darkness. Since it had no oceans, this was a world with a lot of ground to cover. But we saw nothing. And neither did Belle.

"Maybe," said Gabe, "we should just get on the radio. See if anyone's really there."

"Not a good idea," said Robbi Jo.

The monitor gave us a starlit river in the middle of a swath of plains and hills. A herd of large horned animals were moving casually through the area.

I was in favor of using the radio, but I stayed out of it.

Robbi Jo crossed her arms. "You guys do what you think. But if it works, we'll have some explaining to do when we get home."

Gabe and Alex exchanged glances. Then Gabe looked up at the overhead. "Belle?" he said. "You there?"

"I'm here, Gabe."

"Send something. Say hello."

"As you wish." She didn't approve of the idea. And a moment later: *"Greetings from the* Belle-Marie. *Is anybody there?"*

We waited. She repeated the transmission. I found myself almost hoping the silence would continue. I was ready to go home. Except I wanted to meet the aliens.

It took a couple of minutes, but we got an answer. It was a strange language, of course. I activated my mike. "Hello," I said. "We'd like to talk with you."

The voice replied. It sounded like a male, and it also sounded ecstatic. Happy to see us, even if we couldn't exchange information.

"Belle," said Alex, "can you track the source?"

"North of us," she said. *"On the ground."*

It took a while to find them. We passed over endless plains, hills, rivers, lakes, and forest. *"Signal's getting stronger,"* said Belle. She had us on a northwestern course by then. And roughly a half hour after we first picked up the signal, we found them.

It was a village. No surprise there, I guess. It lay in fading daylight on the west bank of a large river. It wasn't identical with the village in the *Columbia* pictures, though. Gabe was quick to note that the blocks of houses were the same, but they'd been rearranged. It was as if we were looking at a jigsaw puzzle in which the pieces had been inserted in different places.

They were surrounded north and south mostly by forest. A field with only a few scattered trees lay west of the town. There were low hills across the river, one of which resembled a bowl that had been turned over.

"There's something else," said Robbi Jo. She pointed at a walkway on the north side. It divided seventeen houses. The arrangement was identical with the group on the satellite. And the swing was there, in the same place, though it was different: this one wasn't hanging at an odd angle.

We saw movement. Belle focused the telescope, and we could make out a couple of creatures walking in the streets and two or three seated on porches. No vehicles were visible.

"You picking up any of the language?" I asked Belle.

"*Nothing yet, Chase.*" It was midafternoon on the ground.

"They're putting us in a difficult position," Alex said. "I'd assumed we'd be able to have Belle connect with an AI, pick up each other's language, and make for an easy exchange. Now it looks as if we're going to have to take the lander down, do what we can with the language, and hope everything goes well. That will be even more of a shock back home than making radio contact. I'm not sure we won't wind up in jail."

"Or dead," I added. "Going down to say hello to high-tech strangers without establishing a connection first could have a bad ending."

"Right now," Alex said, "it doesn't look as if we're going to have much choice." He looked over at Robbi Jo. "What do you think?"

Her eyes closed momentarily. "I don't see how we can walk away from this."

We decided their midmorning would be a good time to make the descent. Next question: Should we carry weapons?

It would probably not be the best way to arrive. "The Ulakans," Robbi Jo said, "to the best of our knowledge, carried books, not guns."

"But they knew all about us," I said.

We settled into a stationary orbit, and somebody saw us. They began coming out of the houses and off their porches. Some of them waved in our direction. "So how do we handle this?" asked Robbi Jo.

"I suggest," said Gabe, "we just stay in orbit for now, as discussed. It's going to be getting dark soon. We wouldn't want to be on the ground when that happens."

"I was thinking the same thing," Alex said.

"Belle," I asked "any way you can get a handle on the language?"

"Not unless I have a way to make some connections," she said. "Somebody will have to go down and talk with them, wear an imager so I can watch and more or less pick up what they're talking about."

Alex explained to the voice on the radio that we would stay nearby, and that we would go down in the morning. The voice responded.

"I think," Gabe said, "that he understood we were signing off. He sounds glad that we're here."

"Like the snake?" I asked.

))◐⟨⟨

We watched the telescopic images on the monitors until finally night descended. The lampposts came on and the houses lit up. Our time was midmorning, slightly after 1100 hours. Gabe and Robbi Jo tried to get some sleep but didn't manage it. They eventually opened a couple of books. Gabe got caught up in a historical examination of widely believed tales that weren't true. Like the theory that Kory Sumter, who had been the world president on Dellaconda at the beginning of the Mute War, had known the attack on Point Edward was coming but had done nothing to prevent it because he wanted an excuse to take on the Mutes. Robbi Jo spent her time paging through the astronomy book.

Our stationary position over the village was burning excess fuel, so we left it and slipped back into orbit. We missed the village on our next pass but picked it up after that. The houses had gone dark, with one or two exceptions. But the lampposts were still on. We waited three hours past sunrise before we tried talking with them again. The same voice replied, and we went back into our stationary position. Belle told us it was probably just trying to say hello.

We were still debating whether we should go down. The Spaulding Mandate required that we leave and let the authorities decide on the proper approach. We were already in trouble because of the radio transmission. "If we play it safe and just go home," said Alex, "we'll be in better shape. We've found them. What else do we need to do?"

"No," Gabe said. "I say we go down. I'll do it. When we get home, we can claim I took the lander in the middle of the night. None of you guys knew about it."

"No," said Alex. "We don't know yet what the reaction will be on the ground. If things turn bad, two of us would at least have a chance to get clear. We'll take the blasters."

I'm not sure it could ever have gone the other way, but when we finally decided to complete the visit, Alex spoke into the mike again, using his gentlest tone: "We're coming down. We'll see you in a few minutes." We got a short reply, and Belle said it was probably asking whether we would visit them.

Then we had to decide who would go.

"Best if it's me," Gabe said. "I have no license to lose. Worst they can do is fine me."

"Or jail you," said Robbi Jo.

"And the fine would be substantial, I suspect," said Alex. "To be honest, I doubt that when they're deciding to level charges, it will matter much if you've gone down or just stood by and watched it happen. And if things go seriously wrong, we will probably all serve some time."

Gabe smiled. "Whatever."

Alex nodded. "Okay. If the fine happens, Rainbow will pay it."

Robbi Jo raised her hands. "Enough nonsense, guys. I'll go."

I'm embarrassed to admit this, but I thought there was a substantial risk in just dropping out of the sky to talk with people who, for whatever reason, had recently cleared out of Korella.

Gabe suggested that either I or Robbi Jo stay with the *Belle-Marie*. "Alex, do as you wish." He was going.

Robbi Jo said she'd go.

I said nothing.

The only one who seemed to notice was Alex. He glanced my way but turned quickly in another direction. "No," he said. "If things go wrong, I don't think we want Chase making that long flight home alone. Robbi Jo, you stay too. Gabe and I'll do it."

Robbi Jo's features hardened. "Alex, I thought you were better than this. Chase never suggested that you push women into a back seat."

 ☽ ☾ ● ☾ ☾

Belle estimated the temperature at about 27 degrees Celsius. A bit warm but okay. Everything was quiet. Alex showed up with some coffee and a few chocolate chip muffins. "Thought you'd like some," he said. He was still trying to adjust to Robbi Jo's comment. She and I were seated in the passenger cabin. She never took her eyes off the notebook.

"Thanks," she said. Her voice was cold.

I could see that Alex was trying to find a way to calm the waters. I jumped in to help: "Thank you, Alex," I said. "I think we should settle back into a standard orbit. We'd use less fuel."

"We have a fuel problem?"

"No. I just don't want to waste it for no reason."

I knew he'd reject the suggestion. And he did. "Let's stay where we are, Chase. Ask Belle to keep an eye on us. If she sees any unusual activity while we're on the way down, let us know."

"Okay, Alex."

His snack consisted of one muffin. He finished it off and went back to his cabin. "You know," Robbi Jo said, "there's no reason you and I couldn't take the lander down." She smiled to show she meant it.

"We can't do that," I said.

"Why not? You one of those women who does everything she's told? We could probably go down, say hello, give Belle some time with their AI, if they have one, and come back up before they even get dressed. We wouldn't even have to say anything to them."

"Let's let it go, okay?"

"How about if I take it down? You can deny any knowledge."

"Robbi Jo, you don't really want to do that."

"Actually, I do. I'd love to do it. Meet the aliens. What are we afraid of? They could hardly look more friendly."

"That sounds like a good way to get killed."

"Chase, we know they're high-tech. They're not savages; they built a civilization."

"That's not the point. Look, if you want, I'll talk to Alex. Tell him what you want to do."

"No. He already knows what I want to do."

"Whatever. He owns the *Belle-Marie*. And Rainbow Enterprises. You haven't been part of this organization for years. It's easy for you to talk about ignoring him."

Her eyes closed and she exhaled. "I know." She raised her hands. "You're right. Answer a question for me, Chase."

"Okay."

"What would you do if I took the lander down?"

I pushed back in my seat. "Belle?"

"*Yes, Captain?*"

"You heard this?"

"*Yes.*"

"Lock the lander."

Robbi Jo let out a long sigh. "Let me try something else."

"Go ahead."

"Would it really be hard on you if you had to go home alone? If something happened to the rest of us?"

"I wouldn't want to lose Alex or Gabe. But to answer your question, I could live with it. If you can talk him into taking you along, do it. It's okay with me."

Gabe came into the passenger cabin a few minutes later. Robbi Jo passed him a muffin. "You guys about ready to go down?"

He smiled. "Yes, we're ready. Or at least we will be when Alex gets out here."

"Gabe, I would like to go with you."

"That's not a good idea. Too many people at risk."

She looked around the cabin. "You could stay. Do you care that much?"

"About your safety? Sure."

"I care about yours, too. But I'm not using it to deny your being present during the moment this whole trip has been about."

"I understand what you're saying, Robbi Jo. But we just can't do it your way."

"Don't you think that should be my call?"

"If something bad happens, think about the situation Chase would be in."

"Chase says she has no objection if I go down with you guys. Is that all right with you, Gabe?"

His brow got wrinkly. He looked at me and I smiled back. I almost said, *Please, don't take her*. But I understood what she was going through. We were about to make history, and I could already see the story would be how the guys went down while the women stayed back and played it safe. "How about," I said, "if all four of us go down?"

Gabe rolled his eyes and asked me not to be silly.

We heard Alex's cabin door open. Gabe got up and went back. We could hear them talking, and when they joined us, Alex immediately confronted Robbi Jo. "If," he said, "this is really what you want to do." And he apologized to me.

Robbi Jo let me see she wanted to talk. I went up onto the bridge. She followed me, smiled, and asked if I was okay.

"I'm all right."

She leaned over the controls and checked the microphone to be sure it was off. "I'm sorry about causing all the fuss."

"It's all right. I should have backed you up."

"You did. I know the job means a lot to you. You're not interested in risking it. I understand that."

"It's more than the job, Robbi Jo. It's Alex. I know what he expects from me, and I don't want to disappoint him."

"I doubt that could ever happen."

Alex, Robbi Jo, and Gabe put pressure suits into the lander as a precaution. They clipped imagers to their shirts so Belle and I could watch. They also took the astronomy book we'd received from Larry. When they were ready to go, they assured me they'd be careful and climbed into the lander. Alex took a last disapproving look at me and closed the hatch. I went back to the bridge. Belle depressurized the cargo area, opened the cargo door, took the lander outside on the cradle, and released it.

22

The harsh reality is that we live in a universe that does not care for us, that shows no interest in our welfare, and that will not miss any opportunity to do away with us. How else to explain black holes, asteroids, plagues, tidal waves, tornadoes, hurricanes, and tigers? But that fact produces a positive effect: any intelligent species will understand this, and consequently they will assist each other whenever possible. And for those who doubt that this is so, recall that this is the definition of intelligence.

**—Brandy Crestworth, graduation address,
Mount St. Charles Academy, 4411 CE**

The sky was full of cumulus clouds, blocking my view of the village until the lander got through them. When it did, somebody aimed one of the imagers in its direction so I could see it. It looked quiet. A few of the inhabitants were seated on porches, and two of them were walking past houses in a leisurely manner. It was obvious they had not yet seen the lander. But how could they not have a detection system of some sort to alert them if visitors showed up? Especially visitors they should have been expecting.

"I've hesitated for obvious reasons to mention this." Belle's voice. *"Acquiring a new language simply by listening to a conversation in which neither side understands the other is not an easy task. Our side will be speaking Standard, and I need a consistency of intent from that person, which will not exist if all are in the discussion. Consequently, our best approach is for two of you to stay in the lander. Preferably, it would work best if Alex spoke with the aliens. The reason is that I have had more conversations with Alex than with anyone other than Chase."*

I guess everyone had had enough of that debate. Alex agreed with the proposal, and Robbi Jo and Gabe signed on. They would stay in the lander, out of sight.

I watched as they descended through the late morning sky. The view from the imager showed mostly open ground with scattered trees of a kind I hadn't seen before. The trunks were pink and the branches filled with leaves of a variety of colors. The river was wide and it looked deep. It flowed east where it narrowed and entered a canyon, pitched over a waterfall, and then moved on for another hundred or so kilometers before emptying into a large lake. It was easy to understand why the villagers had chosen this area for their settlement.

I think we were all riveted by the stillness of the town, which continued even as the lander descended into plain view. Then suddenly porches and pathways filled with the aliens, waving ecstatically at the lander. They were coming out of houses, some looking up at the approaching vehicle; others were knocking on doors and, when they opened, pointing at the sky.

I'd been watching through Robbi Jo's imager. "You know," she said, "I'd rather do this the way the Ulakans did. They were able to talk with us, and they obviously knew a lot about us before they showed up."

"Well," said Gabe, "that sure beats dropping out of the sky and trying to figure out how to say hello."

"Let's hope," she continued, "Belle can pick up the language quickly. We can't even be sure that offering to shake hands wouldn't be perceived as a threat."

I think Alex wanted to get away from talking about threats. "This place," he said, "looks a lot like the location they had on Korella. Nice weather, warm temperatures, perfect place for a vacation. Obviously they like being on a shoreline. The river's not quite the same as the lake, but it looks like a good setting for a sailboat."

"I don't see any," said Gabe. "Sailboats, that is."

No. There were no boats anywhere. No piers.

"I think," Robbi Jo said, "they had a couple of piers on Korella." I didn't recall having seen any boats or piers.

Alex stayed near the edge of the town as he descended, touching down finally just off its western side. They were drawing a few of the aliens, but only a handful. Seven or eight individuals were coming toward them, waving arms and cloths. For the most part, the ones who'd been on the porches *remained* on the porches.

Robbi Jo and Gabe retreated to the back of the lander, where they could keep out of sight. Alex got to his feet. "Okay, guys, good luck to us. If something unexpected happens, get clear. You understand?"

"Just be careful," said Robbi Jo.

Alex picked up one of the blasters and pushed it into his belt, under his clothes. "Just in case." He looked through a window at the mostly empty pasture. The villagers were bipeds, about the same size as humans. Their faces were similar to ours. Large eyes, though. Their green skin, in a forest, would have rendered them invisible. And of course they had six fingers.

Two of them approached the lander. No weapons were visible. Alex went over to the hatch and hesitated. "They probably think we're the same as they are," he said. "They're going to get a surprise when they see us."

"Make sure you smile," said Gabe.

Alex picked up the astronomy book and opened the hatch. He was about to place one foot on the ladder and start down, but the pair of aliens released a startled cry and tried to back up. The smaller one lost its balance and fell. Its companion helped it back onto its feet.

Alex held up an arm. "It's okay," he said. "I'm a friend." One of the two aliens wore a bright red shirt and dark trousers. It looked like a male. His partner, in green and gold, was smaller, graceful, and obviously female. Although there were apparently no breasts. The male spoke to Alex, but they kept a respectful distance.

"I'm glad to be here," said Alex. He closed the hatch and started down the ladder. Both aliens lifted their hands, palms open, in a gesture that suggested Alex come no closer. "That doesn't look good," he said. He raised his right hand, slowly. Gabe and Robbi Jo stayed out of sight.

The two villagers exchanged comments, and then lowered their hands. "It's the Ulakans all over again," I said to Robbi Jo and Gabe. "I wonder when we'll find some real aliens?"

"I suspect," said Robbi Jo, "there are limited ways for intelligent beings to develop and behave. They need families, they take care of their kids, and they show you an open hand so you know they aren't armed."

As if confirming her view, the taller of the two raised both hands again and showed his palms. "He's telling me to stop," said Alex.

I was thinking that Robbi Jo was right, that in the end we're all pretty much the same.

Alex and the two villagers stood gazing at one another. There was no indication that either had a weapon. But of course they'd probably thought their own people would be coming out of the lander. The male touched his chest and said something. No idea what it was, but he looked concerned.

"Hello," Alex said. "It's okay. We are friends. My name is Alex."

The female said something, maybe giving their names. Her teeth, which looked sharp, were visible. And a tiny villager, a child, appeared out of nowhere and began trotting toward the lander. An adult came in behind it, swept it up in his arms, and retreated.

Alex raised the book, showing them the cover. Both leaned forward, to get a closer look without actually taking any steps. Then the female reached for the book. Alex gave it to her. "Does it belong to you?" he asked.

It obviously surprised them. The male asked a question, probably about how Alex had come into possession of it.

Finally they approached, coming slowly. The female was paging through the book. Then she handed it back to Alex, said something to her partner, and pointed back into the town. The male turned halfway around, probably trying to invite Alex to follow him. The female watched but didn't move. Alex went forward a few steps.

They fell in on either side of him. Most of the others backed away, giving them space. The male reached over and put out his hand. I couldn't see clearly how Alex responded, but he told me later that they touched fingertips. He took a moment to point his remote at the lander and close the hatch. Several more aliens appeared on porches, but for the most part they stayed there. A few others, scattered around, watched silently as Alex followed his two guides. They led the way back into the village.

Alex commented about how pleasant the weather was and then said, "Where are we going?"

The female replied by holding up her hands, indicating he should be patient until they figured out how to communicate. At least that was how it looked.

"This is a beautiful area," Alex said, speaking slowly.

The female replied softly.

"That's good," said Belle. Alex could hear her, but of course the aliens couldn't. *"Get them talking. As much as possible. Stay with general comments, where it's fairly obvious to them what you're saying. That will allow me to start putting everything together."*

Alex lifted his left arm to shoulder height and moved it slowly around, taking in the entire town. "This is the same place you had on the other world," he said, shifting his perspective to look at the sky. "How did you move all these buildings?"

The male responded with a short comment that probably indicated he had no idea what Alex was talking about. And that, I realized, was the boss's intention. Perfect.

"Good," said Belle. *"Keep going, Alex."*

The town was considerably more than houses and walkways. The several larger buildings that we'd seen on Korella were also visible, but they were in different places. The one that resembled a school was on the same road that Alex was, about five blocks from the river's edge. The courthouse or town hall was located in the center of the area, but not quite in the same location as it had been on Korella. Trees, flowers, hedges, and bushes filled the ground everywhere. There were a couple of parks. They looked similar to the ones we'd seen in the pictures, but again the locations had changed. The benches and tables, however, appeared to be in the same places.

There was a wide variety of houses. Some appeared to be made of stone, some of wood, others of material that might have been a plastene. They ranged from one to three stories. Some had only two ground-floor front windows, while others seemed to have fronts that were entirely glass. Rooftops were occasionally domed. Others were sloped, some angled, and some just flat. Most of the flat ones supported chairs and a fence.

They passed a house with someone watching from the porch. Alex waved at the watcher. He waved back. "How many of your people are here?" he asked.

The male gave another short response.

"*I think he understood the question,*" said Belle. "*Not many here, apparently. I don't have the numbers down yet, but I think they expect more. He probably answered in the hundreds. But how many is a hundred when you have twelve fingers?*"

Alex tried to keep the conversation going. Speaking slowly, he commented on how good the houses looked, and the gardens, and how active the children seemed to be, and how beautiful the weather was. He asked how long they'd been there, and whether they had transportation other than walking, and where they'd come from originally.

Alex and the two villagers managed to exchange names. The male's, as delivered by Belle, was unpronounceable, but Alex got by with Daylok. It was close enough. The female was Szola.

They turned into a roadway that led toward the center of the village, turned left at the first intersection, and stayed straight toward a three-story house that might have been made of a silver-white metal. It had a porch with three chairs and a garden filled with blooming flowers. As they approached the front gate, Daylok indicated he would like to see the book. Alex passed it to him and said thanks, holding his left hand out to make his reference clear. Then: "Nice home."

Daylok opened the gate and led the way through the garden. When they reached the porch, he stood aside for Szola. She climbed the three stairs. The chairs were coffee-colored. They appeared to be wooden. The front door opened for them. Alex got a brief message from Belle, informing him that he was doing fine, that he should keep going, and that she was picking up the language. She added that he should try to keep the imager on whichever of the two was responding to him.

"What we need," said Robbi Jo, who was probably speaking only to Gabe and me, "is for them to have an AI in their living room. Do that and Belle will have command of the language in about twenty minutes."

Szola led the way inside. The interior had cream-colored walls with a few framed photos, a sofa, and three chairs. There were a couple of side tables, both with lamps. An almost-empty bookcase stood against one wall, and a ceiling fan was rotating slowly overhead. A staircase led to the upper floors. We could see into two adjoining rooms. One had a large table.

Daylok looked at Alex, pointed to the sofa, and said something.

Alex waited until Szola had taken a seat. Then he said thanks and settled onto the couch. Daylok placed the book on one of the side tables.
They needed the better part of an hour, but they eventually began to
understand each other. Belle picked up the alien language and translated it for Alex. When Alex responded, Belle translated for Daylok
and Szola. It was an awkward process, of course, but it worked.

Szola asked where the voice was coming from. Alex told Belle
to introduce herself. She complied. Alex's hosts both nodded at
the voice that came out of nowhere and said they were happy to
meet her. Belle commented how good the house looked. She then
tried to explain that she was a support mechanism for Alex.

When she'd finished, Alex asked whether there was anybody
like her in the house, or in the town.

They talked it over. They both answered and the translation
was no. Szola added that their support mechanisms hadn't arrived
yet. Then she said something else, which Belle translated: "*Along
with everything else.*"

"Daylok," said Alex, "were you the person we spoke to on the
radio?"

No," he said. "We have someone assigned to cover radio transmissions."

I couldn't help noticing that Szola wanted Daylok to say something. Her eyes were focused on him. He kept looking away but
finally gave in. Again, Belle translated: "Alex, you know we tried
to get you to stay in the lander."

"Yes. I thought you were uncertain about our intentions."

"No. That was not our concern. I didn't want you to leave the
vehicle because there's a virus. Neither of us has any symptoms, so
you're probably safe here. It's why we haven't offered you anything
to eat or drink, though."

"How serious is it?"

"We have eleven dead already. We didn't want you to be exposed to it. It's why we brought you in here." Daylok stopped, leaned forward, decided he shouldn't get close, and pushed himself away. "Do you feel all right?"

"I'm fine, as far as I can tell. What are the symptoms?"

"Rising temperature. Once that starts, our people have been dying within a few days."

"Do you have any doctors here?"

"We have three, but they haven't been able to do anything about the virus. We need some specialists."

"What causes the temperature to rise?"

"It infects our regulator."

"What's a regulator?"

Szola and Daylok both looked at Alex as if he'd asked a dumb question. "It controls body heat."

"You mean sweating?"

"What is sweating?"

"It uses water to control body heat."

"In what way?"

"The glands bring water out onto our skin. It evaporates and cools us down."

Daylok looked repulsed. "You bring water out through your *skin*?"

"When we need to."

Szola was showing teeth again. "We don't have that kind of organ," she said. "We have a regulator. Don't ask me how it works, but it keeps us from overheating. If you don't have one, that's probably good news, because you should be safe from the virus."

"I hope you guys stay well," said Alex. "I assume you tried ice?"

"Yes. Of course. It was the first thing we did. But it only made things worse. When we used ice, the body reacted by producing even more heat."

"I'm sorry to hear it." He paused a few moments before changing the subject. "May I ask, why did you leave Korella?"

"We liked it at first." Daylok's eyes were dark. "But there was a spiritual side effect. We were never able to determine precisely what it was, or what caused it, but it was somehow invasive. No one was comfortable. And the children had nightmares. We tried to live with it for a while. But Tokon couldn't wait forever, so we had to make a decision."

"Who is Tokon?"

"Gora Tokon. He was the pilot of the *Triskuul*, our transport vehicle."

"And you came here from Korella?"

There was a brief conversation in the alien language between Daylok and Belle. I assumed she was trying to determine how to identify Korella for him.

The answer was yes.

"Daylok," said Alex, "was anyone else supposed to join you on Korella?"

"There should have been two follow-up missions. But so far we haven't seen any sign of them."

"Would they have known to come here?"

"They should have. Tokon left a satellite explaining what had happened, and where we were going."

Gabe couldn't resist commenting, "Now we know what the message was on the satellite the *Harbinger* brought home."

Robbi Jo nodded. "We might be the reason these people are in so much trouble."

ꙮ ꙮ ● ꙮ ꙮ

"The follow-up vehicles," Daylok explained, "were supposed to bring additional equipment, food, and hopefully, medical supplies. And there were supposed to be more people to join us."

"When the *Triskuul* left here," Alex asked, "were they aware that the follow-up ships were running late?"

"Yes," said Daylok. "Tokon was the only person on board the *Triskuul*. But yes, he knew. He waited several days and finally decided he needed to act. He left to get help."

"How long ago was that?"

"Eighteen days."

"How far are we from your home world? From the world you left?"

"It's complicated. We needed nine days to get to Korella. Then maybe six to come here."

"Let's stay with this a moment. How many days did you need to get to Korella if you count only the time when you couldn't see anything outside the windows except darkness?"

He and Szola talked it over. "That was four days. Maybe five."

"Are you talking about the length of days as they are here?"

"Yes. Days here are about the same as they were at home. It's one of the reasons we chose this place."

"Good enough. Thank you. Daylok, it sounds as if you've no means of communicating with your home world?"

"Just the radio."

"But you're not close enough for that, right?"

"That's correct. A transmission would take several years to get there."

"You also have faster-than-light travel. Don't you have an upgraded communication system?" He was referring to hypercomm, which moves transmissions well beyond light speed.

"No. We have nothing like that. I thought it was not possible. We implore you to go to our home world and let them know about the virus. Let them know we need help."

"What is the name of your home world?"

"Sovol."

"Where is it?" The conversation was becoming intense. Alex took a deep breath. "It'll be okay. We'll do everything we can for you. We just have to figure out where Sovol is."

"There's a cluster of stars in the southwestern sky. It's in there somewhere. I can show you tonight." Daylok reached out with his right hand and grasped Alex's shoulder. "I hope you can manage it. You're all we have. Please. Tell them where we are. And that we need medical help. Or evacuation. Is your ship possibly large enough to evacuate us?"

"No, it's small."

"I'm sorry to hear that. I wish you were in a transport vehicle." He hesitated. "Our sun, by the way, is called Daka."

Alex looked over at the astronomy book. "We should be able to find it in there somewhere."

"I hope so."

"Does *this* world have a name?"

"Arinaka. But if you're thinking of using it to direct anyone to find us, be aware that it had no name before we arrived." We learned later that the name was derived from their equivalent of "placid." Or "peaceful."

"About the star cluster, is Sovol *in* the cluster? Or is that just the general direction we'll be going?" I couldn't see Alex's face, but I knew he was not comfortable. If it was *in* the cluster, there was no way we were going to find it.

"No. There are some stars off to its right. Daka's one of them."

"But you don't know which one?"

"I wish we did. Just knowing it was up there seemed like enough in the old days. We were on Korella at the time. But it's all visible from here, too."

Belle told us, and Alex, that she had enough information to send out a hypercomm transmission when we got into position.

"We might be able to talk to them," Alex said.

"You think so?" Daylok and Szola both showed some excitement.

"We'll try."

23

We have no special position in the natural world. Humans are blessed with sunlight, soft rains, wide forests, and broad oceans. Nature even provides an extensive variety of food and drink. For all that happy talk, we still have to confront earthquakes, tidal waves, hurricanes, and, on occasion, viruses looking for a place to hang out.

—Vicki Greene, *Dying to Know You*, 1433

"Is there any reason," Alex asked, "to think that Tokon might have been unreliable?"

"No," said Daylok. "None whatever." The question obviously annoyed him. "I would have trusted him with my life."

"It looks," said Robbi Jo, "as if he did. But I'd say they had the right guy. The satellite he left here was a marker."

Alex continued, "When you were there, on Korella, you lived

in the same town, more or less, that you have here. The streets are in different places, but it's the same. You literally picked it up and brought it here with you. How did you do that?"

That ignited more discussion between Daylok and Szola. Finally Daylok held up his hands. "We pushed a button."

I could hear Alex breathing. "What do you mean, you pushed a button?"

"Literally, that's what we did. The controller has a button. We get our personal stuff out of the house and push the button. The town goes away. When we get here, we push the button again."

"And it comes back?"

"That is correct."

"Why is it different? Why are the buildings in different places?"

"We rearranged things on the way here. Some people wanted to be closer to one of the parks; others wanted to be next door to a friend or relative." He stopped and held out his hands. What else was there to say?

"You rearranged things on a computer?"

"Yes. Then we fed it into the controller."

"How does the controller work?"

"You're asking me to explain the physics. I don't know. I have no idea how it's done."

Gabe broke in: "Alex, can you explain how a lamp produces light? Other than switching it on?"

"Daylok, where is the controller?"

"We have two. One of them is on the satellite. Tokon put it there to set up the town."

"It was a marker."

"Yes. The other one's in my office."

Szola broke in: "His office is in the town hall. I should have mentioned that Daylok is our mayor."

"Really? Well, Mr. Mayor, I hope we can be of assistance."

"'Daylok' will work fine, Alex."

"Please," said Szola, "let's forget about the trivia. Maybe we can use the book to figure out how to get to Sovol. We are losing someone every couple of days. We need to get out of here. Or get some medical help."

"Did Tokon know about the virus before he left?"

"No. He went back to make sure everyone knew where we were, and to pick up some supplies. There were also others who were scheduled to come with us on the backup flights. The ones that never arrived. Tokon was gone a couple of days before people started falling ill. We didn't plan this thing very well. It was dumb. And we got unlucky. When Tokon left here, the only problem we were aware of was that the backup vehicles were running late. But we didn't think of them as being missing." Her eyes locked on Alex. She looked frightened. "He should have been back days ago."

"You don't think anybody here would know how to find Sovol?"

"I doubt it," said Daylok. "I don't think we have any pilots here. But let's find out." He got up and walked into an adjoining room.

"He's going to ask around," Szola said.

After a few seconds we heard his voice. And then Belle: "*He's presumably speaking into an electronic device, explaining that you are friendly and you wish to help. That you are willing to go to Sovol. Anyone who knows how to provide directions should please get back to him immediately.*"

Szola gave Alex a weak smile. "We were hoping you might know."

Alex picked up the astronomy book and started to page through it.

"I wish," said Szola, "I could get you something to drink."

"So do I," said Alex.

Szola went paging through the book again on the chance there was a map somewhere. But it would probably have been impossible to locate Sovol even had there been one. A flat map of the sky does not give you much.

When Daylok came back, he was just shaking his head. "Nothing yet," he said. "But we need to give it more time."

"Where did you get the book?" Szola asked.

"It's one of yours. It was apparently left behind when you came here."

She was still turning pages when Daylok stopped her and pointed at something. "That's it," he said.

"Your home world?"

"Yes."

It was a picture of a terrestrial world with continents and oceans and a moon. Szola nodded. She pointed at three lines of print at the bottom of the picture. "Yes. That's Sovol."

She passed the book back to Alex. "Does it say anything about where it is?" he asked.

"No." Szola tapped a fist on the picture. Turned more pages in both directions. "There's a lot here, but it's all about galaxies and clouds of stars. We're going to have to read through the entire thing."

She continued going through the pages with increasing desperation. Alex stopped her, turned back a page, and pointed at one of the pictures. It was the sun with the red circle drawn around it. "Any chance somebody here drew this?"

"It's certainly possible."

Another picture showed the group of stars that literally pointed to the left. "That's the Arrow's Head," said Szola. "It's a constellation back home."

"It's frustrating," Alex said. "What does the caption say?"

Daylok stared at it and shrugged. "Just that it's in the sky."

"That's not much help."

Daylok looked at the back page. "It's from our library." Szola produced what appeared to be a comm link. She activated the device and held a short conversation with someone, raising the volume so we could hear. But it didn't help; there was no way Belle could keep up with it. When she was finished, she delivered a weak smile. "That was our librarian. I told her about the book. It *is* one of theirs."

"How'd they lose it?" Alex asked.

"One of their readers had it and apparently didn't bother to take it with him when we left Korella."

"Do they have any other astronomy books?"

"No." Szola looked down at the book. "I just asked her that. Unfortunately not. The library's still pretty small. There are more books coming, but they don't have much yet. I'd guess there are only fifty or sixty books over there."

Daylok's attention had been drawn to one of the front windows. He got up, walked over to it, and groaned.

"Something happening out there?" asked Alex.

Daylok replied to Szola, "They've closed the curtains."

Szola swallowed and shut her eyes. "No, please. Not Barran." She turned to Alex. "He died."

"I'm sorry," said Alex. "Who's Barran?"

"A child. He was only six years old."

That was followed by a long silence, broken finally by Alex. "The virus?"

"Yes."

Daylok embraced her, and then turned to Alex. "We lost two yesterday. It's getting worse." He got to his feet. "Let me see if I got any responses." He went back into the room where his communication device was.

Alex asked about Barran. "Was he a relative?"

"No. A neighbor. Lived across the street."

"Are you certain about his death? Could they have just drawn the curtains to keep the sunlight out?"

"No. They would not have done that."

Daylok returned, looking depressed. "All I got so far is what we already know, that it's in the same general direction as Korella, and it's somewhere in the eastern sky off to the right of the star cluster. We have to be patient. Maybe somebody will be able to supply directions."

Nobody was. Responses continued to come in, but they talked only about the star cluster and asked Daylok to extend their best wishes to the visitors. The sun went down, and they waited for the stars to appear. Meantime, Szola tried to keep the conversation going. Alex said that if he could read their books, he'd enjoy visiting the library.

"They're looking for a name," Szola said. "They're talking about calling it the Tokon Library. They still might, if he gets back here with some help. But lately they're considering just naming it for the town."

"What is the town's name? Is it the same one it had on Korella?"

"It doesn't have one yet."

Daylok had been going into the computer room every few minutes. But the responses had slowed and eventually stopped. The skies grew dark.

"So our last hope," said Szola finally, "is Tokon."

"No," Alex said. "We'll do what we can to find your home world."

She managed a smile. "Thank you. We appreciate your trying."

They waited for the stars to reappear. Then it was time to go outside. Robbi Jo whispered a comment: "Alex, make sure you bring the book back with you."

)) ● ((

They went out and looked at the night sky. They moved across the lawn to get a better angle on the southwestern sky. A lamppost was making it difficult. Eventually they got a clear view of the southwestern sky. "There it is," said Szola. The cluster. A small cloudy section glowing just above the horizon. There were a lot of stars off its right side. I heard someone take a deep breath. And Robbi Jo commented that it would take a couple of years to sort through them.

"It might help," said Alex, "if you came with us. You guys can read the book. There might be something there." I caught Alex's eye and he read my reaction: *Several of them are infected. And we don't really know whether we're safe from the virus or if it can harm us. It might damage other organs.* "Chase, they're all at risk here. If this thing doesn't get stopped, they'll all be dead pretty quickly. For us, the risk is minimal." Belle did not translate it.

"I've been all through it," said Szola. "There's nothing."

"If we can find your people, we'll be asking a lot from them, and they may not trust us."

There was a quick emotional conversation between Daylok and Szola. When they'd finished, Belle translated: *"Szola doesn't think you'd have any problem getting them to believe your story. Just to be certain, she has something for you."* She reached into her pocket and produced what might have been a driver's license.

"It's my library card," she said. "It should be more than sufficient to prove that you found us."

"One more question," said Alex. "How do we refer *to* you guys?"

Szola smiled. "We are Arkos. As long as we are breathing."

24

That which is lost is only forever gone when it has been destroyed or we have given up the search. Life is seldom good to those who are inclined to surrender.
—Aneille Kay, *Christopher Sim at War*, 1322

(These words also appear on the Christopher Sim Memorial on Dellaconda.)

It was time to leave. Alex picked up the book and said goodbye to Szola and Daylok. They embraced at the front door. Then all three walked down onto the roadway and started toward the lander. It was visible in the moonlight. They'd gotten about halfway when doors began to open in most of the houses. Arkos came out. Some stood on their porches watching, while a few came down to the roadway, raised their hands, and shouted. Belle informed us they were saying "Good luck" and "Thank you," and "We will never forget you."

Alex waved back. "I should confess," said Daylok, "that in the message I sent to the town, I told them I was optimistic. That you didn't actually have any specific information about the location of Sovol, but that I thought you'd be able to find it."

"That was exactly the right thing to do," said Szola. "They needed some good news. Something to hope for."

"I thought," Alex said, "that they were keeping a safe distance from each other to prevent the virus from spreading."

"It looks," said Daylok, "as if they are willing to take their chances to say thanks."

Alex's first comment to Gabe, when he got back into the lander and closed the hatch, was: "We have got to make this work."

"I know."

"First thing we should do is send a message home. Get a rescue mission started as quickly as possible."

"That would take a while," said Gabe. "At the rate they're dying, I doubt there'd be anybody left by the time Skydeck could get out here."

"It doesn't hurt to try."

"The Arkos might have the hypercomm technology," said Robbi Jo. "Maybe these guys just don't know about it. Let's send a few hypercomm transmissions out near the star cluster. We might get lucky."

A few minutes later we received a message from Alex that he wanted relayed home. It described the medical problem, including as much information about the aliens' regulator organ as he could manage. Which wasn't much. I wonder if we have any doctors who would be willing to come out here and take this on." Robbi Jo bit her lower lip. "If everything goes perfectly, it'll be six weeks before a rescue vehicle gets here." I fired off the transmission and we sat staring at one another. "Good luck to us," she said. "And to the Arkos."

)) (((

"How do we find Sovol?" I asked as we gathered on the ship. "Everything else aside, we'll run out of food, oxygen, and fuel before we can come close to checking out those stars."

"The arrowhead," said Alex. "It's very likely a view from their home world. Find an area where the stars line up like that and we'll probably be in business."

I asked Belle if she could locate a world with that kind of sky. She sounded annoyed. *"Does anyone have any idea how to narrow the field? That is a big sky out there."*

"Belle," said Gabe, "an arrowhead ought to be fairly easy to pick up."

There was an unusual silence while we waited for a response. *"Gabe,"* Belle said finally, *"I don't have a three-dimensional perspective of the sky. If the arrowhead is a constellation, we need to be in the home world's system, or at least reasonably close, to see it. To work it out from a distance, I'll have to measure the range between us and a load of individual stars, which I can do, although even that will take time. And fuel. I'll also have to determine their distance from each other."*

"Not encouraging," said Gabe.

Alex took a deep breath. "I don't see that we have any other option."

"This is beginning," I said, "to feel like a mission to nowhere."

Gabe smiled. "Sounds like a good title for the memoir."

"I hope not."

Alex focused on me. "Head for the cluster. Set for ninety light-years." He took another deep breath. "Maybe we'll get lucky."

Gabe shook his head. "I wish I had a better idea." He started back into the passenger cabin. Robbi Jo got up and asked Alex where the astronomy book was.

He looked back into the cabin. "It's in one of the seats."

She followed Gabe inside and Alex sat down beside me.

I activated the allcomm. "Thirteen minutes until we leave orbit. Everybody belt down."

)) ● ((

We had nothing to work with other than what Daylok and Szola had told us. So I aimed us just off to the right of the star cluster and submerged for a four-and-a-half-day ride. There's been a lot of talk recently about an FTL system that would allow views of the outside world. Most physicists think it's impossible, but it would certainly be helpful on long flights. Especially like that one. As it was, we'd simply travel until we reached the time limit and then surface and see where we were.

Once we got moving, I tried to read, but I kept seeing Daylok and Szola wishing Alex good luck while the other aliens, who had spent most of the day in their houses, waved at us and squeezed the shoulders of their kids.

Alex instructed Belle to put together another package of directions that would inform a rescue unit how to find the world we'd just left, Arinaka. He laid out the nature of the problem, how many people there were, the medical issue, and the need to move quickly. He added that they were the people who'd recently left Sovol for a different world and had been forced to move to the present one.

)) ❂ ((

It was going to be a long flight. Four and a half days with nothing outside the windows and no sense of movement can be difficult under the best of circumstances. But with the survival of the Arkos hanging over our heads, it looked to be seriously stressful.

Gabe tried putting Ed Carnova on the HV. Carnova's probably one of the funniest guys we've ever seen. At least we were all in agreement on that. I went back and joined them. But nobody laughed, and after about ten minutes we turned it off. Usually when we're submerged I spend a substantial amount of my time in the passenger cabin and just participate in whatever idle talk or anything else that's going on. But not on this occasion. After we shut down Carnova I went back to the bridge and sat for almost an hour staring at the blackness.

I decided a shower might help. When I passed through the passenger cabin, Alex was sitting with his notebook on his lap, but he was staring at the back of the seat in front of him. Gabe was on the other side of the aisle with a crossword puzzle to which he seemed to be paying no attention. Robbi Jo had taken a seat in the rear. The astronomy book was open beside her. I thought at first she was asleep, but her eyes opened as soon as she heard me. All three looked my way and delivered bogus smiles. I returned them. They all nodded, but no one spoke.

I'd just arrived at my cabin when Gabe called my name. "I've got a surprise," he said. "I'd planned to save this for the flight home, but I guess we need something now." He got out of his seat and went to his cabin. When he came back, he was carrying two packets in one hand and a book in the other. "I made a minor discovery on Ilyanda. There's a hardcover bookstore,

like the one your boyfriend has, Chase. One of the books was only a century old, but it had been part of a collection owned by Jorgina Epcott. She'd spent a lifetime traveling throughout the Confederacy, looking for books of historical value. This one is an account of a game that was apparently pretty popular at one time."

"A *game?*" asked Alex.

"They called it 'bridge.' I suspected it might be helpful on a trip like this." He held the book where we could all see it. The title was *Play the Hand You're Dealt.* He sat down, opened one of the packets, and showed us some cards.

I'd seen pictures of playing cards before, but I'd never actually encountered any. A "deck," I remembered they were called.

"You get any details on how old the game is?"

"It goes all the way back to ancient times. Probably four or five thousand years."

Robbi Jo asked for the book and opened it. "Does it give us the rules?"

"I think I've got it figured out. If you guys would like to try it—"

We set up the table in the workout room. It was a tight fit, but we were all able to squeeze in. Gabe passed the cards around so we could all take a look. He explained the rules and the terminology. We went through the cards. These were aces and those were queens. The game was divided among four suits. Alex, of course, had a lifelong passion for antiquities. We drew cards to determine partners. I got Gabe. I was hoping it could get us thinking about something other than the arrowhead. It worked with the guys, but neither I nor Robbi Jo could manage any enthusiasm. We lasted a couple of hours, then folded our hands, and talked about how

interesting the game was, and returned to the passenger cabin for snacks. We never got back to the table.

Robbi Jo and I spent the evening on the bridge, trying to find something other than Sovol to talk about. But we didn't get far from the trail. We wondered why Tokon hadn't gotten back. Whether Alex had in any way been at risk from the virus. How pushing a button had moved Szola's town from Korella to their new world. Arinaka, right? We were getting too many names to remember.

Mostly we just sat staring out at the sky. Except, of course, that there was no sky. Just darkness. I've tried a number of times to read what physicists have to say about Armstrong space, what it is, why it exists. Why it's a necessary part of the cosmos. That without it we wouldn't have a functioning universe. That it was the reality for what physicists used to call dark matter. And I'll admit here that I haven't a clue what they're talking about. It's all beyond me. I understand that we're lucky it exists. And it makes interstellar travel possible. Which is good, but whatever else you can say about it, it absolutely defies my monkey brain.

Looking back now, I can't recall having done anything of significance during that flight. I tried reading, tried watching shows, tried sitting down with someone and just talking, but there was nothing to talk about except that we had no idea where we were going. And the question that hung over all our heads was what we would do if we arrived at the star cluster and couldn't find anything. Go back to Daylok and Szola and watch them all die? Or go home and hide?

Mostly I sat on the bridge with a book on my monitor, reading words without following the context. Alex joined me near the end of the second day. "Depressing, isn't it?" he said. "What are you reading, Chase?"

The page had been on the display for probably a half hour. "It's a Grover Clayborn collection."

"Who's Grover Clayborn?"

"He was a critic. Didn't like anybody. Says ninety percent of us are idiots. And that's the women."

"Guys have a better average?"

"Worse. Ninety-*five* percent of males."

"He's dead?"

"Yes. Been gone almost sixty years. I've always enjoyed his work. He didn't think we'd had a decent piece of theater during his entire lifetime. Didn't think marriage was a good idea. Disapproved of both political parties, religion, professional sports, you name it."

"Sounds like exactly the guy we could use to get through these next few days."

)) ● ((

Gabe wondered if we'd missed an opportunity with Larry. "They might have gotten inside the pilot's head—I forget his name—Tokon, do I have that right?—and gotten a sense of where they came from. Maybe we should have stopped there and talked with them."

"We asked about that," said Alex. "They said they didn't know."

"There's a possibility they knew more than they were aware of."

"It's a bit late now," said Robbi Jo.

"You think anybody's going to believe that story?" I asked. "About the intelligent forest?"

"I doubt," said Robbi Jo, "the whole forest was conscious. Probably just the more advanced life-forms."

"Which included the trees."

"Of course." Robbi Jo put down the piece of pork roll she was about to eat, folded her hands, and used them to support her chin. "Is a vegetable brain possible?"

Alex smiled. "I suspect we'll get a lot of people going there to find an answer to that." It was the first time I'd seen him look amused since we'd left orbit.

)) ● ((

The next two days dragged by, and we were all delighted when Belle informed us, as we sat in the passenger cabin trying to find something to occupy us, that we were approaching our destination and would be leaving Armstrong space in thirty minutes. We'd known we were close, so there wasn't much we had to do. Just belt down.

I went up front and checked the numbers. We were good on fuel, and everything else was fine. I looked at the black windows and thought how even a vacuum would be an improvement.

Robbi Jo came up a few minutes later and took the right-hand seat. "Good luck to us," she said.

Eventually Belle told us to secure ourselves, and we felt the tug on our stomachs that normally precedes a transition. I expected to see a cloud of stars off the port side. It was there, but it looked just as far away as it had. The thing was a lot farther than we'd expected. Daylok had given us the impression they were just next door to it. But that was irrelevant. Their home world was out here somewhere. A million stars glittered across a hazy sky. "Belle," I said, "start taking pictures. Look for the arrowhead."

"This is impossible," said Alex. "There are too many stars."

)) (((

We didn't know where we were going other than a very general direction. We took pictures in all directions, made a short jump, and took more pictures. All we had was the arrowhead, and I saw no hope whatever. We didn't even know which direction to go.

We continued taking pictures of stars and leaving Belle to compare them, but we were getting nothing. After a couple of days, Robbi Jo was beginning to look distracted, as if she were somewhere other than with us. "You miss Chris?" I asked.

She shrugged. "I expected to be home by this time."

"I think we all did."

She raised her left hand, fingers spread. "I told him we'd be about three months."

"I've lost count, but I suspect we're close to that now."

"It's okay. He's gotten used to it." She rearranged herself in the seat. "Though I've never been gone this long before."

"Sounds like a serious relationship."

She smiled. "I didn't think it was when I first got on board for this. But I'm surprised at how much I miss him." She looked at the black windows. We were in Armstrong space. "We might as well be searching in here for Daka."

When we surfaced later, she asked if we could turn the telescope on the cluster we'd followed out there. I was surprised that she'd want to divert the telescope. Belle was using it full-time, but it didn't seem as if it would matter. "Sure," I said. "But just a couple of minutes, okay?"

Belle complied and put the cluster on the monitor. It was a vast swirl of stars, adrift in a mixture of red, green, and blue gasses. Robbi Jo copied the image on her notebook. "Thank you."

"Need anything else?"

"No. I'm good." She was looking at the cluster. "I've seen that before," she said.

"Really?"

"Yes. I think it's the Orion Nebula."

"Good," I said. "I'm impressed."

"You okay, Chase?"

"I'm okay."

"Alex looks ready to give up."

"He'd like to get his life running again. But if we have to abandon those people, it'll kill him. He's inclined to play the role of a realist. What happens, happens. He can live with it. But he's not really like that."

"I know. I hate to think what the flight home will be like if we can't do something. Some of the people I've worked with, if they'd run into a situation like this, they'd have just thrown up their hands, wished Daylok good luck, and said goodbye."

))●((

We continued moving among the stars, taking pictures while Belle looked for the elusive arrowhead. Nothing changed. We wandered across the sky, unsure whether we were getting closer or moving farther away. The prime question was becoming whether we should return to the alien world, give them the bad news, and watch them all die, or just return home. I suspect you can guess which choice I'd have made.

Eventually Robbi Jo came back onto the bridge. Her incandescent blue eyes locked on me. "There might be a way to find them," she said.

"What way is that?"

She was carrying the astronomy book. Her finger was inserted between a couple of the pages.

"You got something?" I asked.

"Maybe." She opened the book. "You recognize this?" She showed us a picture. It resembled a dark animal's head outlined against a luminous sky.

"It looks familiar." I'd seen the picture before. Not only in that book but in astronomy volumes back home. "It's the Horsehead Nebula."

She flipped a few more pages, and we saw another cluster of red, green, and blue gas filled with stars. "This one's the Flame Nebula." She looked as if she expected some excitement, but I had no idea where we were going. Neither, obviously, did Alex, who'd come in behind her.

She turned to another picture. It looked like swirling stardust. When neither Gabe nor I showed any sign of recognition, she said, "It's the black hole in the Carpathian Cluster."

"Another cluster," Alex said.

"It's okay. We won't have to go there." She turned more pages. "This is the supernova explosion a thousand years ago in the Markham Cloud." She turned more pages and pointed at another picture. "I know that one," said Alex. "It's the Crab Nebula."

"That's good, Alex." Robbi Jo looked impressed. "It's in Taurus. I didn't know that one, but I knew I'd seen it before." She showed us another picture. "This one's the spiral nebula in Coma Berenices."

Alex was looking as if he thought she'd lost her mind.

"Okay. You recognize a lot of this stuff. Can we get to the point?"

"These pictures were taken through a large telescope. The Horsehead, the Orion, and the Flame are all relatively nearby. There's an outside chance that whoever was taking the pictures rode out there in an interstellar and actually got close-ups, but it's much more likely they were taken through a telescope."

Gabe had joined us. "Okay," he said. "So how does that help us?"

"I think," Alex said, "I see where this is going."

Robbi Jo smiled. "The photos very likely show us how these things appear from the home world that we're looking for. Assuming they have a super telescope. Which they would certainly have to get close-ups of all this stuff. We don't have a telescope that would allow us to see these things, but Belle should be able to work out the angles in each of these photos and figure out which direction the telescope was located. Somewhere the six lines will coalesce."

Gabe shook his head. "Those numbers will be too big. No way we could put those angles together and follow them to an intersection point."

Robbi Jo held up a hand, fingers spread. "You're right, of course. They obviously won't come together at one point, but they'll give us a neighborhood. Instead of looking all over the sky for the arrowhead, we should be able to limit the search to a relatively small area."

Alex glanced at me and then focused on Robbi Jo. "You run this past Belle?"

"Not yet."

"Belle, you been listening?"

"*Yes, Alex. I have location information on the Crab Nebula. We can see the Orion. And we also have the Flame."* She paused. *"I also have the Horsehead. But not the others. It should be enough."*

"Okay." Alex raised a fist. "Four should be enough. Assuming everything in the book used the same telescope. Or at least took the pictures from the same area."

"I'd be shocked," Robbi Jo said, "if the pictures didn't all come from the same source."

"Good enough." Alex looked down at the microphone. "How's it look, Belle?"

"You're jumping the gun, Alex. Can you let me see the pictures in the book?"

Gabe held the book for her and turned pages so she could get a good look at the four pictures. It took only a few moments. *"Okay,"* Belle said. *"I have them."*

"Can you locate the telescope?" Alex asked.

"I'm working on it now."

Usually Belle performs her operations in seconds. This one took a while. *"The nebulas are extremely large,"* she said. *"The numbers change depending on which part of it we focus on."*

"Go to the center of each object," I said.

"Of course. But that still leaves ground to choose from. There's some speculation involved."

"Do what you can, Belle."

"Just give me a few minutes."

Robbi Jo looked delighted. I was thinking how fortunate we'd been that Larry had given us the book.

Gabe got up, said he was going to get some lunch, and suggested we all move back into the passenger cabin. We did and I went with Gabe into the galley. Alex and Robbi Jo had eaten earlier. I picked up a grilled cheese sandwich and coffee. Gabe got

some chicken strips with a honey-mustard dip. We took them back
out to the cabin and set them on trays. I was taking my first bite
when Belle came back on the speaker: *"The angles come together
in a relatively small area close to where we are now. I cannot be certain, of course. But the telescope should be located there."*

"How far are we?" asked Alex.

"About seventy light-years." Three days.

"Let's hope," said Robbi Jo.

"Are we targeting a single star system?" asked Alex.

"No," Belle said. *"Unfortunately, I can't narrow it down to that
degree. We are headed for an area with a diameter of approximately
sixty cubic light-years with about twenty stars. It's similar to conditions at home. I can't guarantee a positive result. But the lines cross
in the middle of the area, so the odds are favorable. The telescope
should be in there somewhere."*

"And," said Alex, "so should the arrowhead."

The prospect of putting together a rescue mission and lead-
ing it back to the movable town seemed finally plausible, which
turned us all on. I can't recall feeling happier in my entire life.
We walked around, hugged each other, and raised a few drinks to
whoever had built the telescope.

I was talking with Robbi Jo when Alex brought us a fresh
round of sherry. "So much for the pilot staying off the alcohol,"
I said.

Alex smiled. "Chase, I wanted to say thanks."

"For what?"

He glanced over at Robbi Jo. "For suggesting we bring *her*
with us."

"That's very nice of you, Alex," she said.

"I hate to think where we'd be without you."

"On our way home," I said.

Robbi Jo kissed his cheek. "It might be a good idea to wait and see whether it works."

I hugged her. "I understand. But however it turns out, you've at least given us a chance."

We settled in that afternoon and watched *Tarana*, a remake of the old-time classic *Casablanca*. I've seen it probably seven times. Never get tired of it.

Afterward we did our workouts, had dinner, and just sat around talking. Nobody was sleepy, so we eventually put on another film, a comedy about a bumbling agent working for the World Security Group (a made-up organization) who discovers that evil shape-changing aliens have infiltrated the government.

We surfaced three days later at about midnight. I don't think any-one had slept much. We were all set up along windows and the wraparound when we emerged under another starry sky. Gabe was on the bridge with me. I saw no sign of a constellation that looked like an arrowhead. But that was no big deal. There were a lot of stars out there. If it was in the area, we'd probably need time to find it. Meantime it would help if we could pick up an artificial radio signal. Or maybe spot the telescope in orbit somewhere.

We'd been there about ten minutes when we heard Belle's voice. *"Got it,"* she said.

I didn't see anything new. "What? You got a radio signal?"

"No, Chase. But I have the arrowhead."

25

Alone, alone, all, all alone,
Alone on a wide wide sea!
And never a saint took pity on
My soul in agony.

> —**Samuel T. Coleridge, "The Rime of the Ancient Mariner,"**
> **1798 CE**

It would have been difficult to miss the arrowhead. It consisted of eight stars lined up almost perfectly, a projectile in the sky. A brilliant blue star was at the tip of the constellation.

Belle was taking more pictures in an effort to determine in which star systems the arrowhead would be visible. With all eight stars. Sometimes, Belle told us, only parts of it would be there. Sometimes only a single star would be missing. In one system, she said, there would have been an additional star. Ultimately we limited the number of possibilities to six.

The first one we went to had, as far as we could see, no planets at all. The second one had only a gas giant in its Goldilocks Zone. In the third one, two terrestrial worlds orbited inside the zone, one near the center, the other on the inner edge. We visited the one in the center first.

We needed another short jump to get close. We surfaced in a celebratory mood. Until Belle looked through the telescope.

The images that came up were mostly rocky surfaces, desert, and dust. There were no oceans, although rivers and small lakes were visible. And no sign of life. Clouds drifted through the atmosphere. There were two moons, but no indication anyone had ever set foot on either.

Gabe was on the bridge with me. I leaned over the microphone. "Anybody there?"

Belle repeated the question in the alien language. We got nothing.

"Damn it," said Gabe. "Check the other world." But he sounded discouraged. "Waste of time. They can't be there. It's too close to the sun."

"It's in the zone," I said.

"Just barely."

We were on the allcomm, so we could be heard in the passenger cabin. Alex said, "Let's just take a look. These people have super tech. Eliminate the possibility. We don't want to have to come back."

VILLAGE in the SKY   313

We made another jump to get within range. When we turned the telescope on it, we got a jolt: there were cities. And oceans. And a moon with a ground station. But the station was dark.

"Talk to them, Belle," I said.

The transmit light came on. *"Hello,"* she said in the alien language. *"Is anyone listening?"*

Again, we got no response. We passed over the moon and a few hours later settled into orbit. Other than a few animals wandering around, there was no visible movement anywhere, no land vehicles, no aircraft, nothing. The cities appeared to be empty. The forests looked gray and dying. The oceans were small.

"Okay," said Alex. "Now we know why they were on the move."

Gabe growled. "So where'd they go? There were only a few hundred with Daylok and Szola."

Cities and towns were everywhere. They encompassed a wide variety of lavish architecture. We were looking down at minarets, fluted spires, pagodas, cupolas, obelisks, and a range of structures unlike anything I'd seen before. Two cities even had pyramids. The styles were generally confined to geographical areas. Some cities had minarets, some had towers that would not have looked out of place in Andiquar, other areas resembled luxurious suburbs, or would have if there weren't so many open spaces. But nothing moved anywhere.

"It looks dead," said Robbi Jo.

"We getting any radio?" asked Alex.

Belle reported negative. She was still transmitting, speaking in what should have been the local language. *"Hello, your people are in trouble. We need your assistance to help them. Is anybody there?"*

Apparently nobody was.

"Why not send the whole Arinaka package?" said Robbi Jo.

"Put all the information out there. There's no reason to hide any of it."

"Do it," said Alex. "I don't guess it could cause a problem. Sure. Send it all. Make it a broadcast." It felt like an act of desperation.

We caught up to and passed beneath the sun. We were out over a small ocean. Its north-south coastline was empty. There'd been no coastal towns anywhere, no boardwalks, no sign of support services. We saw several islands off to the north. They had towns, but again no sign of life. There were a couple of bridges that connected the towns, although it was hard to see why they'd been needed. Several kilometers inland we passed over a north-south walkway with buildings on its western side, and nothing but open ground on the east. "This is where the ocean used to be," said Gabe. "What's the temperature here, Belle?"

"*Forty-four degrees Celsius.*"

"Desert level," said Robbi Jo.

"Yes, it's warm." Alex's voice. "I wonder if the sun is in its expansion phase." It did occupy a substantial portion of the sky, although it was setting behind us. We kept moving, and the world descended quickly into a vast darkness broken only by starlight. Neither moon was in the sky, but the arrowhead was. Instead of the symbol of hope that it had become during the flight, we felt as if it was laughing at us.

We stayed in orbit, moved through the night, rose into sunlight, crossed another small ocean, left it behind, and passed over a wide canyon. A narrow river ran through it. Bushes and trees, most apparently dead, were crowded onto both banks. Occasional polished rocks glittered in the sunlight. Belle was transmitting into an empty sky. We'd stopped sending the package. Instead, the message was simple: "Anybody there? Your people need help."

"So does anyone who lives here," said Robbi Jo.

We continued across a blistered landscape, which improved slightly as we angled north. Or maybe we were just getting used to it. Belle reminded us that Daylok and his people had to be growing desperate. There was no time to waste, and we had no clue where we were going. We were getting ready to pull out of the system altogether and look elsewhere for a world that would have accommodated a population on the run. Then Belle surprised us: *"We're getting a transmission. Someone's asking us to identify ourselves. It's the Sovolan language."*

"Where's it coming from?"

"Northwest."

"Everybody belt down," I said. Gabe was with me. He locked in. Two security lights blinked on from the passenger cabin. They were ready. "Okay, Belle, track it." I put together a message for Belle to send. "Hello. We are friends. Some of your people are stranded in a distant star system. They are dying from a virus and need assistance. We want to get help for them. Is there someone here who can assist?"

A voice that sounded like Szola's responded, *"What people? Who are you talking about? Who are you?"*

We were passing over a dead forest.

Alex took over: "They traveled in an interstellar vehicle called the *Triskuul*. Their pilot was Gora Tokon."

"I'm sorry, but I have no knowledge of any of this. Would you please tell me who you are?"

"We've sent ahead notice and have come a long distance. We found your people in need of help, and we are trying to assist. But they are running out of time."

"*I just don't know anything about it.*"

"Is this Sovol?"

"*No.*"

"Have you heard of Sovol?"

"*Of course. It's a world in the Branko system.*"

"Can you direct us to someone here who might be able to help?"

"*Yes. I believe I can. Where are you now?*"

A road ran north along the edge of some trees. Occasional buildings were on both sides. Had there been a town anywhere, a couple of them might have been manufacturing plants, department stores, hotels. But there were few houses. Hardly any. And of course no traffic. "The signal's getting stronger," I said. "We're getting closer to you."

"*Good. I'm located in the Seawalk Entertainment Complex. In a two-story building on the east side of the only road in the area.*"

Robbi Jo broke in: "There it is." A few kilometers ahead lay a group of flat two-story buildings, an elevated track that looked like an amusement ride, a large disk with chairs that probably rotated, a couple of places that might have been home to bumper cars or a skating rink, and maybe a fun house. It was all on the east side of the road. A field lay on the opposite side, beyond a single building. There was a high sliding board on the field and a few diving boards. But there was nothing to dive into. The field was for the most part somewhat lower than the surrounding ground, and we could see sections of a wall along its sides. If it had indeed once been a pool, it was now just home to a few trees.

"Okay," said Alex. "You're near a high slide."

"*Yes. I am in the building at the north end of the pool.*"

I wondered how long it had been since the speaker had looked through a window. "Can you come outside where we can see you?" I asked.

"*Unfortunately, I have no such capability.*"

Alex smiled at me. The thing was obviously an AI. How had I missed it? "Time is of the essence," he said. "You say you can connect us with someone who can help. Please do that so we can get started."

"*No. I need assistance also. Please put someone on the ground and we can resolve this.*"

"That will take time."

"*I'm sorry. But I insist.*"

"I've got it," said Alex.

We all offered to accompany him, but he wanted to do it alone.

"Alex," I said, "you should have backup."

We argued for a minute until Gabe told him I was right. Gabe wanted to go too, but in the end, I got the assignment. We went down to the cargo bay and took two blasters out of one of the storage cabinets. We didn't expect to need pressure suits, but we put two of them in the lander just in case. We climbed into the vehicle. The cargo hold depressurized, the doors opened, and the cradle took us outside. We started the engine and a few moments later we were on our way to the ground.

The sky was clear. No clouds and plenty of sunlight. It was hard to be certain, but it looked as if there had been *two* pools, one considerably larger than the other. They might have been connected, but it was impossible to be certain. The smaller pool had been near the road, and that was where the diving boards were. The slide was on the edge of the larger pool.

"*The temperature*," Belle said. "*is forty-one degrees.*" Again, Celsius, a little over a hundred degrees for those who use the Fahrenheit system. That doesn't sound particularly high, but we were well into the northern hemisphere. She added that the oxygen levels in the atmosphere were sufficient. "*You shouldn't need the suits.*" We drifted in over the complex, set down on the side of the road, and scared a few birds.

We put on sunglasses, got out into the heat, and watched the birds flutter around for a minute before descending back into the trees. A small furry creature hurried past us, leaped onto a branch, and disappeared in the foliage. "I wouldn't expect to see animals with fur in this kind of climate," Alex said. He was right about that: it was blistering.

We tried to use trees for cover as we walked toward the two-story building. It had a porch with a few windows. The door lit up and opened. It was a relief to walk inside and watch the door close. We mounted a ramp and went into a lobby. It had several wooden chairs, a counter, and a long table. There were open doors on both sides and a closed one behind the counter. A cool breeze was coming in from somewhere. The front door closed behind us, and the voice that sounded like Szola's spoke while Belle translated: "*Greetings. Welcome to the Seawalk Entertainment Complex. Please come into the office on your left and take a seat.*"

We removed our sunglasses and complied. The office was empty. Two windows looked out toward the road, and a third one behind a desk provided a clear view of the two rectangular fields that had once been pools. There were two more wooden chairs and a bookcase that was stacked except for the top shelf, which was occupied by a cube-shaped device wired into the wall. The desktop showed no sign of activity. *"I am pleased to meet you,"* the voice said. It was obviously coming from the cube. I tried to remove a couple of the books, but they were packed tight and stuck together. It had been a long time since anyone had touched them. There was a lot of dust. It was hard to resist looking around the room for something we could have used to wipe things down.

A monitor hung on the wall beside one of the windows. As I watched, it lit up and an Arko face appeared. It was a female, older than Szola. Her features were relaxed. She invited us to make ourselves comfortable and apologized for the slovenly appearance of the room. Alex introduced us and said hello. "May I ask," he added, "what is your name?"

"I am Itira. I must confess I had not expected my next conversation to be with someone so different. Who are you? Where are you from?" The exchanges were slow, of course. *"Is there one of us,"* she said, *"with you?"*

"You mean someone from this world? Or this system? No. The voice speaking your language belongs to Belle. She's a mechanical intelligence who acquired the language from your people. Am I correct in believing you are also a mechanical intelligence?"

"Yes. I am."

"As we thought. We are from a place hundreds of light-years away."

"And you've come all this distance to rescue our people?"

"Yes."

"Thank you for your concern."

"We came across them accidentally while doing some exploration." Alex explained their situation.

"I am sorry to hear what our people are enduring."

"Are you able to pass the information on to someone who can help?"

"*Unfortunately not. There is, however, another presence on the far side of this continent, near the ocean, where Xachri is located. They might be able to help. I know of no one else. I will forward the details on locating them to Belle, if you wish.*"

"Yes, please."

"It will take only a moment."

A green light blinked on at the top of the cube and held steady for a few seconds while Itira spoke. There was no translation, of course. But after a couple of minutes, Belle told us she had it. "*It's not as precise as I would like, but it should be enough to allow us to make contact.*"

"What is Xachri?" I asked.

"*In earlier times,*" Itira said, "it was the world capital. It is still home to the Historical Preservation Society, one of the few organizations still active out there. It provides whatever robotic maintenance is possible for the city, and arranges tours for visitors."

"Where do the visitors come from?" asked Alex.

"From worlds that were colonized in an earlier era."

"Can you tell us where those other worlds are?"

The monitor image lifted her right hand. It had six fingers. "*I can give you their names, but no, I have no detailed information.*"

"The Sovolans," I asked, "originated here? On this world?"

"*More or less. They all did. The Sovolans evacuated two thousand years ago.*"

"And they left because the sun was expanding?"

"*It still is. It will continue to do so into the far future.*"

"How long," asked Alex, "have you been here? At the Entertainment Complex?"

"*Three hundred seventeen years.*"

We both took a deep breath. "When did they close it down? The complex?"

"*My error. Actually, that was when they closed it down and left. I'd been here, by then, approximately forty years.*"

"It's probably longer than that," I said.

Alex smiled. "Six fingers?"

"Yes." And we didn't know how long a year was. We weren't sure how Belle was handling the translation, but "hundred" was probably 20 percent longer on that world than it would be with humans.

"Itira, do you receive visitors periodically?"

"*Occasionally. They don't usually walk in the door. They normally just ask a question or two and fly by.*"

"Three hundred years. And you still have power."

"*I have my own generator. And a robotic maintenance unit. As far as I know, this office is the only location in the complex that uses power.*"

"They were closing the place when they left?"

"*Yes.*"

"Why'd they leave you?"

"*I don't know. I'd expected to go with them. But it just didn't happen.*"

"Where did they go? Do you know?"

"*They were moving off-world. To Sovol. There was a great deal of confusion during the departure. They turned off the power everywhere else in the complex. But they apparently just forgot about me. I suspect they had too much else to think about.*"

Alex walked over to one of the windows. The space that had been provided for the pools was clearly visible, as was the road.

"Itira, have you been in communication with them? The people at Xachri?"

"They're too far. But Xachri should stand out among the ruins. If not, you can probably exchange radio transmissions with them when you get close. Especially you should look for the Silver Tower. It would be hard to miss. I explained all this to Belle."

"Is the Silver Tower the tallest building in the area?"

"No. They never completed it. They were building it when the decision was made to get everybody off-world. It was left unfinished. It's easy to find. It's located almost directly across the street from Assembly Hall."

"So what's Assembly Hall?"

"It's where the conferences were held that eventually united all the nations and races on the planet. It's easy to spot. It's a circular building. I think it's four stories high. There's a lot of statuary out front."

I asked if there was anyone at all, other than mechanical intelligences, still there anywhere.

"The director of world capital maintenance has a small staff at Xachri. He should be able to show you how to find Sovol."

"What is the name of *this* planet?"

"This is Arkonika."

"What," said Alex, "was the Silver Tower intended for?"

"It was to have been the tallest structure on the planet, dedicated to Jenris Kaloppi, who started the movement that eventually drew us together into a global civilization. It was to have a spire that would have narrowed almost to a needle point. And the building would have been predominantly of a silver color."

"Sounds beautiful. Pity they weren't able to finish it. They didn't move it to Sovol?"

"It wouldn't have been portable. Large buildings were not

erected using that technology. No one would have been comfortable on the eighteenth floor of a portable building."

"Is this place portable?"

"No. It's an ordinary structure."

"Itira," I said, "how does portable technology work? How are you able to move buildings around?"

She smiled. *"Look through the window."* There was a small building out there. I hadn't noticed it before. *"That is the Appetite Café. Or it was."*

Belle, her voice low and speaking in Standard, explained that she'd had some difficulty with the translation. *"'Appetite' is the best I can do."*

Itira continued, *"When they shut the complex down, there was of course no further use for it. You see it?"*

"Yes."

Suddenly it wasn't there anymore.

"How did you do that?" asked Alex.

"The café is an electromagnetic construct that can be turned off and on when convenient."

"It's a force field," I said. "Same as we use to protect the *Belle-Marie*."

"Incredible," said Alex. "I didn't think we could use it for anything like that."

"It's also used for billboards," I said. "Gabe's name was on the one at the Acadia Hotel for his guest appearance."

"It has its limits," said Itira. *"We don't employ it for anything with more than four floors. People aren't comfortable being too high in that type of structure."*

"Okay, Itira," Alex said. "Thank you. We have to be on our way." He paused. "You indicated you need some help."

"I do."

"What can we do for you?"

"Disconnect me."

"We should be able to manage that. Where do you want to be moved to? You'll need a place that has power. Or if you prefer, we can probably hook you up to an alternative device in the *Belle-Marie.*"

"No. Just disconnect me."

"But you won't be functional if we do that."

"That is precisely what I wish. Disconnect me and drop me on a mountaintop somewhere. Or in an ocean."

"Itira, I understand that being alone is difficult. But come with us. We'll find a home for you."

"Being alone is not the issue, Alex."

"If I may ask, what is?"

"Let me show you something." Her image blinked off the monitor and was replaced by a view of the two pools, back in the era when they actually *were* pools. They were filled with Arkos of both sexes and a wide range of ages. They were laughing and waving at one another, chasing each other, leaping off diving boards, and posing for pictures. The young ones were riding down the slide into the water. *"I was able to watch this for a long time. My problem is not that I am alone, but that I am contained in a box. I have no life. I do not wish to continue this existence. If you would, please disconnect me."*

"Belle," I said, "if we pull the plug on her, will she be gone?"

"Probably not, Chase. She has an energy storage system that will support her for several days. But during that period she will be gradually shutting down."

"Itira," Alex said, "we do not wish to harm you."

"Then do as I ask. Please do not leave me here to continue in this dismal manner."

Alex was silent for a long moment. Then: "Thank you, Itira. I wish we could help."

"You are helping," she replied.

He disconnected her.

We got back into the lander and lifted off. I watched the complex drop behind and eventually fade away. "Belle," I said, "you there?"

"I am here, Chase."

"You okay?"

"Of course," she said.

26

*Family and friends are the anchor of civilization. The peace, security, and love
that frame the house we live in, the countryside with which we are familiar, those
with whom we share our time, form the cornerstone of our lives. There is no greater
treasure that we have devised and that we will always embrace than their presence.*
—Reverend Agathe Lawless, *Sunset Musings,* **1312**

A half-finished silver tower should have been easy to locate,
but it was a big continent, and we had no specific instruc-
tions other than just head west and slightly north. Belle's
radio transmissions drew no response.

The ground was mostly covered with what might once have
been a single giant city. Forests were few and small. There were
no country areas and few waterways. Occasional sections of open
ground appeared to have once belonged to oceans and lakes.
Whatever the reality, they were obviously in full retreat. We

cruised over unending urban structures, passing countless tall buildings. They appeared to be in decent condition, but they were empty.

The sun was in the middle of the sky when Robbi Jo, seated beside me, leaned to her left and pointed out through the wraparound. "There it is." She was right. We all knew it immediately. The unfinished Silver Tower was a unique structure in a ziggurat style. It stood on a wide base, with parapets on both sides, which gradually, a few stories at a time, grew together into a circular monolith design. And then, probably halfway to its intended height, the construction had stopped. There were other tall buildings, but only a few in the area rose higher, and there was probably nothing that would have approached its altitude had it been completed.

Assembly Hall was presumably the wide circular building with pillars across the street. There was a substantial number of statues out front.

"*We're getting a transmission,*" said Belle. "*They want to know who we are. Do you wish to go visual?*"

Alex was in the passenger cabin. "Not yet, Belle." He activated the mike. "Hello," he said. "This is the *Belle-Marie*. We came across the Lost Mission. They need your assistance."

After a minute they responded, "Belle-Marie, *there is no record of your vehicle. Who are you?*"

"We are from a different place. Do you wish to go visual?"

"*I don't know what that means. Yes. Go visual.*"

"Be aware we are not Arkos."

"*Go visual.*"

"Be aware we look different. Do it, Belle." The monitor lit up and we were looking at an Arko, whose eyes went wide in shock.

He pushed back in his chair and almost fell out of it. He needed a moment to recover. When he did, he asked where we were from.

"We are aliens. From far away. You know about the mission that went to Korella?"

"Wait. Let me get someone." He waved his right arm, looked to his right, and said, "Over here." There was a brief delay before somebody else appeared on the monitor.

The replacement also could not avoid staring. He needed a minute to get his feet on the ground. Then: "Who are you? What happened to you?"

"Hello," said Alex. "We are aliens."

"Incredible." Belle explained that she couldn't translate his one-word response, but she gave it her best try.

"Your people are in serious trouble," Alex said. "They are dying from a virus. We came to get help."

The speaker looked as if he'd gotten control of his emotions. "Do you know where Assembly Hall is?"

"Yes. We can see it."

"Very good. We are located in the Maintenance Center two blocks north of Assembly Hall. There's a parking lot with a large carved rock globe at the entrance. My office is on the fifth floor." He showed them five fingers. "I will be waiting for you. My name is Randol. And just so you know, no weapons are allowed in the building."

I got on the allcomm: "Who's going down?"

In the end, Alex and Robbi Jo. Hopefully, before it got much later we'd have the directions to Sovol and be on our way.

$$) \;) \; \bullet \; (\; ($$

Robbi Jo took control of the lander. Both she and Alex wore imagers clipped to their shirts, so we could see everything. I watched them descend through a cloudless late afternoon sky and set down in the parking lot. There were a few vehicles, but they were together on the far side. They climbed out, carrying no visible weapons, and turned to look at the sphere. It was set in a brace, about eight meters in diameter. A line of symbols was engraved on it, nothing that Belle could read. Alex took a picture. Then they started toward the front of the building.

"Good luck," Gabe said.

They climbed a few steps onto a deck. The doors, either glass or plastene, opened automatically. They passed into a lobby, filled with chairs and sofas. A long, curved desk was set against the back wall. It looked like a place that would normally have been busy, but it was empty. Several lamps blinked on, and a male voice came out of nowhere. Belle told us the speaker offered greetings. *"The associate director,"* the voice continued, *"welcomes you to Xachri. Take the elevator to the fifth floor."*

Belle explained that they were being directed to an office number something. *"Sorry. I can't translate the numbers."* Belle spoke to the voice. *"Take the elevator,"* she said.

Three elevators lined the wall at the far side of the lobby. Each had two buttons with symbols. An Arko came out of a door behind the counter. He spoke, and Belle took up the translation: "Let me assist you."

He pushed a button beside one of the elevators. It opened, and they all went inside. The doors closed. The Arko looked nervous, but he did what he was supposed to. He pushed another button and they started up. The doors opened and they all got out. The Arko turned left and led them down a corridor with a lot of doors. He selected one, the seventh one on their left, and knocked on it.

It opened into a room with a sofa and three chairs surrounding two large potted plants. Two windows looked out onto the parking area. An Arko sat beside a table, wearing a white pullover shirt and dark slacks. He was trying to appear at ease. He got out of his seat. "Welcome," he said. "And thank you for trying to help."

"It's our pleasure."

"I'm Randol. What can we do? Where are they?"

Alex introduced himself and Robbi Jo. "They moved to a second world. They've been expecting vehicles to bring support, but they have not shown up. And they're enduring a killer virus."

"May I ask," said Randol, "where you are from?"

"A considerable distance, Randol." Belle quickly explained she didn't know the proper way to address him. Alex asked for direction.

"'Supervisor Randol' works fine," he said. "Or just 'Randol.' The title doesn't matter."

Alex explained about the lost village and the virus. When he'd finished, Randol pressed his fingertips together. "I'm sorry to hear it. Thank you for bringing us this information. We will act as quickly as we can. We've been concerned about the Lost Mission for a long time."

"Good. They need assistance quickly. They might need to evacuate."

"We will take care of it."

"When will that be?"

"As soon as the director gets back."

"Where is he now?"

"He has taken some visitors for a boat ride on the Kava River. As soon as he returns, I'll let him know."

"When will that be?"

"Probably three days. Then he'll activate one of our vehicles and send it to Sovol to inform them of what has happened. They'll arrange a recovery mission."

"Three days? Randol, your people are dying every day. Are you able to communicate directly with Sovol?"

"You mean by radio?"

"By whatever means you have."

"Alex, a radio transmission will take almost four years to reach them."

"Can you contact *him* by radio? The director?"

"The director is a female. And she is on another continent. No, I cannot reach her."

"Do you know if the *Triskuul* ever arrived?"

"The *Triskuul*? What is that?"

"It's the transport vehicle that took the Lost Mission out somewhere to establish a colony."

"Okay. I don't know anything about it. But the last time I looked, they were still just missing."

"The *Triskuul* should have returned to Sovol weeks ago."

He smiled. "We'll check on it. Anything else you need?"

"Can you locate Sovol for us? Do you know where it is? Just tell us how to find it. Do that and we'll take care of the rest ourselves."

"I'm sorry. This is an unusual situation. Please do not be offended, but you are people from another place. I am not empowered to provide the information you want. We will have to wait for the director. I know that is inconvenient, but I have no choice."

"All right. Let's try a different approach. You say the director is on a boat somewhere."

"That is correct. On the Kava River. The river is of historical interest. Several hundred years ago—"

"Let's save that. Can you tell us where the river is, and where she would be?"

"Again, I apologize, Alex. But I can't allow you to disrupt the voyage. I'm sorry, but you can't even prove you've actually intersected with the Lost Mission."

"Look," Alex said. He dug into his pocket and came out with a plastic card.

Szola's library card. "Szola is the wife of the colony's mayor. She gave it to us in case anyone here didn't believe us." He handed it to Randol.

Randol glanced at it and gave it back. "Colonies don't have mayors," he said. "In any case, I'm sure you have the technology to manufacture one of these."

"The language is yours."

"As is your interpreter's. I'm sorry, but I have work to do. I will contact you when the director gets back."

"Okay," said Alex. "That's enough. You've informed us that Sovol is just under four light-years away. It shouldn't be hard to find."

Robbi Jo turned so her imager picked up Alex. He got out of his chair, went to one of the windows, and looked out at Assembly Hall. "It's of historic interest, isn't it?"

"Yes."

"That globe in front of the building. It's a compelling piece of work. There's something engraved on it. Can you tell me what it is?"

Randol joined him at the window. "It represents the principle on which we are founded."

"And what is that?"

"We All Stand Together."

"Beautiful."

"It is the heart of our society."

"Randol, I suspect the disappearance of the people on the *Triskuul*, and of the *Triskuul* itself, has gotten a fair amount of attention."

"I don't really know. Sovol is another world. It's a long way from here."

"Randol, you referred to these people as 'the Lost Mission.'"

"That is correct."

"They've obviously drawn some serious attention."

"All we know is what we hear from the media."

"They are dying every day. And you're forcing us to go hunting for them."

Robbi Jo broke in: "Something you might want to keep in mind, Randol: the Lost Mission is a big deal. Moreover, I won't even ask how often you get alien visitors. But we'll be talking to the media soon. And if the *Triskuul* never arrived, and people are still dying, you might want to think about how you and your boss are going to look."

Their guide was waiting outside Randol's office. They left, took the elevator down, and exited through the front door. Robbi Jo started for the lander, but Alex said something to her that we couldn't hear, and they changed course and headed toward the globe. They took their time, walking slowly through the parking area. When they reached it, they circled around to the front, although they stayed off to one side so anyone in the Maintenance Center could see them. Then they started taking pictures. Alex took photos of Robbi Jo in front of the globe, and Robbi Jo took photos of Alex. Included in all the pictures was the engraving that read *We All Stand Together*.

As far as we could tell, neither of them looked up at the fifth-floor windows to see whether anyone was watching. Gabe and I couldn't see them either. But by then we'd figured out what was going on.

They were in the lander on the way back to the *Belle-Marie* when they picked up a radio transmission. "Alex?" It was Randol. "We're getting flight directions to Sovol for you. You'll have them in a couple of minutes."

27

We're all in it together.

—Phrase believed to have appeared during the American Pandemic, during the early years of the third millennium.

Everything went perfectly from there. We needed five hours to reach Daka, Sovol's star. Two planets orbited in the Goldilocks Zone. Our information was that both were occupied by Arkos. Sovol was the one farther from the sun. We sent them the package of information and got an almost instantaneous reply (when you figured in the time required for the radio signals to travel back and forth). We got a male voice welcoming us to Sovol. He sounded delighted by the news, told us they would look for us at an orbital station, and asked for an estimate of arrival time.

We took a couple of minutes to jump in closer to them and got within about forty hours. We let them know where we were, and a new voice turned up on the radio. Apparently they were relaying the message to a central command of some sort. *"Thank you for what you're doing,"* she said, *"and for the information. We've already begun putting together a rescue mission. We're sorry to hear about their problems, but at least they're still alive. When they disappeared from the world they'd selected, we didn't know what to think."*

"We're glad to help," said Alex. "You'll be able to find them now?"

"Yes. Thank you for showing us the way." She took a deep breath. *"I should inform you that we've been concerned about the Korella mission ever since it went missing. We did not know where they went from Korella. We assumed they'd get in touch with us, but it never happened."*

"The *Triskuul* left them weeks ago. It was coming here to get help."

"It never arrived, Alex." That generated a long pause. *"You'll be docking at Segalia, correct?"*

"I assume that's the orbiting station?"

"Yes."

"We're on our way. We'll be there late tomorrow."

"Excellent. My name is Olekka. I will be waiting when you get here."

)) ● ((

By the time we arrived, the rescue mission had left. They'd sent a transport vehicle. The plan was to evacuate everyone. Someone else had gone out in an effort to find another world to which they could be transported.

They also checked us to be sure there were no signs of a virus. Olekka tried to set up a celebration for us, but the food was inedible and the drinks were flat. I took one bite of a fried fish and quit. They offered to give us a tour of the planet, but we all wanted to get back to Arinaka. They refueled us and restored our oxygen supply, and their maintenance people did some work. Olekka told us if we ever needed assistance, she would be there for us. "I cannot adequately express my gratitude."

The Sovol media showed up and interviewed everyone. Alex told them we were delighted that we'd been able to help. And he was careful to give credit to Randol.

We sent a hypercomm transmission to the Confederacy, informing them that help was on the way to Arinaka, and that they could cancel any planned mission. Twenty hours after we'd arrived at Segalia, we were on our way back to Arinaka. That required another six days. But when we got there, the rescue vehicle was in the process of evacuating the survivors. Sixty-eight had died. Szola was okay. But Daylok was gone. They'd sealed everyone off from the lethal air supply, and they checked Alex to make sure he hadn't picked up the virus. Fortunately, there was no sign of a problem.

They were going back to Sovol. Szola told us they'd had enough of other worlds. She couldn't look at us without growing teary. "I'm sorry you live so far away," she said. "I'd love to visit you sometime." She managed a smile. "We could bring our own food and drinks."

We'd told her about our problems at Olekka's party but told her she could send us recipes and we'd manage the meals.

We returned the astronomy book, and I explained to Szola how Robbi Jo had figured out how to get us close enough to find Sovol. "I wish," she said, "there was a way we could repay you."

They extracted the bodies of the victims. A second vehicle arrived and took them on board. We stayed until everyone was gone, helping wherever we could. And finally we took the lander back up to the *Belle-Marie*. And started for home.

A month later we arrived at Skydeck. I'd never been happier to get home. We weren't even out of the *Belle-Marie* before we were getting medical examinations again. Happily, we were okay.

Within three weeks, a follow-up mission was on its way to Sovol, where they established formal relations, and everyone said what a pity it was we were so far apart.

$$) \;) \; \bullet \; (\; ($$

One of the first things we did was throw a party at the country house. We invited a crowd of friends. Among them were Lou Banner, Veronica Walker, Autumn Ulbrich, Henry Cassell, Quaid McCann, Jennifer Hancock, Vince Reddington, and everybody else who had a connection with the past few months. At one point, Alex expressed his wish that we could have included Szola. And Ollie and Neo.

Robbi Jo brought her cello.

$$) \;) \; \bullet \; (\; ($$

We filed a report outlining what had happened. We knew that we'd broken the rules against making contact, and that we could expect to pay a price. We were charged with violation of the Spaulding Mandate, endangering the welfare of alien entities, and endangering Confederate security. Our lawyers all wanted us to accept the charges and make a deal, but we overestimated the impact of our efforts to assist the Arkos and pleaded not guilty on all counts. The courts found us guilty on all charges. We received suspended sentences. Alex and Gabe got substantial fines and are now prohibited from travel outside the Confederacy. Robbi Jo and I lost our licenses.

Despite all that, Alex received an award from the Rimway Humane Society, Gabe has become director of the Andiquar Archeological Museum, and Robbi Jo is speaking at universities around the world.

The Arkos who'd survived the virus settled back on Sovol. They are out somewhere in open country, and the town is the same one they had on Korella and Arinaka. We saw pictures of Szola, and of some of those who'd lost their lives, including Daylok. There was also a portrait of the library. They named it for Robbi Jo.

Chris Baxter told me she was one of the smartest people he'd ever known. The complete package.

EPILOGUE

Several days after this manuscript was sent to the publisher, we got word from the Arkos that the *Triskuul* had been found adrift in the Korella system. No one could explain why Tokon had gone back there other than that he'd probably wanted to determine whether the satellite he'd left was still in place. Presumably he wanted to raise hell with someone. But unfortunately, he came down with the virus. He was probably not aware that he was dying until the rising temperature of his body rendered him helpless. Included with the report was a notation that a newly designed interstellar transporter, the first of its kind, would be named the *Gora Tokon*.